CHRISTMAS AT THE LAKE

Autumn Macarthur

ABOUT THE AUTHOR

Autumn Macarthur is a USA Today bestselling author of clean Christian inspirational romances with a strong touch of faith. If you love happy-ever-afters, sweet romance, and Hallmark movies, chances are you'll enjoy her stories!

Originally from Sydney, Australia, she now lives in a small town not far from London, England, with her very English husband (aka The Cat Magnet), and way too many rescue cats for our tiny house! A recent addition to the family are two baby guinea pigs. For such small creatures, they have amazingly huge personalities.

When she's not feeding cats, she hand sews, reads, and most of all writes heartwarming stories of love and faith. With every story, God teaches her the exact same lessons her hero and heroine need to learn to commit to their forever love.

She's also blessed with a chronic health issue that has changed her life in the way it limits her. It hasn't been easy, but she's come to give thanks for the gift hidden in the illness — the way it's taught her patience, brought her into a greater dependence on God, and given her a far deeper appreciation of His love and provision.

Sign up for her reader newsletter at her website http://faithhopeandheartwarming.com to get insider news and exclusive offers. Or you can visit her on Facebook as Autumn Macarthur.
She'd love to hear from you!

Faith, hope, & heartwarming –
Real romance, real faith.

Christmas at the Lake

BY

AUTUMN MACARTHUR

Copyright 2016, 2017, 2020 © by Autumn Macarthur

First Print Duet Edition, August 2020

ISBN-13: 9798671774740

Published by Faith, Hope, & Heartwarming
http://faithhopeandheartwarming.com

All rights reserved. No part of this publication may be reproduced, stored in a retrieval system, or transmitted in any form or by any means— for example, electronic, photocopy, recording— without the prior written permission of the author. The only exception is brief quotations in printed or broadcast reviews. Your support and respect for the property of this author is appreciated.

This book is a work of fiction. Names, characters, places, and incidents are the product of the author's imagination or are used fictitiously. Any resemblance to actual events, locales, or persons, living or dead, is coincidental.

BIBLE VERSION COPYRIGHT NOTICES

Easy-to-Read Version (ERV) Copyright © 2006 by Bible League international

New International Version (NIV): Holy Bible, New International Version®, NIV® Copyright ©1973, 1978, 1984, 2011 by Biblica, Inc.® Used by permission. All rights reserved worldwide.

The Voice (VOICE): The Voice Bible Copyright © 2012 Thomas Nelson, Inc. The Voice™ translation © 2012 Ecclesia Bible Society. All rights reserved.

OTHER COPYRIGHTS

Wild Mountain Huckleberry Muffins recipe copyright © 2013 The Rowdy Baker and used by permission. All rights reserved worldwide. Not to be reprinted or reused without The Rowdy Baker's written consent.

"It Came Upon a Midnight Clear" Christmas carol by Edmund Hamilton Sears, Public Domain.

CONTENTS

CALM & BRIGHT   page   1

MIDNIGHT CLEAR   page 127

CALM & Bright

HUCKLEBERRY LAKE #1

*"You know what I say about Christmas.
You can never have too many lights on the tree, too much love in the
home, or too many cookies."*
Liz Calder

…*be kind and compassionate. Graciously forgive one another just as
God has forgiven you*…
Ephesians 4:32

DEAR READER

I adore Christmas! Yummy food, fairy lights, decorating the tree, giving and receiving gifts—the big kid in me delights in all that! Plus it's a time for family, faith, and love, all things that mean a lot to me. And they're all important elements of my new novella Calm & Bright, too. It's a story of finding home, a second chance at love, and the greatest gift of all—the gift of a second chance with God.

I've wanted to write this story since my spring release in 2015, Forget Paris. Brad appears in it briefly, and unfortunately he's a bit of a jerk! Okay, a LOT of a jerk! But I love knowing none of us is such a jerk we can't be redeemed by love and faith. That earlier story woke Brad up that he needed to change, and in this story, God helps him find his heart's true home.

This book begins a new series, set in beautiful Huckleberry Lake, Idaho! Every book is a complete romance, following a different couple through the trials and joys of a developing love, deepening their faith in the process, until they're ready for the happy-ever-after God has planned for them.

I've enjoyed writing this story so much! And I hope you'll enjoy reading it, too.

CHAPTER ONE

December 23

"I FELL FOR YOUR LINES too many times before, Brad. Never again."

Maddie Calder Hughes wouldn't fall for her ex-husband's charm this time.

No matter how honest and convincing he sounded. No matter how her heart raced and her body trembled simply being in the same room with him. She'd been swept off her feet, crazy in love when she said, "I do." But she was smarter now.

Too many broken promises. Too many shattered hopes.

His smile didn't falter. She must have imagined that flash of hurt in his eyes, the way the lines around them deepened for a moment. Because nothing wobbled Brad's self-confidence.

When she asked Brad to come to Huckleberry Lake for Christmas, the last thing she expected was he'd ask her to consider a reconciliation. But he had, almost as soon as he arrived at Gran's cottage.

Part of her hadn't expected him to even turn up, despite his promises things would be different this time. She'd longed to tell him to forget it, to stay in the city and work through the holidays as he usually did. But though Brad had betrayed her and their marriage vows, she couldn't deny their son a visit with his father.

Especially at Christmas.

At least this time she'd insisted on it being on her terms. No sterile, child-unfriendly hotel room in L.A., hardly seeing him because he couldn't take time away from his high-powered healthcare management job. This Christmas, Brad came to them, or he wouldn't see Jacob.

Huckleberry Lake, Idaho. The opposite of the big-city hustle Brad thrived on.

Here, in the place she'd lived her whole life, she could resist the treacherous tug of her emotions, everything in him that still called to her. Here, she knew who she was.

A Calder of Sunset Point.

But what she hadn't considered when she asked him to come here was how seeing him in Gran's living room flooded her with memories. Last time he'd been here, their love was new and clean and bright. Back then, anything seemed possible. The cozy cluttered room felt so much smaller, filled by his vibrant presence.

"It's not a line." Brad reached out to her, a gesture of apology. "I simply wanted to be honest and upfront with you."

Looking away, she shook her head. His gesture was as empty as his words.

Standing behind the upholstered wingchair while he sat in Pop's old recliner had been wise. She clamped her fingers to the chair's upper edge. Safer to keep her distance. If she took his hand, if she touched him, she'd be lost.

Brad's hand dropped to his side, and he loosed a long, low breath. "I wish you'd believe I've changed. I'm going to church again, doing counseling with my pastor. Won't you give me and our marriage a second chance?"

She risked a glance at him. His steady gaze and his clear hazel eyes seemed so sincere. Maybe he really had changed. With God, all things were possible, right? A small, hopeful part of her wanted to believe it, wanted to rebuild her trust in him. He'd come back to Huckleberry Lake, where they'd first met, after all.

"Maddie…"

Just her name, yet his voice washed over her, sweet and warm as maple syrup on pancakes. And his smile. Oh, his smile.

The summer they met, she'd fallen instantly in love with him, because of his smile. One curve of his lips, one hint of his beguiling dimple, one twitch of his eyebrow, and she'd melted.

Older and wiser now, she was immune.

She hoped.

Annoyingly, his smile still made her heart flip over, though that instinctive response was far from welcome now. Brad's smiles came too easy. He could turn that confident grin on anyone. Use it to win a deal in business. Or to charm other women. She wasn't the only one to respond to his smile.

As she refused to respond, his beautifully sculpted lips drooped. His broad shoulders sagged. It looked so much like disappointment and sorrow.

But it couldn't be genuine. But despite knowing the truth about him, Louise's email confirming her doubts and fears, she so badly wanted to believe his act.

To trust him again.

Her back straightened. Whenever her resolve weakened, she needed to remember how things had really been. How many promises he'd broken. How many nights and weekends she'd been on her own. And what he'd done since their marriage ended.

She'd given him time. She'd waited for him to come to her. And he hadn't. He was only back now because his plan B didn't work out. He didn't want *her*. He simply didn't want to be alone.

That wasn't enough to base a life together on.

"Brad, you need to accept that our marriage is over. We're Jacob's parents. Nothing more." Though she kept her voice gentle, her hands sliced a cutting gesture, underlining how she meant her words. She felt nothing for him now. Zero. Zip. Zilch. Nada.

Maybe if she repeated it often enough, she'd believe it.

He nodded slowly. "If that's final, I have to accept it, though I don't want to." A hint of a smile curved his lips. "I have ten days to convince you to change your mind."

Brad never did let setbacks get him down. Resilient as a rubber ball, he bounced up again. Like his charm, it was an asset he knew how to use. If one plan didn't work, he simply moved on.

"I won't change my mind. I can't go back to living the way we did." Her flat tone held finality, but more than a hint of regret.

Without meaning to, her arms crossed over her chest and clasped her shoulders, as if she needed to hug herself. She wasn't proud of the way their marriage ended. The way *she'd* ended it. When she made those vows, she'd fully intended them to last for life.

But she hadn't known then how tough her marriage would be.

He stood and took a step toward her, hands outreached. She stiffened. Seeming to hear her unspoken message for once, he subsided back into Pop's old leather-covered recliner, shaking his head.

Something—anger?—glinted in his eyes, and his jaw tightened. "You never told me you were unhappy. Then you rushed up here when your gran had her stroke and needed looking after. I understood that, she means a lot to you. But next thing, I'm served divorce papers, and a Fed Ex parcel arrives containing your rings. What was I supposed to think? For all I knew, you'd met someone else."

"*I* respected our marriage vows!" Antagonism sparked her voice.

Puzzlement creased Brad's brow, and he raised his hands, almost in surrender. "So did I."

"Did you?" Hurt disbelief wobbled her. They'd strayed

into territory she wasn't sure she wanted to discuss. Would knowing what really happened be even worse than her suspicions and Louise's tip-offs? "We can't talk about this now. Gran and Hiram will be home with Jacob any minute."

Brad's shoulders slumped. "I don't want us to argue over the past, Maddie. I'm different now. Let's look to the future. I'm willing to see my part of why things didn't work out, and do what I can to fix it. I want us to be a family again."

Her heart ached to believe he was the different person he claimed to be, so badly. Something in her still yearned for him, still felt that soul-deep attraction that brought them together and carried them through a long-distance engagement. That had made her so sure he was "the one".

He certainly looked different, as if he'd been indoors more, out of the California sunshine. The boyishly handsome features were the same, but his golden tan had faded. The natural sun-streaks in his hair were subtler, darkened to copper rather than beach blond. The fine lines around his eyes had deepened. He appeared to have a new maturity.

But if she weakened and said yes, she'd be back where she was then.

Always coming second to his job, alone with Jacob in an apartment with no yard and a tiny kitchen. A thousand miles from home, in a city where the fast pace felt like another planet. No one seemed to have time to make friends and be neighborly, though she'd tried, really tried.

Always working, Brad hadn't noticed how homesick she was, and she hadn't wanted to trouble him by telling him. She'd waited in their apartment, night after night, never knowing when he'd come home. Never sure if he'd be back before Jacob's bedtime or if he'd turn up for his son's birthday parties or if she'd have to go to church on her own again.

The pitying glances she fielded from the other women there made her wonder if they believed she even had a husband. He'd been missing when she needed him with her so often, she'd felt just as much a single mother when they were married as she did now.

But far worse had been wondering if he was *really* working late nights and weekends, or if he was with some other woman. Calling someone else "Princess" and making her feel as if she were the only woman in the world.

Now she had confirmation, those fears would be even stronger.

Firming her resolve, she shook her head. "You'll need to work harder to convince me. Nothing you've done so far has changed my mind."

He came here, a quiet whisper sounded in her mind. *He says he's regained his faith. What do you have to lose by giving him a chance?*

Her heart. That's what she stood to lose.

In just a few minutes with Brad, she'd begun falling for him all over again. Already her determination not to trust him or allow him past her defenses crumbled.

As if he sensed her softening, an optimistic grin lit Brad's face, and he jumped up from the chair. "Just keep an open mind to the possibility, Maddie. That's all I ask."

Meeting again here, where they'd tumbled into love, was such a bad idea. Memories she'd spent all year trying to forget filled every place she looked. Next thing, she'd be falling into his arms, like she had that summer. Heedless and headlong.

That. Mustn't. Happen.

Just like before, she'd fall hard for him, and then get her heart broken.

All over again.

And Jacob would be upset again, by his daddy's broken promises. He wasn't a toddler anymore, easily distracted by packages of new toys in the mail. He wanted his daddy.

She'd take the risk for herself, even knowing another heartbreak was inevitable. But she couldn't risk their son. His precious trust was too important and too fragile. She'd seen him disappointed by his father too many times.

If that wasn't enough to strengthen her against the way

Brad walked in the door and hooked straight into her feelings, she had another reason to bolster her determination. Straightening her back, she lifted her head.

"Nothing you say or do will make any difference, Brad. Even if I want to give you a second chance, I can't. Gran's having more mini-strokes. She insists she can manage, but she needs me here. Her doctor says she can't live alone."

CHAPTER TWO

SO MADDIE STAYED WITH HER grandmother because she had to, not because she wanted to? That possibility never occurred to Brad.

He'd already thought only a miracle would soften Maddie's heart. Now this bombshell put a serious kink in his hopes to win her back.

Lord, surely You haven't convinced me to work toward reuniting my family if there isn't a way! Help me to keep trusting You.

"Me moving here isn't an option. I have to be where the hospitals are, or I don't have a job to support us. The nearest large healthcare facility is what — a hundred miles away?"

"Bonner Health in Sandpoint is a little over fifty miles. Then the big hospitals in Spokane or Coeur d'Alene. Nothing nearer." Triumph edged her voice. As if she celebrated proving they had no future.

"What about your dad? Could he help?"

A quick headshake set her thick dark braid bouncing on her shoulder. "No."

"Hasn't he retired from the mission field now?"

Maddie's lips tightened. "Yes, but Dad's still working. He's found a whole new mission among the Florida snowbirds. And Gran won't leave. She's lived here since she married Pop. All her memories of him are here. She says moving back to town again would kill her."

He raised an eyebrow. "Really? Or like my second stepmother would 'Simply *die* if she didn't get that new purse'?" He mimicked Dionne's nasal whine perfectly. Not that Maddie would realize. Dad had moved on to wife number four by the time they met.

"I know people say that, but I don't think Gran's exaggerating." Maddie loosed a sigh, turning her mouth downward. "They had to release her early from the hospital, because she pined so badly for the lake she stopped eating."

Brad rubbed his chin. "I didn't know that."

"No. You wouldn't. You didn't come up here to visit. Not once." Maddie's tone hardened, and the sizzling glare she threw him could fry bacon.

She didn't understand. She'd never understood. And yet for some crazy reason, he still loved her. Still wanted her to be his wife as much as he had that summer they'd met. Despite his foolish lapse when the divorce became final, Maddie was the only woman for him.

"I couldn't." He tried to explain. "I was under so much pressure, finishing up my MBA. And at work. Taking a couple of days off would have risked my chances at the promotion I was up for."

"Winning promotions isn't all there is to life. I needed you. Jacob did, too. And you weren't there for us. Ever." She emerged from behind her armchair barricade and stood facing him, chin raised, hands on hips, eyes narrowed. Color flared in her cheeks.

He stared at her, wordless for once.

This wasn't an appropriate time for him to notice the way her faded jeans and bright blue sweater hugged her curvy figure.

But he *did* notice.

Even years later, without a trace of makeup, Maddie was as heart-poundingly beautiful as the night they met. She still wore the same sweet perfume. He'd caught the delicate floral scent as she'd opened the door and hurried him inside. It accelerated his pulse just as much as it used to.

But she seemed different, too. The Maddie he'd married

never got angry. She sure looked furious now.

Like a brick hitting the side of his head, he realized.

Maybe she *had* been angry. She'd just never let it show.

That explained a lot. Like why he'd had no real clue she'd been unhappy in their marriage, let alone unhappy enough to divorce him.

Help me to understand, Lord. Then help me make things right.

The words she spoke now were important. More important than reminders of physical attraction, no matter how much a good marriage needed that.

Maddie was finally telling him why she'd ended things.

Battling the temptation to meet anger with anger, he kept the edge from his voice. "We needed the promotion. As husband, my task was to provide for you and Jacob. It still is. Only the monthly child support I send lets you stay here and care for your gran. A community of less than two hundred can't offer much in the way of employment opportunities."

Her eyes flashed, though he'd simply stated a fact, not been accusatory. Surely even a stubborn dreamer like Maddie had to admit he was right.

"I do shifts in the store for the new owners now and then." Her lips twisted. "I still think of it as 'our' store, though it's years since Pop died and Gran sold it. In the summer, there's plenty of work waitressing at the resort across the lake."

Waitressing for three months of the year wouldn't possibly earn enough to support her and Jacob. But he didn't intend to argue. Instead, he smiled, as memories surfaced.

"You were working there when we met. You looked so adorable in your blue and white uniform. It matched the color of your eyes. Remember how I kept making excuses to call you back to our table? Then I came back the next night, hoping you'd be there again."

His heart warmed, remembering that summer he'd stayed with his grandmother at her rented vacation place for a few weeks. She'd been horrified when he fell for a mere waitress.

But he had. He'd fallen hard and fast, so sure it was God's will for them to be together. The week after he graduated, they'd married, thinking the world was at their feet and they'd live happily ever after. Enrolled in a fast-track MBA and with his new hospital management job, their future seemed bright. Then his marriage went the same way as all of Dad's. The fairy tale ended fast.

Just like Dad, he hadn't had a clue about commitment.

Now, he had to convince Maddie he did.

Though what good would it do when his career and her gran's needs put them so far apart?

Maddie's face and posture softened, her anger seeming to evaporate as fast as it flared. She dropped into the chair opposite him, eyes distant and dreamy. "Yes. I remember." Then her shoulders sagged and her gaze dropped. "I'll need to arrange child care for Jacob before I can waitress next summer. At least at the store, the living quarters are right there. Pat and Susanna don't mind him coming with me."

The urge to protect and care for his family swelled in him. "You won't need to. I promised you'd be able to stay home with our children. Once I get this next promotion, I can increase the monthly check."

Maddie lifted her head, something he couldn't quite read shadowing her blue eyes. "Is this the Chicago job? Permanently in head office? You'll be even further away. Nearly two thousand miles."

"Still a flight and a car ride." His lips twisted, and he shrugged. "Anyway, there's no guarantee I'll get it. I'm up against some heavy competition. My boss warned me taking time off now was risky."

"I'm not sure whether to be sorry or glad," Maddie admitted with a cute rueful grin, much more like the girl he fell in love with. "But I didn't intend to hurt your chances. I just wanted to make sure Jacob got more time with you."

"Let's just say it would have been better for my career if you'd come to L.A. But I missed seeing Jacob at

Thanksgiving. I couldn't miss Christmas, too."

"When you see Gran, you'll realize why I can't leave her. She's still feisty, but so much frailer. Thankfully our neighbor Hiram is wonderful. He went with her to Jacob's nativity play rehearsal this morning, so I could stay home to wait for you."

He smiled, looking forward to seeing his boy. "What role is Jacob playing? I seriously hammed it up one year as Joseph."

It still stung that Dad was never there to see him. Facelifts and Botox in his plastic surgery practice came first. But he wouldn't mention that. He and Maddie had never spoken of things like this. So much they still didn't know about each other.

"I'm sure you did ham it up." The laughter in Maddie's eyes belied her dry tone. "I've been Mary. And the angel, another year. But far from hamming it up, I was so nervous I forgot my lines. This is Jacob's first time, so he's a shepherd. Next year, he might graduate to Joseph. Here, the part with the speaking lines is the angel, and the oldest kid gets that role." Her antagonism melted as she talked about their son.

Gratitude flooded him, sweet and warm in his chest. He leaned forward in the chair, feeling close to Maddie. "You did right insisting I come here. His first nativity play isn't something I want to miss. I've missed so much else."

As if he'd pushed a button, the laughter in her eyes vanished. She sat straight up in her chair, arms folded over her chest. "You *chose* to miss so much. Right from when he was a newborn. You didn't even take the full paternity leave you were entitled to."

"Entitlement was one thing," he jumped to defend himself against her resentment. "Taking it was something else. The hospital corporation's so-called family friendly policies apply far more on paper than in reality."

At his words, she bristled even more.

He'd fallen right into the trap. Getting defensive. Those solo, marriage-counseling sessions with his pastor focused on the need to listen.

Not something he'd had a lot of practice at yet.

Before things escalated, he quickly said what he should have said. "I'm sorry I wasn't there for you."

And he tried to sound like he meant it. Because he did.

He wouldn't intentionally have chosen to hurt her, then or now. He just hadn't realized. Maddie never said anything. If she had, maybe he could have done things differently.

It worked. She sank back into the chair, her anger visibly deflating. "Thank you for acknowledging that." Raising her hands, she scrubbed them over her face. "Let's let it go now. You'd better get your bags inside."

He was only too glad to let go of the topic. Though he'd learned more about Maddie and what she wanted from him in the past ten minutes than in four years of marriage and almost a year of divorce.

This communication stuff wasn't easy. No wonder Dad was on wife number five.

It didn't take long to cart most of what he'd brought with him into the house and up the stairs to the guest room Maddie showed him to, overlooking the frozen lake. One bag of clothes. Everything else in the trunk of the SUV, rented at the airport, were Christmas gifts for Jacob, Maddie, and her grandmother.

Apart from one tiny box in his luggage. Praying he'd be successful, he'd packed the wedding and engagement rings she'd returned. God willing, he wouldn't leave with them still hidden in his bag.

Averting his eyes from the red-and-blue quilt-covered double bed, he forced his mind from thoughts of how different this Christmas would be if they were still married. If they were sharing this room and this bed, rather than being separated by an expanse of hallway.

And an even bigger expanse of misunderstandings and broken dreams.

Maddie swallowed audibly and peered out the window. "More snow on the way. You got here just in time."

Her overly cheerful voice suggested she'd shared similar thoughts. Satisfaction warmed him. If she had, maybe she still felt the spark he did.

They'd need more than attraction to rebuild their damaged relationship. They'd need faith and prayer and willingness — and a lot more listening skills than he was sure he could muster. Then there was the problem of her gran.

But that spark wasn't a bad place to start.

CHAPTER THREE

AWARENESS FLOODED MADDIE, heating her cheeks. When they were still married, she'd hoped they'd share this room. When she'd tried to get Brad to come to the lake for vacations, and again when she asked him to visit after Gran's first stroke.

Thankfully, Brad had no way of guessing that. Or of knowing how her unwelcome desires bothered her.

Because he'd never visited. They'd never been in this room as man and wife. He'd put his job ahead of his family too many times.

Finally, that triggered the divorce.

The room still stirred unwanted memories. Her foolish daydreams during their engagement, imagining life together while they were still a thousand miles apart. She'd sat in the window seat watching birds dance across sunset waters and the stars come out over the darkening lake, as they spoke on the phone well into the night. Losing those hopes ached like a broken bone.

She'd do her best to ensure they weren't alone again, especially here.

The sooner they got downstairs, the better. The sooner Gran and Jacob came home, the better.

Where was Gran, anyway? The constant worry chewed at her. Far too independent-minded, Gran refused to accept any limitations. But Hiram would take care of her.

"Maddie, this is for you." Brad's voice broke into her

pointless anxiety. He held out a beautifully wrapped, ribbon-tied box, eight inches by six inches.

Moving away from him, nearer the door, she eyed the gift as if he offered a bag full of rattlesnakes. "I don't want presents, Brad. They didn't make things better when we were married, and they won't now, either."

She winced over sounding so bratty and ungrateful, but then straightened. It was true. Too many times, he'd tried to plaster over their problems by spending on her.

He pushed out a tight, hard breath, and his shoulders slumped. "I wish I'd known what you *did* want from me. I wish I knew now. I can see I messed up, and messed up badly. I still don't know why, and it isn't for lack of trying to get it right."

Pausing with her hand on the doorknob, she shook her head. Sadness rather than anger tightened her throat. "I wanted quiet time together, not expensive gifts. I wanted to linger chatting at the table after a home-cooked meal in the evening, not rushed dress-up dinners in the latest trendy restaurant, where the music was always too loud to talk. I wanted you home with me, and with Jacob."

This honesty felt too close, too personal.

If even half the rumors she'd heard about him were true, how could she believe or trust him again? Brad didn't like being alone. That was the only reason he tried to get her back. Being second best to his work was bad enough, being second best to other women… that broke her heart.

Even so, shouldn't she give him a chance? She believed in a God of forgiveness.

But forgiving Brad wasn't so easy.

Please, Lord, show me what to do. I really don't want to forgive him. But if You tell me to, I guess I need to try.

"I'm sorry, Maddie. I didn't realize." He swallowed. "When you made excuses to get out of going to dinner, I thought you didn't want to be with me."

She shook her head, regret tightening her tummy. How

had they got things so wrong?

Brad extended the box to her with both hands. "I hope this present is different from the others. I thought about what you'd truly like. It's fragile, and it won't last long." He smiled ruefully. "A bit like our marriage."

This was a new Brad, a man she almost didn't recognize. With his apologies, his honesty, his willingness to take responsibility. They'd strayed into unfamiliar territory.

It felt as wild and potentially dangerous as the snow-covered forest surrounding the lake.

"Could we go downstairs? I'll make coffee. You must be ready for a cup after your drive from the airport." Without waiting for him to reply, she headed for the stairs, needing to escape the intimacy of talking this way in the room she'd once hoped they'd share.

Their marriage was over. It had to be. She couldn't dare permit herself to hope.

Gran's sunny yellow kitchen felt so much safer. She filled the coffeemaker and set it working. Brad hadn't forgotten his gift. He set it on the scrubbed pine table in front of her.

"Please, Maddie."

She couldn't resist the entreaty in his eyes, though her fingers trembled as they reached for the bow. Then the front door squeaked open, and voices carried from the hall.

Gran, at last. And Hiram's deeper voice as well as Jacob's high-pitched chatter.

"Maddie, we're home!" Gran bustled into the kitchen, rosy-cheeked from the cold, her left leg dragging just a little, and then turned to talk to someone behind her. "Jacob, you take off those boots before you come in here."

Jacob groaned. "I can't get them off."

Maddie stepped toward the door. She hadn't told the boy his father was coming today, in case Brad didn't turn up. He'd let Jacob down so many times before. She could tell him now.

"I'll do it." Gran raised a hand and returned to the hall. "Hiram, you go through."

Maddie smiled as the hearty gray-haired man entered the kitchen. She loved their neighbor, Pop's old school friend, as if he was another grandfather.

"Maddie, you'll be pleased to know both Jacob and your gran behaved themselves at the rehearsal."

Before she could introduce Brad to Hiram, Jacob exploded into the kitchen and launched himself at his father. "Daddy, Daddy, Daddy!" The hundred-decibel squeal shook her eardrums.

Brad scooped him up. Their son's arms wrapped tight around his father's neck.

Her hands clenched as she suppressed a sharp stab of jealousy. Of course Jacob was pleased to see him. This wasn't a parenting popularity contest.

Even if it felt that way.

When Brad touched Jacob's blond hair, his hand shook a little. "I'm so glad to see my little guy again! Though not so little now. You must've grown six inches and gained six pounds since I saw you in the fall."

Something uncertain yet proud in Brad's voice hit her hard. Maybe he really *had* changed.

"Daddy, now you're here, this will be the best Christmas ever!" Jacob's excitement accentuated his lisp. Christmas, adorably, came out as Cwithmath.

Something yearning and strong haunted Brad's face for a moment, and her heart compressed. She'd wanted him to prove he valued Jacob more than work, for once. Wanted him to give their son the gift the boy craved most. The gift Jacob deserved.

His father's time.

Not a fraction of Brad's attention while he fielded business phone calls and emails. Not promises he'd be home by bedtime, always broken.

And now, he was doing it. Here, away from work, with his son.

Thank You, Lord!

But even as silent thanksgiving echoed through her, anxiety niggled. Jacob would miss Brad when he left. Ten days together, then long months without his father.

Gran hurried into the room. "Brad! It's good to see you again after all these years. You should have visited sooner. Now you know I want you to call me Liz. None of your Mrs. Calder nonsense." Her wide grin up at him belied her scolding tone. Barely five foot tall, her tiny frame held a heart as big as Idaho. She turned to Hiram. "This is Maddie's Brad. You and Lucille were away last time he was here, so you didn't meet him."

"Not *my* Brad." Maddie couldn't stop the words escaping her. "He's my ex-husband," she explained. "Jacob's father. Though you probably already guessed that." She forced a chuckle.

Gran pouted. "Oh, I know you're divorced, but that's man's law, not God's. In my eyes, you'll always be married. I wish you two would kiss and make up."

And I wish you'd stop treating our divorce as some childish spat, easily fixed with an apology and a kiss. Maddie tightened her lips to hold back the words. Taking a deep breath then letting it go, she forced her tense muscles to loosen and prayed for calm.

"The coffee is fresh. I'll pour some for us all. There's gingerbread, too." She busied herself getting out mugs, pouring a cup of diluted juice for Jacob, and arranging cookies on a plate.

"Ah, lovely." Gran sat at the table and released a satisfied sigh. "You know what I say about Christmas. You can never have too many lights on the tree, too much love in the home, or too many cookies." She touched the unopened ribbon-clad parcel and raised an eyebrow at Maddie. "Or too many gifts, either."

"That's something small I picked up for Maddie," Brad said to Gran. "It won't wait till Christmas." He smiled at Jacob, still held tightly in his arms. "I have presents for you, too."

"Why don't you unwrap it for me, Gran?" Maddie lifted the coffee jug, using it as an excuse. Too many times Brad's impersonal gifts left her feeling let down, as if one of his office staff chose, not him. She didn't want to feel that again. Especially now.

As Gran lifted the box, her sharp gaze darted between Maddie and Brad. Maddie didn't even want to imagine what she was thinking. The older woman didn't simply add two and two and get five, like everyone else. Gran could easily make it six and a half.

"It's fragile, so don't shake it!" Brad warned, reaching out to stop her.

Gran's merry laugh rang out. "How did you know I was about to do just that? I like to guess what's inside."

"Sorry to spoil your fun. It's fragile." He smiled as he settled opposite her at the table. "You'll need to open this one to find out."

Maddie poured them each coffee while Gran, excited as a child, pulled off the ribbons and tore through the blue foiled paper to expose a cardboard box. Inside that waited a solid-looking white foam container.

"Oh, the suspense! This is like those Russian dolls." Chuckling, Gran glanced up at Brad. "Don't tell me it's a trick and there's nothing inside."

He shook his head. "I don't play that sort of mean joke. There's something in there. The box is in two parts. Lift the top one off. Carefully!" he added as Gran tugged at it.

She handed the container to Maddie. "You'll have to do it. My old fingers can't manage."

Maddie eyed her. Almost certainly, this was a ploy to ensure she opened Brad's gift. But she couldn't argue, despite the wily sparkle in Gran's eyes. Hands a little unsteady, she picked up the box. Easing the foam sections apart revealed a circular opening, protecting a bunch of sweet peas in soft pastel colors. She gasped and stared at him.

Sweet peas in winter.

Most florists didn't stock the delicate flowers, even in season. A cellophane wrap inside the smoothly curving green ceramic vase held water, so they weren't the least bit wilted.

Lifting them to her face, she inhaled. Something hard and defended in her melted as she breathed in the old-fashioned scent she adored. He'd gone to a lot of trouble to get these flowers to her.

Brad never gave her sweet peas when they were married. He'd always brought home huge long-stemmed bunches of flashy but scentless roses. Each time, she'd tried to appreciate his gesture. But it left her heart untouched. The roses were conventional, expected. As if he'd walked into the florist shop and asked for whatever most women wanted, not considered what *she* wanted.

The sweet peas were different. It couldn't be coincidence he chose these particular flowers or this particular vase.

He must have remembered how much she loved sweet peas. How they'd chatted and laughed while she picked big bunches in Gran's garden, the long hot summer they met, arranging them in a ceramic jug much the same color green. The sweet peas flowered abundantly that year, and their scent held extra sweetness, gently pervading the room they were placed in.

Did he also recall how she'd peeped over the top of the bunch at him, just the way she did now? As her eyes met his warm hazel gaze, her heart had stuttered with a wild ecstatic joy.

Exactly the way it stuttered now.

And it mustn't. She couldn't let herself feel like this for him. Not now.

She set the bouquet on the sink with a clunk. She hadn't known then what a disaster their marriage would be. How much worse it was to be lonely in a marriage than to be alone. How Brad would betray her.

Pain twisted in her gut. No matter how badly she wanted

to believe he'd changed, nothing could change the facts.

Her joy in his thoughtful gift shriveled and died as surely as in a few days the delicate blossoms would also shrivel and die. And as surely as in ten days' time, Brad would be back in the city and out of their lives again.

CHAPTER FOUR

WHAT JUST HAPPENED?

One minute, Maddie seemed delighted with his gift. Their eyes met as she gazed over the pretty blooms, and something real and warm and sweet had passed between them.

Brad wanted to jump up and do a two-handed victory punch in the air. He'd gone to half a dozen florists before he found one with sweet peas, but if he'd finally got it right with her, it was worth it.

Then her expression changed, hardened. She turned away from him to plunk the vase onto the kitchen sink. "Thank you, Brad. I'll freshen the water and think where to put these so they'll last a little longer."

Her thank you held little gladness. Instead, the brittle words carried something bitter. Something hurt.

Staring at her rigid back, he wished Maddie would tell him what she really felt. The real reason she'd divorced him then turned so sour. A man could go nuts trying to figure it out.

Hurting and angry, he hadn't asked why. He'd accepted the divorce, let her have what she wanted. Jacob needed his mom, and if she didn't love him anymore, what was the point contesting it? Getting those divorce papers told him they had nothing worth fighting to save.

Now, he knew better.

If they were to have a chance of becoming a family again, he had to understand her reasons. Even though creating peace and goodwill between the hospital's doctors and insurers would be an easier challenge. Or convincing his dad healthcare management was a worthy career choice.

Still, he had to try with Maddie. And then do what he could to fix things.

"The florist said keeping them cool would help them last longer," he offered. "Maybe a windowsill?"

"You said you had presents for me, too, Daddy!" Bright eagerness shone in their son's face.

At least Jacob, he could probably please. Brad swallowed hard, but the pressure on his throat didn't shift. It was surely only Jacob's stranglehold on his neck choking him, not a lump of emotion as solid and indigestible as raw steak.

Lifting the boy higher loosened his tight grip. Brad reached out to ruffle baby-fine blond curls, just like his in photos at that age, before they darkened to brown. His fingertips felt clumsy and rough against that silky smoothness. Awkward protectiveness swelled in him, filling his lungs till he could hardly breathe.

Lord, please show me how to be a good father to my son. And a good husband to Maddie, if she'll let me.

Liz waggled a finger at the boy. "Jacob, it's not polite to ask. You have to wait until you're offered."

"But this is *Daddy*. He always brings me presents. And he said." That raised a chuckle from everyone, even Maddie.

Brad grinned. "I did say I had presents." He glanced at Maddie as he spoke, gauging her response. "Maybe I could give you one now, if your mom agrees. There's the one I left in the back of the SUV."

She nodded, though her brow creased. "One now would be fine."

"Presents!" Grinning, Jacob punched his hands in the air.

Maddie lifted a warning finger. "Only one. The rest have to wait till Christmas."

"I'll go get it." Brad lowered Jacob to the floor, but the boy clung to him.

"Take me too."

Maddie shook her head. "No. You'd need to put all your cold-weather clothes back on to go outside. Coat, hat, gloves, boots."

Jacob pouted, lips pursing and then opening, ready to argue back. Maddie sighed, and her shoulders sagged.

Brad crouched to Jacob's level. "You need to do what your mom says. I'll be back with your present before you get halfway done with all that."

Maddie shot him a grateful smile, full of way-too-obvious surprise he'd backed her up.

As he quickly pulled on his boots and coat in the hall, another realization smacked him hard. Had he unintentionally undermined Maddie's mothering? She'd done the discipline, while he'd spent his time with Jacob having fun. Making up for seeing so little of the boy. She must have felt she had two kids to deal with, sometimes.

Out in the driveway, the icy wind bit through his thin down coat. He took barely more than a minute getting Jacob's gift from the back of the SUV. Even so, by the time he ducked back into the house with the package in his arms, Jacob waited in the hall, dancing with impatience.

"That's for me?" The kid's eyes widened at the size of the parcel. How the toy store in Spokane had paper big enough to wrap it, Brad had no idea. But he'd wanted to make Jacob happy with his gift, and as soon as he saw it, he knew it was the thing.

He hoped.

"It is." He grinned at Jacob's excitement. "Want me to carry it into the kitchen so everyone can see you open it?"

"I can carry it." Jacob's arms spread wide, and he struggled to half-carry half-drag the gift. Stifling another grin, Brad held the door open for him.

It shamed him to admit he didn't know for sure whether Jacob would like what he'd bought. Busy with work, he'd seen way less of them than he wanted back in August when he'd paid for Maddie and Jacob to fly to L.A. for the boy's birthday. They spoke weekly via Skype, but four-year-olds weren't the best for phone conversation. It wasn't really being part of his son's life.

Truth was, even when they'd lived together as a family, Jacob's Sunday school teacher probably knew as much about his son as he did. Those years after Jacob's birth had been grueling. Establishing himself at work, as well as doing his MBA evenings and weekends.

This trip to the lake for Christmas was a chance to change that. Though it risked his promotion, maybe Maddie had been right insisting he come here. Even right insisting he stay till New Year's Day.

In the kitchen, Hiram and Liz oohed and ahhed at the size of the package. Maddie's lips tightened a little, the same way they'd done when she'd seen the parcel filling the back seat. Impossible to guess what she was thinking.

Maybe if he could, they wouldn't be in this mess, living over a thousand miles apart.

Jacob tore into the wrapping, and then squealed when he saw the huge, blue soft toy. "It's an elephant! Like the one at the zoo. Can I really have him now?" He looked to Maddie for permission.

She nodded, and Jacob ran over to hug Brad. "Thank you, Daddy. He's the bestest present ever ever ever."

Her glued-on smile bent out of shape. Brad gave her an apologetic shrug. It wasn't like they were competing for Jacob's love.

Or at least, he hadn't consciously intended it that way.

Jacob grabbed the toy, towering over him by twelve inches and three times as wide, and hugged it tight. "His name is Trunkie. He can sleep on my bed with me."

Maddie surprised Brad with a sudden laugh, sweet and merry as bells. The genuine smile she gave Jacob warmed her eyes. "I'm not sure you and Trunkie will both fit in the same bed. He's a lot of elephant."

"Maybe he can stand beside your bed and watch over you

while you sleep?" Brad suggested.

"Yes. That too." Jacob gazed up at him. "Daddy, I wish we lived with you all the time."

A hard knot tightened in Brad's chest, and he swallowed. There wasn't a trace of blame or recrimination in Jacob's voice or in his glowing face, but he felt it anyway.

He'd hoped the outcome of this trip would be exactly what Jacob asked for. Remarrying Maddie, being together as a family wherever he was working. Now, with her grandmother's health complicating things as much as Maddie's attitude, he couldn't see an answer.

All he could do was trust God had a plan.

Lord, help me to be a better father than mine ever was. I haven't done too good a job so far. I don't deserve that the kid loves me so much.

Glancing at Maddie, he chose his words with care. "I want to be with you all the time, too, Jacob. But I have to work, and that means I need to be in the city. I'll be here with you for a whole ten days, and I'll see you as often as I can next year."

Though how often that would be if he got the promotion, he couldn't guess.

Before Maddie said anything, the phone rang, and she answered it. Maddie mostly listened and spoke very little, but her worried expression and her dejected slump into a chair suggested whatever the caller said wasn't good news.

"Uh huh… uh huh… Oh, I'm so sorry to hear that.… No, of course, I don't mind. I'll come over straight away."

She hung up the phone, shaking her head as she loosed a sigh. Tears gleamed in her eyes, and she rubbed a hand across her face. "That was Pat. Their daughter's at the hospital, with pregnancy complications. He and Susanna need to go to Coeur d'Alene to care for the other children. He's asked if I'll look after the store for them."

Brad knew who Maddie meant. The fifty-something couple who took over the store after Maddie's pop died. He and Maddie spent hours there that summer, chatting over ice creams and sodas.

Liz's face crumpled. "Oh no. It's far too early. She's what, six months? We need to pray for them."

Hiram took her hand, bent his head, and began to pray out loud for the family. Surprised, Brad closed his eyes and joined them.

As Hiram's resonant voice filled the room, asking God's care for the family and for the unborn baby, Brad felt a deeper sense of peace. God's presence right there with them. He wasn't used to being around people who prayed just like that, but the impromptu prayer was so right and so natural. When two or more are gathered…

The outcome was in God's hands, and they could trust His will would be done.

After Hiram ended, Liz and Maddie both looked more comforted, though Liz still clung to the older man's hand.

Maddie raised her head to Brad, face creased in apology. "I'm sorry. You've only just arrived, and I need to go. There's really no one else who can take over there." She grimaced. "It could mean I'll be working there the whole time you're here."

"Pete and I used to *own* the store, not just work in it. I want to help out, so you two have some time together." Liz stubbornly tipped her chin as if daring Maddie to argue.

Maddie replied with a smile, though an edge of sorrow loosened it. "That was ten years ago, Gran. Anyway, I'll need you here to help with Jacob."

Ouch. Brad hoped that was a ploy to keep her gran safely home, and not a dig at his parenting ability.

"I planned to sit and visit with your gran for a while, Maddie," Hiram said. Brad didn't miss the hint of a wink he flickered her. Reassurance he'd be there for Liz, if needed? "You and Brad could both go to the store."

Brad shot the older man an assessing glance. Was Hiram creating an excuse for them to spend more time with each other?

"What a good idea," Liz chimed in with a sunny smile.

"You could be there together while I watch Jacob. Knowing there's backup would comfort Pat and Susanna. I have Hiram right next door if I need anything. These winter days, the store closes early. You'd be home hours before Jacob's bedtime and still have plenty of time with him."

The tight smile narrowing Maddie's lips confirmed his suspicion. They were being railroaded.

Not that he minded.

He needed all the help he could get.

CHAPTER FIVE

MORE MATCHMAKING. Just what Maddie needed.

With Hiram aiding and abetting Gran's scheme to push her and Brad together, avoiding the man would be a bigger challenge than she thought. There'd been a mischievous twinkle in Gran's eyes ever since she heard he'd agreed to come for Christmas. Maddie warned her not to even think of it.

Their marriage was well and truly over.

So her suspicion had been correct. So what? Gran would realize soon enough she was wasting her time. After Christmas, Brad would go back to his big-city, high-flying life, chasing his latest promotion or his latest blonde, and leave her and Jacob behind at Sunset Point.

Exactly where she intended to stay.

She'd lost herself once before, when she left to marry Brad after one summer of shining romance. Then she discovered their married life had as little substance as the shimmer of moonlight on the lake.

Much as she wanted to, she couldn't spend time arguing. Pat and Susanna needed to get on the road.

"Okay," she said. "See you later, li'l guy." She bent to kiss Jacob, perched on Trunkie's broad back chattering away to the elephant in some unintelligible language only Jacob and his toy understood. She doubted he'd miss her. Typical of Brad to give such a huge gift.

She could one-up him though, come Christmas Day. The

local carpenter had refurbished Gran's vintage sled, and it hid under her bed, packaged up in five rolls of gift wrap.

Gran followed them out to the hall as they bundled into their cold-weather gear. She picked up the edge of Brad's black down coat and squeezed it critically. "Your coat might be fine for Southern California, but it won't cut much ice out here." Diving to the back of the closet, she pulled out a different coat and handed it to him. "Wear this instead. It's a proper man's coat for these parts."

As Maddie saw the heavy red-checkered wool and the thick padded shearling lining, her fists involuntarily clenched. "No, Gran! Not Pop's lumber jacket. You can't let Brad wear it."

Gran pursed her mouth and raised her hands to her hips. "Maddie Calder Hughes, I hoped your pop and I raised you to have a heart with more Christian charity than that! Pete hasn't needed his coat for a long time now. He'd want your husband to have it."

Maddie bristled. She did have charity. For everyone but Brad. "He's not my husband." Even as she spoke the words, she knew how childish they must sound.

"And you know what I think about that." With a quick headshake sending salt-and-pepper curls bouncing, Gran straightened to her full four foot eleven and poked a finger at Maddie's chest. "I'm sorry you coming up here to help me when I was ill separated you two. I feel so responsible."

Maddie huffed, narrowly avoiding an eye roll. "*You* aren't responsible."

She didn't add the words, *Brad is*. Gran didn't understand. How could she? Her marriage had been so different. She and Pop had been true partners, in everything.

Concern creasing his brow, Brad broke in. "Don't blame yourself, Liz. Maddie did the right thing, looking after you. If our marriage had been stronger, a couple of months apart wouldn't have made any difference."

He had that much right.

The glance she threw Gran begged her to drop the topic. As much so she could escape the uncomfortable prickle of her conscience, suggesting she'd been equally responsible, as to get going to the store.

Gran ignored her unspoken message, turning to Brad instead. "Humor an old lady. At least wear Pete's jacket this once. Then you can decide whether your smart city coat is better."

Brad shook his head, giving Maddie a rueful smile, just genuine enough to melt her resolve all over again. "I don't aim to upset Maddie. If the coat holds special memories of her grandfather, I can understand seeing me wearing it would be hard. Besides, city slicker though I am, my coat will be good enough for the ten days I'll be here."

He chuckled, and his dimple flashed. He gave every appearance of warmth and liking for the older woman. Or was it just the almost-irresistible Bradley Hughes charm at work?

If only she could be less cynical about his motives. But it was hard not to be.

Finally, they escaped Gran's good intentions and got out the door. The snow piled on the sidewalk hindered her frustrated stomp as she headed off, past snowmen in yards, and clapboard houses decorated for the holidays. Brad made a move that might have been to hold her hand, but she pulled hers out of reach.

"Not much has changed," he observed, his words puffing steam into the cold air.

Maddie wasn't in the mood for small talk, but she couldn't be impolite, either. "There are a few new houses, further around the bay. But thankfully, Huckleberry Lake hasn't been 'discovered' yet. I like how things here have stayed the same."

They turned onto Main Street, and a gust of wind fresh off the frozen lake whipped her coat and hair.

Brad crossed his arms and gave an exaggerated shiver. "Maybe your gran was right about offering me your pop's coat."

"I don't want you wearing it." Hurt constricted her throat. Pop had been everything Brad wasn't. Honest, faithful, there for his family.

"Maddie, I wish I knew what I did to upset you so badly. I never meant to, I promise you." Confusion deepened Brad's low voice and shadowed his gaze.

Her churned-up emotions boiled over in a sound that was almost a growl. "So many things. But for now, I want the answer to just one. Did you fly to London this spring trying to get Zoe back, or not?"

An ugly, strident note sharpened her voice, but she didn't care. Impressing Brad scored zero in her priorities. She'd only been in love once in her life. But as soon as he had the divorce papers, he'd run back to his first love. And he'd contacted Zoe long before that.

Brad's cheeks reddened, and his shoulders tensed, but he didn't avoid her angry stare. His eyes stayed fixed on her, tempting her to duck her head instead. With every ounce of her resolve, she lifted her chin and met his steady regard.

He nodded slowly. "Yes, I did. I'm sorry." His hands reached toward her in entreaty and apology.

Hot tears stung her eyes, and she accelerated her pace. All she wanted was to get away from him as far and as fast as she could. So it *was* true. She'd hoped it was gossip, with no basis in fact, despite the details Louise gave. Her heart weighed heavy, a dark frozen boulder in her chest, icy as the winter lake.

Brad caught up with her, grabbed her arm. "I went a little crazy when the divorce came through. I wasn't thinking straight." His jaw flexed, and a muscle twitched in his cheek. "I've always been the golden boy, the one who got everything I wanted. From Christmas presents to girlfriends to promotions. But I couldn't have you."

"No. You couldn't then, and you can't now." She yanked her arm away.

"I felt like I'd lost everything when I lost you and Jacob. Everything." Passion and sincerity vibrated in Brad's low voice. "Crazy, I know, but I felt if Zoe still loved me, I'd have something." A humorless smile twisted his face. "Second best, but something."

Her mouth tightened. "That is such a lie. The whole time we were together, *I* was the one feeling second best. You broke off things with Zoe within a week of us meeting and then asked me to marry you. I always questioned whether you regretted that hasty decision."

He shook his head. "Never."

"You truly never wondered 'What if?' I know you emailed her, stayed in contact." She swallowed, choking back tears. "I didn't want to be jealous. I tried to trust you. But then you went to her the moment you were free. If she hadn't sent you away…" Biting her lip, she trailed off.

Something in his reaction almost broke her heart. The droop of his broad shoulders. The remorse shining in his clear hazel eyes. The downward turn of his lips. Such deep sorrow.

If this was an act, he deserved an Oscar.

"I can see how falling in love with you while I was as good as engaged to another girl wasn't the best way to convince you I'd be faithful. But from the day we met, it was always you. It's only ever been you."

She shook her head again. "How can I believe that?"

Brad sighed. "I made a stupid mistake. I *did* run to Zoe, and I thank God every day that she was wise enough to send me away." Wry humor curved his lips. "Easy to see why. I spent the whole time I was with her talking about you and Jacob. I showed her all the pictures of you on my phone. She saw straight away I still loved you."

Maddie wanted so badly to trust he was telling the truth. But it wasn't just Zoe.

Straightening her spine, she stiffened her determination, too. "So Zoe sent you away. And then you moved on to

Louise. How many more women turned you down before you came back to me?"

His puzzlement looked every bit as real as his regret had. "Louise? What's she got to do with anything?" He held out his hands, palms uplifted. "I've seen her exactly once in the last year."

"That's the problem. What happened that once. And other times, before that."

He looked down, and sucked in a slow breath, brow creased. She had him now.

So why instead of feeling triumphant did she feel miserable?

Brad raised his head. "I have no idea how you know about it, but I've done nothing I need to feel ashamed of."

Antagonism rose in her, hot and sudden — overwhelming. "Right, so you didn't invite her to your apartment, give her alcohol, and then make a pass at her? If you see nothing to be ashamed of in that, your morals are shakier than I guessed." She almost spat the words.

His jaw set and his eyes darkened, became hard as stones. "Is that what Louise told you? And you trust me so little you believed her?" His gloved fists clenched. "It was the other way around. She turned up uninvited, and she'd been drinking. More fool me, I let her in. Then she got nasty when I wouldn't play. You have to make your mind up who you want to believe, her or me."

Maddie stopped walking and stared at him. How could he look and sound so sincere? Her stomach swirled uncertainly. Soft, troubled words slipped out with the vapor of her breath. "Why would she lie to me?"

The question hung between them, almost visible.

"I told her I loved you. How going to Zoe helped me realize my marriage vows were for life. I guess causing trouble with you was her payback." His lip curled. "Or maybe she hoped if she could stop you considering a reconciliation, she still had a chance. She hinted once or twice while we were still married that if I wanted an affair, she was available."

"No." Pain twisted Maddie. Had she really got it so wrong?

Brad's eyes met hers, clear and transparent as the lake shallows in summer. "Was it her who told you I'd flown to London, too?"

Wordless, she nodded, biting her lip. It all made a kind of horrible, crazy sense. Brad's old classmate, Louise, had seemed her only friend in L.A. But Louise subtly poisoned her trust, and encouraged the divorce, too. She twisted the toe of her boot in the snow. "I'm sorry. I guess because I was already angry with you, I *wanted* to listen to her lies. I was wrong." Her admission choked out, small and quiet, and lingered there.

Brad took her arm, and this time, she didn't pull away. "I'm sorry too, Maddie. Sorry I didn't do a better job of showing you I loved you. If I had, you might not have fallen for her lies. I see how you might not have felt able to trust me, or believe our love would last." He barked a short laugh, edged with regret. "It took Zoe to tell me that. I never realized...."

"Okay, now I believe you *did* spend all your time talking about me." She laughed shakily. "I was always that bit jealous of Zoe, that you loved her first. She's pretty and smart, and I'm—" She broke off to wave her free hand up and down herself. "I'm just me."

"Yes. You *are* just you. That's why I fell in love with you. That's why I *still* love you." He drew her closer. Despite the snow, his nearness sent a surge of warmth along her skin and stole her breath. Her head tilted back, as she gazed into his darkening eyes.

The week they met, he'd almost kissed her, right here on this corner. And now she felt eighteen again. Felt the same tremulous anticipation. The same dancing heartbeat. The same hope their fairy-tale romance would end with "happily ever after".

But knowing the truth about Zoe and Louise didn't change

anything else. The lives they lived were just too different. Nothing could change the things that pulled them in opposite directions.

Yet still, her eyelids fluttered closed, waiting for his kiss.

CHAPTER SIX

INTENSE LONGING TO LOWER his head and kiss Maddie's sweetly parted lips swept Brad.

There were so many sensible, logical reasons he should let her go. He'd rushed her too much already. They'd freeze if they stood here much longer. They needed to get to the store ASAP.

But still, he lingered, holding her close as the silent moment stretched and her eyelashes trembled on her cheeks.

Awareness hung in the air between them. Did the same unforgettable memories crowd her mind?

He knew in this instant, she'd willingly let him kiss her. But how would she feel about it later? Taking advantage of her vulnerability wouldn't change the huge gap of trust and faith between them they still needed to bridge. Let alone all the other things keeping them apart.

Somehow, he found the will to let her go and step back.

Maddie's eyes flew open, reflecting the sense of loss he felt. Saying nothing, she looked away, out to the lake, obscuring her face.

"We'd better get to the store." Raw emotion roughened his voice.

So much for trying to play it cool. But he didn't want to hide how he felt from Maddie, not after she'd opened up and told him more than she ever had. As they started to walk again, he took her hand.

Even through two pairs of thick gloves, he felt her hand

shake.

"Yes." The same quiver shook her single word.

He clasped her hand more firmly. "Maddie, thank you for talking about things that bothered you. I'm grateful you did."

She'd thrown a mountain of accusations at him, and he'd battled an instinctive urge to go on the defense, fight back against her unfairness. But though she challenged him, he preferred this more assertive Maddie. She'd spoken so little during the final years of their marriage. Better to know where he stood, than have to guess what he'd done wrong.

And then it seemed he'd gotten that wrong, too.

Her quiet stillness had been one of the things that attracted him, tranquil and deep as the lake. Only with the divorce had he realized the depth of unhappiness her silence hid.

"Talking about these things feels strange. When we were married, I didn't want Jacob to hear us argue, I worried it would upset him. And I always thought letting you know I was angry would scare you off." Raising her eyes to his again, she gave a laugh and a wobbly smile. "Doesn't seem to have worked."

She'd been honest, and he owed her the same honesty in return. He smiled. "It won't. I've done some growing up this past eight months. We *need* to talk about this stuff. We both want to be good parents for Jacob, without disagreeing all the time. So we have to resolve the problems that split us up. Even if it's scary and tough to talk about."

He wanted more than just being Jacob's Mom and Dad. He wanted her as his wife again, for the rest of their lives. But now wasn't the time to push.

Maddie sucked in an audible breath. "Okay."

Soft and uncertain, but she said it.

That single word surprised him so much, he nearly toppled into a snowdrift and pulled her with him. As he straightened, a grin cracked his face. Sounded like she'd agreed to try. Or at least, to discuss their issues, something she'd refused to do before. Far from agreeing to come back to him, but a big step forward.

Thank You, Lord!

Winning Maddie's love again meant honoring his marriage commitment. Acting like an adult, not a spoiled kid. Being willing to wait for what was important. Opening his heart and mind to following God's will.

God had ways of telling him that. Like when he'd looked into the blue eyes of his waitress at the lakeside restaurant all those years ago, and knew he'd found the woman God intended for him.

He couldn't push her into loving him again. Maybe, for her, their marriage had problems beyond fixing. But he *could* go all-out to give them the best chance possible.

Maddie accelerated her pace. "Here's the store." The relieved "Phew!" she didn't add out loud echoed in her tone.

He studied the building she'd grown up in. The first time they came here, she'd enthused about the history of the store, opened by her great-great-grandfather in 1906. Relic of the days Sunset Point was intended as the railhead for a westbound line that ended up diverting, the big two-floor clapboard structure now seemed way too large for the size of the town.

It hadn't changed much. A new cream-colored paint job and masses of Christmas lights replaced summer's hanging flower baskets and the softly yellowed paint he recalled. As they pushed through the wide double doors to the store's welcome warmth, a bell jangled overhead. It didn't look much different inside, either. Crowded to the rafters with backwoods necessities like snowshoes, paraffin lamps, hand tools, and fishing and hunting gear, half the stock looked as if it could have been there over a hundred years.

The grocery section had changed some. The fresh-bake bread machine was new. A mouthwatering odor from the morning's baking persisted. The ice-cream stand he remembered still stood in one corner.

A traditional Christmas carol played softly. His favorite,

"Silent Night". *All is calm, all is bright*.... He wasn't too sure about the calm. Maddie's worried expression looked anything but, biting her lip as she glanced around the store. A tall stack of unopened boxes suggested a recent delivery hadn't been packed away.

The bright part, they had. Apparently, they followed Liz's rule on Christmas lights — you can never have too many. Twinkling strands hung everywhere. He blinked at the tinsel and bauble overdose filling one corner. The heavily decorated backdrop to the Christmas goods section glittered and shone in purple and blue.

Not that he cared how it looked or sounded. They were here to help Maddie's friends.

A door at the back of the store marked Private opened, and a gray-haired man peered out. This must be Pat, though his worry-lined face appeared far older than the active enthusiastic man Brad remembered.

"Praise the Lord! It's Maddie," he called behind him. He hurried into the store, letting the door to the private quarters swing closed. "Susanna's nearly done with packing. I'll go through a few things with you and give you the keys. Then we'll get on the road. I can't tell you how grateful we are to you." He shook his head and sighed. "The one time we can't lock the door and hang out a Closed sign. The Christmas turkeys were just delivered, and then there's the carol singing tonight. We've been so concerned about Ruth...we haven't even started preparations. I hate leaving you to deal with all this."

Maddie hugged him. "Pat, you know I love being back in the store. It's like home to me. I'll help here for as long as you need."

Rather than easing, Pat's frown intensified. He shook his head. "I don't know how long it will be before we'll make it back. If the doctors can't bring Ruth's blood pressure down, she'll need a C-section. But the baby will be too small for Kootenai Health's preemie unit to manage. They're talking about transferring her to Spokane."

"You and Susanna must take as long as you need. Please don't worry about the store." Soft compassion made Maddie's lovely face even more beautiful. "You've lived in Sunset Point long enough to know what people are like. I won't be able to keep Gran away. And half the town will offer to help once news gets out." She grabbed Brad's arm, drawing him into the conversation. "You've met Brad Hughes, my husband. He's here till the New Year, so that's another set of hands."

Something warm and sweet swelled in Brad's chest at hearing her call him "husband", for all he knew it was only to reassure Pat.

Pat nodded welcome, and then switched to rattling through store logistics with Maddie. Grabbing a pen and paper, Brad took notes. Maddie might remember all this, but he wouldn't.

So he had an MBA. Retail was a whole other world.

By the time Susanna emerged from the rear of the store, her hair still colored the same unlikely dark red he recalled, his brain was stuffed full. Running a store seemed every bit as complex and challenging as running a hospital, though on a smaller scale. At least no one died if you got it wrong. He hoped.

Susanna smiled gratefully at them both, though anxiety creased her face. "Thank you so much, Maddie. And you must be Brad." Taking her husband's hand, she tugged him away. "Pat, we're all packed. I'm sure you've covered the essentials. You can email Maddie anything you forgot. Or call her."

Maddie's hand wave exuded reassuring confidence. "I have your contact details. Trust me, I'll be in touch if I have any questions. You need to let the store go now."

Pat nodded, his face clearing. "Right. It's in God's hands, like everything else. Don't feel you need to keep regular opening hours. Even a few hours a day will let folk get the essentials. And you could cancel the carol singing if you have to."

Maddie laughed. "You're kidding. Gran and Jacob would never forgive me. They've been looking forward to it for weeks. Go to Ruth. We'll manage." Maddie hugged them both, and then gave Pat a gentle shove toward the door.

He needed no more encouragement. Within minutes, Brad and Maddie stood on the store's wide porch, under the overhanging balcony, waving the older couple goodbye.

Maddie kept her smile pinned in place until their pickup rumbled out of sight. Then she slumped against the wall, shaking her head. "Hoo boy. I hope I can do this. We're probably talking weeks, not days here. Maybe even months, especially if the baby has to go out-of-state. Ruth's a new widow, her husband died in the fall, so there's no one else to care for their other kids."

Months. Brad gulped. His hopes of Maddie giving their marriage another chance plummeted to the worn timber floorboards beneath his feet.

Then he manned up. Those concerns had no place here. Maddie was worth waiting for, no matter how long it took. His job now was to support her. "We'll pray for them. And like you said, once everyone knows what's happened, you'll get help."

Clasping Maddie's arm, he led her into the store, out of the cold. A native Californian, "Let It Snow" wasn't in his vocabulary. Even at Christmas. The Chicago promotion he hoped for had just two drawbacks. Distance from Maddie and Jacob, and winter.

Maddie shucked her coat and hung it beside his on the hook inside the door. "True. This is Huckleberry Lake, not L.A. People *do* help." She smiled. "And this time of year, it shouldn't be too busy once we get through Christmas. No tourists or summer people to deal with."

She probably hadn't intended the slur on his hometown, but it stung.

"Were you really so unhappy there?"

"Where?" She glanced up from logging onto the computerized till, her surprised question showing no awareness of what she'd said.

"L.A."

Crinkling her nose, she nodded reluctantly. "I'm just not a city person. It's too rushed and busy for me. All people seemed to care about were looks and possessions and money. Even in church, I never had a sense of community, like I do here."

"There's community." His protest emerged automatically. Then he stopped to think, rubbing the back of his neck. Was there?

The church she'd attended near their condo, the one he'd gone to occasionally when he wasn't too busy, didn't do any outreach to the needy. People were quick to say they'd pray, but few did anything real and practical to help. "Okay. You're right. Our neighborhood and that church weren't the best examples. But not everywhere in the city is like that. The church I go to now is different."

Maddie looked up, and her lips twisted. "Maybe. But I'm not sure I'm willing to take the chance and go back. Jacob is happier here, and so am I."

He searched for an argument to convince her, but before he found one, his cell phone rang. He hadn't known if his network had signal here. The number on caller display made him almost wish it hadn't.

His boss.

Reminding Maddie that his life and his career were in the city might not be the best thing right now. But he couldn't afford not to answer. Taking time off already risked the promotion he'd worked hard for.

It was about providing for his family, giving them a better future. Surely Maddie could see that.

He picked up the call.

CHAPTER SEVEN

MADDIE'S JAW CLENCHED and her hand tightened on the computer mouse. Brad's phone conversation clearly involved his job.

Forcing her tense shoulders to loosen, she tried to concentrate on matching the items on Pat's scribbled list with the online grocery order form he said *must* go in by tomorrow. Get this wrong, and the store could run out of essentials before New Year's Day.

It didn't help. The screen blurred, and her fingers slipped on the keys. All she could hear was Brad's voice. This was it. Once work called, he'd be gone.

"No, I'm out of town all next week.... I'm aware of that.... Yes, I do have my laptop with me.... How urgent is it?... Okay, send me the paperwork, and I'll see what I can do."

She'd heard this so often. What came next would be him disappearing behind his laptop screen to spend hours working when he was supposed to be on vacation. Ignoring her, and worse, ignoring Jacob.

Just like he had when they were married. And whenever they'd visited him since.

No matter how many times she told herself she was being selfish and childish and any other -ish she could find to call herself, she hated how his career meant so much more to him than his family. When he had to decide, he'd always chosen work.

Despite his talk about having changed, he'd probably *still* choose work.

"I'm busy right now. But I'll download the files you send me when I can, and once I've reviewed them, I'll get back to you." He ended the call.

Maddie looked up from the screen and tried to smile. Tried to keep her resentment from cooling her voice. "The office?"

He nodded as he slid the phone back in his pocket. "Hospitals don't close for the holidays, unfortunately. An issue has come up on something I've been dealing with. I'm sorry. I know you'd rather I put work aside while I'm here. But my job isn't like that."

His clear gaze and downturned lips seemed truly regretful. She needed to give him a chance. He'd told them he was busy, hadn't run straight back to his computer. That was a first. Could be, he *was* trying to do things differently. But still…

"I know you need to work. I appreciate how you're a good provider. Thank you for that." She chose her words carefully. "But isn't there some way to find a balance, instead of your job being the most important thing in your life?"

He raised his head and met her gaze with clear, steady eyes. "It's not. You and Jacob were always more important. And now God is, too."

Anguish surged through her like a river flooded with spring runoff. "It didn't feel like we were more important when we were married. When you didn't come to visit us here, I felt like you didn't care. And when you cut short your paternity leave after Jacob was born…"

"I had to. The big project at work…." Brad trailed off, as if he realized that excuse wouldn't cut it.

Her hand rose to cover her mouth as she gulped back painful tears. "I know. But you had no idea how I felt. In a city where I knew no one, alone with a new baby, C-section wound hurting, hormones going crazy, and you — gone up to sixteen hours a day. Then when I said I needed help, you hired a cleaner. I think I cried as much as Jacob did the first few weeks home from the hospital."

"I'm sorry. I should have been there for you." He left the stacked boxes and moved to her side, cupping a gentle hand over hers. His strong arm slipped around her, offering solace and support.

Somehow, she forced words through her constricted throat. "I felt so selfish wanting you home more. You were working hard, I know."

"Yes. But I should have heard what you were trying to tell me." The arm holding her tensed. "I wanted to look after you and Jacob, and it felt like the best way to do it was to concentrate on earning more. So that's what I did."

She shook her head. "I thought you didn't want to be with us. I even worried you'd found someone else, you were away from home so much."

"It wasn't that at all."

Brad's sincerity melted her. She relaxed against him, resting her cheek against his shoulder, allowing herself to draw comfort from his embrace. The pain seeped away little-by-little, and her tense muscles softened. As the air escaped her burning lungs, she breathed in Brad's clean fresh smell.

"Maybe if I'd said more, tried harder to get you to understand what I needed from you, we could have worked things out." She released a shaky chuckle. "All this — the drama and tears — is so not like me. It's as if the lid has come off everything I bottled up. I don't know why. You being back here in Huckleberry Lake again, where it all started?"

Brad laughed, low and soft. "Could be. Everywhere here is full of first-time memories. Reminding me how it felt to fall in love with you." His chin bumped the top of her head, his words ruffling her hair.

"Me too," she confessed.

His arm tightened around her. "Or maybe it's God, working in our lives. Even if we can't be together again, what went wrong between us needs to be healed. Seems I made a mess of being a husband, but I can at least be a good ex-husband."

Regret twisted through her. If only he'd been there for her like this then. When Jacob was born. When Gran had her stroke. All the other times she'd needed him. Everything would have been so different. They might still be married.

But he hadn't, and it was too late now. Her life was here with Gran and Jacob, and Brad was Chicago-bound.

They could never be husband and wife again, but as Jacob's parents, they'd always need to see each other. Brad *had* changed. Become more solid, more compassionate, more committed, more willing to be honest. More the man she'd thought she was marrying. Maybe with God's help, they *could* heal their hurts, find a way to be friends.

"And I'll try to be a better ex-wife." She drew away from him and smiled truce. "Less bitter and twisted and angry."

"Deal." Releasing his clasp, he held out a hand.

She gave his hand a firm, decisive shake, as if they were sealing a business arrangement. "Deal." Good. They'd simply be colleagues in the job of parenting their son, not competitors.

So why did it feel like she was agreeing to so much more?

Quickly letting his hand go, she stepped away. "We need to get to work. There's a lot to do. All those turkeys to get in the cooler, and then matched up with the folks who ordered them, for starters." Her attempt at a businesslike tone didn't quite succeed. Certainly not enough to fool Brad.

Lips twisting, he cast a tiny eye roll heavenward. "I'm not going to pretend this conversation didn't happen, Maddie. But okay, now probably isn't the time or place." He nudged the big stack of boxes. "I'm guessing these are the turkeys. Where do they need to go?"

Relief swept her. If they didn't lighten the intensity, they'd never get through the next nine days. "In the back storeroom, the big cooler there." She gripped a box ready to carry it through.

He took it from her. "I'll move them. You just show me where." She showed him, and he easily hefted the box into place.

"Are you sure you don't need to go sort out that work problem?" Not that she wanted him to leave, but Brad had always jumped whenever his boss called.

He smiled his easy smile. "It's not urgent. It can wait till tonight."

So if it *had* been urgent, would he have left her here? She pushed away the unwanted thought that work still came first. He was here now. That was what counted.

While she went back to completing the stock order, he moved the turkeys in half the time it would have taken her.

"So this carol singing Pat mentioned. Is it a community thing?" he called through from the cooler.

"Yes. Everyone comes. It's a big holiday event here. I'm a bit worried about —"

Heavy feet stomped on the porch, and the front door jangled. Ryan Connor's broad frame filled the doorway.

"Maddie! I heard you'd taken over here, for Pat and Susanna. Now, what can I do to help?" He strolled toward her, stopping just a fraction too close. His wide smile gleamed, just a little too happy to see her.

Clearly, he hadn't noticed Brad yet.

"News got around fast. Thanks for coming over, Ryan." Her return smile cramped her cheeks, more forced than she liked. Ryan's growing attraction had become impossible to ignore. The carpenter was everyone's go-to person. Solid, reliable, always there when help was needed.

And a complication she didn't need or want. She had no intention of getting back with Brad. Her divorce papers said she was legally single. But a whisper in her heart reminded her — she was not free.

Life would be so much simpler if she'd fallen in love with a good, kind, straightforward local man like Ryan, back at eighteen.

He grinned. "I brought a load of firewood for the stove. I noticed Pat's woodpile was getting low. Especially with the carols this evening, I figured you'd be busy, and I didn't want you out gathering wood in this cold."

Before she could thank him, Brad stepped out of the storeroom. He smiled his most charming smile, but if he was a dog, his hackles would be raised. Ryan backed away from her, but eyed Brad as if sizing up the competition before a fight.

Lord, please don't let things get difficult here!

Pretending the air wasn't stiff with tension, she made her best introductions. "Ryan Connor, Brad Hughes. Ryan is Sunset Point's Mr. Fix-It. Brad is Jacob's father." She hesitated a moment, then raised her chin and added, "My husband." A gentle way to discourage Ryan.

"Your *ex*-husband," Ryan corrected her.

Brad rested a light but possessive hand on her arm. "My goal is to change that."

Managing to chuckle as if Brad had joked, Maddie closed her eyes, hoping maybe they'd both go away and she'd be left in peace to get the work done. When she opened her eyes, they were still there.

"All I have time to think about now is praying for Ruth, looking after the store, and making sure tonight goes well." She edged sideways, away from both of them.

At this rate, they'd probably end up chasing each other around the counter like some silly sitcom. She didn't want *any* man in her life. So why did she now have two?

The pair stood facing each other. Neither appeared willing to be first to concede.

"I'll unload the firewood for you. Maybe your 'husband' can help." Looking Brad up and down and no doubt assessing him as soft, unused to any physical labor, Ryan laid down the words like a challenge he knew he'd win.

"Sure," Brad responded, grinning with a confidence she prayed wasn't misplaced. "I'll grab some gloves." He picked up a pair of heavy-duty work gloves from the display and waved them at her. "I'll pay for these when I get back in."

Watching him shrug into his cold-weather gear, she hoped he knew what he was letting himself in for. His gym-gained fitness wouldn't necessarily help here. And she should have let him wear Pop's jacket. That expensive down coat might be perfect for a city stroll, but even a quarter cord of firewood would shred it.

Once the two men slammed out the door and their boots pounded on the porch floorboards, she resumed the order forms. The rhythmic thunk of wood hitting wood offered a powerful distraction, especially as the syncopated tempo accelerated. Were they actually competing to see who could outpace the other?

Please keep them from injury, Lord!

Though really, as long as no one pulled a muscle or otherwise hurt themselves because of their one-upmanship, the sooner the job was done, the better. Then maybe they'd call truce and stop bristling at each other like dogs fighting over a bone.

She'd just finished and hit Send on next week's order when soft footsteps padded on the porch. Too quiet to be either of the men. Claire Robinson entered the store, pulling off her hat to uncover her mane of red hair.

"Hi, Claire." Maddie grinned. There weren't many twenty- or thirty-something women in the small community, so she'd been overjoyed to find a kindred spirit when Claire moved to the lake as the new elementary school teacher.

"Maddie!" Her friend's face lit up, and she threw her arms around Maddie in a warm hug. "I came to collect a recipe from Susanna. I'm trying my hand at huckleberry muffins for tonight, and she told me she had a good recipe. I didn't expect to see you here."

"They had to rush to Coeur d'Alene to be with Ruth. So I'm filling in." She brought up a search box on the computer and typed in one of her favorite baking websites. "I know the recipe she uses. I'll print it off."

"Thanks!" Claire frowned. "I thought you'd be busy today. If you're here, does that mean your rotten so-and-so of an ex didn't turn up after all?"

Laughing, Maddie shook her head. "He's here." She bit her lip. "And I've only been with him a few hours, but I'm starting to wonder if he's way less rotten than I thought. We've cleared a few things up already."

Claire's eyes widened. "Don't tell me that mystery hunk out there stacking wood with Ryan is your ex?"

She nodded.

"Phooey! I hoped he was single." Claire sighed. "He's off-limits now, of course. No matter how much people say it's over, it never *really* is."

Instinctive knowledge jerked through Maddie, smacking her so hard she almost expected to hear the thwack. It was far from over. And not just because of Jacob.

She still loved Brad. She always would.

But she couldn't go back to being his wife.

CHAPTER EIGHT

BRAD RACED TO STACK as much wood as he could carry into the store's woodshed. Logs, ready split for the stove, had solidly packed the back of the carpenter's big pickup.

A *lot* of logs.

But the local guy wasn't going to beat him. Not if he could help it.

He'd seen how the man's gaze lingered on Maddie. Heard the challenge in his voice. No backing down. This was a best-man-win situation. Not to win Maddie, of course, he wasn't that stupid. As they'd marched out the door, her almost-scowl suggested she wouldn't have either of them.

Though it hurt to admit it, maybe a guy like Ryan would be better for her in some ways. Someone who could give her the life she wanted, who wouldn't ask her to leave the place and the people she loved. Someone who hadn't done what she'd as good as accused him of, betraying her by being emotionally unfaithful.

She'd nailed him. He *had* wondered "what if" a few times during their marriage.

The contest wasn't for Maddie. This contest was for respect. And not just the other man's respect.

Self-respect.

He'd keep the pace up if it killed him.

By the way his lungs burned and his back ached, it just might. No wonder there were no gyms out in the country. Who needed them?

Finally, they reached the last piece of wood. Grinning, he stretched out his longer arm and beat Ryan Connor to it by inches. It landed on the top of the woodpile with a triumphant clunk.

The burly man eyeballed him, pulling off his gloves and slapping them together in a sawdusty puff. Then he clapped Brad on the shoulder. "For a city guy, you did okay. So if she takes you back, you'd better make sure you treat Maddie right this time."

Nothing grudging about the way he conceded. Not what Brad was used to in business deals, where they smiled to his face but sharpened knives behind his back. He had the sense of being accepted as an equal. It felt good. Satisfying as winning a big contract.

"I intend to." *If she'll have me.*

Not that he'd say it out loud. Only to God.

They strode to the store side by side, stomping the snow and ice off their feet before going in.

Maddie broke off from chatting with a petite red-haired woman, a touch of concern for him in her eyes. Ignoring the way every muscle in his body ached, he poured all the love and reassurance he could into his smile. Something zinged in the air between them, invisible but real and strong.

The breath went out of him. He'd never get used to the jolt of tenderness and longing seeing her gave him. How could he have been stupid enough to imagine he could love another woman? It would always be Maddie for him. If she refused to have him back, he'd stay single.

Small consolation that living alone and being a part-time dad would give him more time to focus on progressing to the top in hospital management. Though at least when he did, maybe he'd finally win his father's respect. Or maybe not. According to Dad, anyone who wasn't a doctor was nothing.

Winning this small battle with Ryan had been easy in comparison.

Maddie's friend didn't wait for introductions. "You must

be Brad. I'm Claire." She eyed him, as if assessing whether he measured up to her expectations for Maddie. Then she grinned and nodded. Seemed he'd passed her test. "Two men at your bidding, Mads! Lucky girl." She picked up a shopping bag and a sheet of paper from the counter. "Now I have the recipe and the ingredients, I'll scoot home to see how I go with these muffins. Mrs. Parks and I will be back later to set up for the nativity play." Pointedly ignoring Ryan, she hurried off, turning at the door to wave to Maddie.

"What do you want us to do now?" Brad asked.

Holding her face in both hands, Maddie looked around and shook her head. "I don't know what should come next. Store stuff, setting up for tonight, there's so much to do. I didn't anticipate getting thrown this today."

Overwhelm seemed imminent.

Store management, he knew nothing about, but project management, he understood. The first thing was to prioritize. Stepping beside her, he pulled out the notes he'd made while Pat talked, and spread them on the counter. "Let's decide what has to be done today and what can wait till tomorrow or next week."

"We can cross that one off. Pat said it was most important, so I did it first." She pointed to the item he'd written in all caps, the online order with the grocery wholesaler. "And the turkeys are in the cooler, so we won't cause a mass outbreak of food poisoning. The rest of the list can wait. All we need to do now is prepare for tonight." Her laugh had a hollow ring, and she rolled her eyes. "*All* we need to do. Prepare to feed and entertain almost every man, woman, and child in the area."

He rested a hand on her arm, intending to offer encouragement. "We can do this. Would you like to take a moment to pray?"

Even though he touched her sweater, not her skin, every contact carried a reminder of a time they'd been more intimate. Her sudden intake of breath and startled glance showed she felt the same warm awareness. He expected she'd pull back, look away, but she didn't. As their eyes connected, sudden knowledge hit him, as strong as an earth tremor, as sure as God's grace.

Maddie still loved him, despite being so unhappy in their marriage she'd divorced him. She. Loved. Him.

Joy flooded every cell of his body. *Thank You, Jesus!*

It didn't mean things would work out. It didn't mean he had any more hope she'd agree to marry him again than he did sixty seconds earlier. But it did mean whatever he'd done wrong, however he'd failed her, he hadn't lost everything.

They stood gazing at each other, in an eternal moment, lifted outside of time.

Ryan noisily cleared his throat, snapping whatever wordlessly connected them with an almost audible twang. If he wasn't leaning against the counter, Brad might have staggered. He released his clasp on Maddie's arm.

"Come on, you two. There's work to do!" Ryan shook his head and huffed, though he smiled.

"Yes. We do." Maddie laughed, a touch shakily. "Give me a moment to pray." After a silent pause, she opened her eyes and smiled. "Okay. I'm fine now."

Brad longed to support and encourage her, with an intensity that surprised him. Maddie had rarely allowed her vulnerability to show. She'd always seemed so self-sufficient and capable, so able to cope. Now, he saw she hadn't wanted to let on she needed help. And he'd been too tied up in his work to think of asking her.

Just as he had, she'd changed since they last met.

"You're doing great. You didn't expect you'd need to do this."

"No, I didn't. My great-grandmother began hosting the carol singing and nativity here, in the 1930s. I've helped out with this event almost every Christmas of my life. But I've never been responsible for it before." She grinned, though like her laugh it wobbled at the edges. "Gran and Pop used to start setting up for it days in advance. Pat and Susanna are clearly a bit more last minute. I wish they'd asked for help. Until they called, I didn't know what they'd been dealing with."

Her words echoed what he'd been thinking about her.

As she flattened her hands on the worn timber countertop, Brad had a powerful sense she drew strength from her heritage. From all the other Calders before her who'd stood at the same counter, in the same way. That continuity was something he'd never experienced. Had she felt somehow reduced, less than her full self, when she'd lived away from this place?

Along with the prayer, it seemed to boost her. Drawing in a deep breath, Maddie stepped away from the counter. "The first thing we need to do is rearrange the furniture in the café." She pulled back the big folding doors dividing the store from the dining area.

They got to work, frequently interrupted by the jangle of the bell over the front door. The event preparation turned into an event of its own as people turned up to offer help, or came to shop and ended up staying. Maddie broke out sodas and cookies for the helpers. As he stopped to munch on a cookie, making up for his missed lunch, Brad watched her swirling through the group, smiling, laughing, organizing.

He loved seeing this new side of her. Changeable as the lake in summer, but always beautiful.

Finally, she stopped, looked around, and released a satisfied sigh. "Great work, guys. Thank you. I never imagined we'd get it done so fast." Glancing at her watch, she grinned. "Hours to spare. I'll close the store now and go home for a bit. I hope Jacob napped, or we'll have one very grumpy little shepherd later."

At last, the others left, and they were alone together.

"You did a great job." He meant it.

"I had good help." Maddie smiled up at him as she shut down the computer. "You see what I mean about Sunset

Point? It's a community."

He nodded, switching off the lights around the store. "I do see it."

And it sank his hopes even deeper.

More and more, he wondered if he'd be wrong to ask her to leave again. But his life and his work were in L.A. Or Chicago, if he scored the promotion. Apart from Maddie and Jacob, there was nothing for him here. No way to provide for them financially.

Bonner General, fifty miles away, had an excellent reputation, but was small. He might wait ten years for a management opening there, and it would be a hefty demotion. Everything in him screamed out against the idea.

He'd been trained to climb the ladder, not slide back down it.

For now, changing the subject was best. He'd pray about the situation with Maddie later. He eyed the woodstove. "Do we need to feed this thing? You'll need to explain how to work it."

Maddie smiled. "Not much call for these in L.A. The store has backup heating, so it won't freeze if the fire goes out. But a woodstove gives a welcoming, comforting heat. Gran and Pop always kept it burning in the winter." Putting the wire fireguard to one side, she showed him how to open the door and bank the split wood in the firebox.

So many country skills he had no idea about.

At least he could manage the grunt work. "Want me to refill the log basket now?"

"Please."

Outside, the cold air bit harder than earlier. Maddie's gran had been right about his coat. It didn't cut it here, and the splinters from the wood had tattered the surface.

Barely four p.m., but the sun had already set behind the mountains. He paused to appreciate the colors flaming in the western sky and tinting the snow-covered hills and lake. Sunset Point was well named. No one seeing a sunset here could doubt the existence of a Creator.

It didn't take long to fill the big basket with firewood and haul it into the store. Maddie finished shutting everything down and stood waiting by the door, keys in hand, ready to lock up. Her smile lit her face with a radiance brighter than the sunset. "Thank you for all you did this afternoon. I appreciated it."

"I wanted to help. I enjoyed it." That wasn't a lie. Not even a polite exaggeration.

She raised an eyebrow. "Even your woodchucking contest with Ryan?"

"Even that." He rubbed his back and pretended to hobble. "Though I may be sorry later."

Her laugh rang out, merry and clear as a Christmas bell. "I hope not. Now, home to discover whether Gran and Hiram survived an afternoon with Jacob. I really *do* hope he napped." She peeked at him, a mischievous glint in her eye. "I don't know where he inherited his tendency to get grumpy when he doesn't sleep enough. Couldn't possibly be me."

"Of course not." Brad couldn't resist rolling his eyes. Maddie woke like a bear if disturbed before she was ready, while he was an easy napper.

As they walked back along Main Street, she surprised him by tucking her hand into his, the way they used to walk. The icy wind tugged at him, but nothing could chill the warmth her sweet closeness raised.

Not even knowing that a pile of paperwork his boss wanted back first thing tomorrow morning waited on his laptop, and he probably wouldn't get the chance to look at it till midnight.

CHAPTER NINE

MADDIE HELPED JACOB with the jeans and long-sleeved T-shirt they'd agreed should go under his shepherd outfit. Excitement about the carols and the nativity play had him hyped up — before tonight's inevitable sugar overdose.

Thankfully, Gran and Hiram had managed fine. Hiram stayed until she and Brad came home from the store, and Gran even managed to bake a batch of her prizewinning huckleberry pies.

"I have to wear a dress," Jacob pouted to Brad in a disgusted tone.

Maddie smiled and shook her head. "It's not a dress. It's a Middle Eastern robe. All the boys in the play will be wearing them." Looking up from tying sneakers, she pointed at the costume she'd stitched, hanging over his chair. "Ask your daddy what he thinks."

Brad picked up the homespun robe and made a big deal of examining it. "Nice." He whistled. "Definitely not a dress. I wore the same thing when I was in a nativity play, too."

"You wore one? For real?" Wide-eyed Jacob gawked up at Brad, who nodded.

"Sure did."

A grin spread across the boy's face, and he gave a thumbs up, the gesture so comically adult on his small hand she had to stifle a chuckle. "Okay! Mom, when can I put it on?" Enthusiasm replaced his former reluctance.

The power of Daddy. She didn't know whether to be

relieved or irritated.

Relief won. Something shifted in her attitude today. Something big. So many times in her marriage, she'd been resentful. She'd done the hard work of parenting, yet all Jacob had eyes and ears for was Daddy.

But Brad was here with them now. He hadn't used work as a reason to hide behind his laptop and avoid them. That meant so much.

"You put the costume on just before the play." She patted Jacob's foot and stood. "There. You're all done."

Jacob jumped up. Brad was already folding the robe, along with the cloak and headgear. This was how it should have been. The three of them, together. She'd longed for this, immeasurably more than jewelry she didn't wear, presents she didn't want, and meals at fancy restaurants.

Part of her wanted to hold back, resist surrendering to this blessing. Why bother, when he'd be gone so soon? Another part wanted to enjoy the sweet gift while she could, store up memories for when they were apart. Wasn't it time to put on praise instead of despair? She'd spent so long angry over the disappointments in her marriage.

Jacob deserved to see his parents happy together, even if only briefly.

Lord, I don't know how to feel or what to hope for. When we were married, I didn't feel Brad loved me. He didn't seem to want to be with me or Jacob. But things are different now. I don't want to stay angry with him anymore.

She and Brad followed after Jacob's headlong rush downstairs. Gran sat at the kitchen table, head bent over her hands. Praying? She looked up and smiled as they entered, but her face lacked its usual apple-cheeked glow, and something shadowed her eyes.

Fatigue? Anxiety? Or something more serious?

Maddie hurried over to hug her. "I'm sorry for asking you to take over from me today. You had enough to do. Jacob can come to the store with us tomorrow."

Gran straightened. "He was no trouble. Hiram was a wonderful help." A hint of color tinged her cheeks. "I know we always walk, but he's offered to drive me to the carols tonight. Easier to get the pies there that way."

Concern tightened Maddie's chest. Gran never accepted a ride anywhere she could walk. Observing carefully, she checked the older woman. Was she using both hands? Did both sides of her face move evenly? Gran's doctor instructed Maddie in what to look for — the signs of further strokes.

An unwelcome reminder. If she wanted to return to the city with Brad, she couldn't. Not when it meant leaving the beloved woman who'd raised her.

"I'm fine, child." Gran chuckled, opening and closing both hands in front of her and exaggerating a toothy grin. "Just feeling my age."

Laughing, Maddie hugged her again. "You weren't supposed to notice! Okay, I'm reassured. Brad and I should go soon, to finish setting up. When is Hiram coming to collect you?"

"I asked him to come any time now. I know you worry about leaving me alone. No need, of course!"

The mudroom door thudded. Hiram, a backdoor friend. Maddie found him in there, pulling off his snow boots. Smiling thanks, he padded into the kitchen. "Your gran told me you'd want to leave earlier tonight. Would you like us to bring Jacob along with us?"

Maddie hesitated. The gleam in Hiram's eyes suggested he and Gran cooked up the plan to push her and Brad into more time alone. She wasn't sure how she felt about that. Knowing she'd never stopped loving him didn't alter the fact they now lived separate lives. And the point of Brad being here was father-son time. They'd missed a chunk today already.

Jacob decided it. "I want to be with Daddy." More than a hint of mulishness jutted his lower lip.

Gran chuckled. "Maddie, I saw that same look on your face whenever your dad was home on furlough and I tried to separate you."

She remembered. Just like she remembered crying herself to sleep every time her now-and-then Dad breezed back out of her life again. By divorcing Brad, had she done the same to Jacob? Her heart clenched painfully as guilt twisted her.

No. She stiffened her spine. Brad had hardly been home when they'd lived together. Jacob spent more time with his father today than he'd had in a week back then. And life here at the lake was so much better for him.

Somehow, she wasn't quite convincing herself.

When Brad left after New Year's Day, Jacob would cry. The same way she had for her dad.

"Okay, Peanut. You can come with us." She couldn't resist ruffling his soft hair while he was still young enough not to mind.

When they donned their cold-weather clothing before leaving, it was Brad who knelt to fasten Jacob's coat and snow boots. Brad who pulled the thick knitted hat down over Jacob's ears. Brad who helped him on with his mittens.

Once, she would have been jealous. Without her even realizing, it seemed God had healed that. Seeing Jacob's happiness at Brad doing these little things for him, she couldn't feel anything but gratitude.

Brad reached for his coat, a sorry wreck after his work at the store. She stilled his hand, catching her breath as the contact trembled through her.

His head tilted and his eyebrow lifted in a question.

"Gran, is that offer of Pop's old coat still open?" Somehow it felt right.

"Of course. It's hanging right there in the closet." Unmistakable surprise colored Gran's voice and her curious eyes, as she peered around the kitchen door.

"Thanks!" Maddie rested a hand on the red woolen check, remembering that roughness against her face when Pop carried her home as a child. Smiling, she picked up the coat and handed it to Brad. "If you want."

Flashing his dimple in a heart-melting smile, he slid his arms into the thick fleece-lined sleeves. "Thank you."

Stepping out into the moon-bright evening, she took Jacob's hand, as she always did, and Brad grabbed the other. Jacob happily jumped and swung between them. As they crunched their way to the store on the ice and snow, they felt like a family again, for the first time in years.

She glanced over at Brad, and he dimpled again as he met her eyes. Her tummy turned a delicious little somersault.

Jacob wouldn't be the only one to miss Brad when he left.

Thankfully, no one waited outside the store. She unlocked the separate entrance to the café, switched on a blaze of Christmas lights inside and out, set carols softly playing through the sound system. She'd just closed the folding doors separating the café from the shop, when Claire and Mrs. Parks arrived to set up for the nativity play.

Perfect timing, though she always felt slightly nervous when Mrs. Parks was around. The retired teacher had brought most of Sunset Point to the Lord over the years. She watched over her former students with a critical eye and a loving but bluntly opinionated voice.

Anxious to know how Ruth was, Maddie sent Susanna a quick text when she had a moment to spare between running from one end of the building to the other. The reply wasn't encouraging. Her OB transferred Ruth to Spokane, so her twenty-six-week preemie could be whisked to their Level IV neonatal intensive care immediately after birth. Maddie's heart ached for the family.

Oh, Lord, please be with them all. Keep Ruth and that tiny baby safe! My worries are so small in comparison.

The café filled as people added their food donations the counter, then stood chatting. Brad's presence was an unexpected blessing. He kept an eye on things when she was busy elsewhere, and took care of Jacob. Not that he had much choice. Only Claire gathering the children in readiness for the nativity play peeled Jacob away from his father's side.

For a guy who claimed he didn't know what to do around children, Brad sure seemed a kid magnet. Not just Jacob, but the others, too. He'd always been able to turn on the charm, but this went deeper, a new substance she hadn't seen before. He truly *had* changed.

Maybe, more than she had. So much easier to blame Brad than take responsibility for her own part in things. She winced as the troubling whisper hit home.

Hiram and Gran arrived, and Maddie hurried to take the pies from them, assessing Gran as she did. She smiled, silently thanking God. Whatever was wrong earlier seemed to have passed.

"You've done a good job. Everything is set up nicely." Gran beamed her approval as she glanced around the crowded room. "It must feel like old times for you, being in charge of the store. I know you never wanted me to sell it."

Maddie's smile stiffened. She hadn't, though she'd known they had no choice. How could a widow in her seventies and a schoolgirl in her teens have managed? But she'd loathed the cottage when they first moved there, simply for not being the old familiar store with its quirky rooms and its memories of Pop.

Maybe why Gran had needed to leave? "It's okay." She gave Gran a quick hug. "You did what was best at the time."

"I did, child. But I know you felt it. Any news from Pat or Susanna?" Gran steepled her fingers against her lips as if already praying for the family.

Tears stung her eyes. "Not good, I'm afraid. Ruth's in Spokane. They expect the baby will be born tonight. Susanna asked us to keep them in our prayers."

"We have a good gathering here tonight. We'll use the opportunity to lift their needs to the Lord." Hiram surveyed the room and sighed. "Joe isn't here yet? Every year, I wonder if this time he isn't going to make it." He glanced at his watch, and then raised his voice. "Welcome to the Sunset Point Christmas celebration. Please, everyone, be seated. We're ready to begin."

They'd moved the café chairs to one side of each table, facing the makeshift stage. Though they used all the chairs Maddie could find, they didn't have enough to seat everyone. No matter. Standing at the side with Brad, she could still see Jacob.

She nodded with satisfaction. It all looked good.

Claire and Mrs. Parks had hung a black curtain at one end to be the night sky, with a big silver star glowing at the top, and laid artificial turf on the floor. A flock of knee-high paper mache sheep stood on the left. Claire had been all for using real sheep and a donkey. Imagining the chaos, Maddie gave thanks her friend let the idea go.

On the right, they'd assembled a stable from a portable gazebo, cardboard, and straw, held together with plenty of hot glue. The wooden manger, the one her great-grandfather made for the first nativity play here, took pride of place. The children clustered off to one side.

Hiram opened his Bible and cleared his throat. After a few nervous giggles from the performers, the room hushed. Then noisy footsteps echoed on the porch, the street door opened, and old Joe sidled in, ducking his head as everyone turned to look at him.

So the trapper made it through another year. Good. Maddie waved to him in welcome, and he moved to stand beside them. Joe lived in a hut up in the hills like a hermit. Unfortunately, he looked and smelled like it, too. She made sure to breathe through her mouth.

Nodding to the old man with a smile, Hiram began. "Remembering the true meaning of Christmas, the birth of our Lord, let's read from the Gospel of Luke. In those days Caesar Augustus issued a decree that a census should be taken…"

Brad pulled out his phone and started videoing.

The old familiar words rolled out, resonant and deep. "So Joseph went up from the town of Nazareth in Galilee to

Judea, to Bethlehem the town of David, because he belonged to the house and line of David. He went there to register with Mary, who was pledged to be married to him and was expecting a child."

Christopher Mullins and young Sally Parks, holding her tummy, trudged across the stage to the stable and flopped on the straw.

"While they were there, the time came for the baby to be born, and she gave birth to her firstborn, a son. She wrapped him in cloths and placed him in a manger, because there was no guest room available for them."

Sally produced a swaddled baby doll from under her cloak, cuddled it, and then rested it on the manger.

"And there were shepherds living out in the fields nearby, keeping watch over their flocks at night."

The three shepherds, including Jacob, the smallest and youngest, wandered among their sheep, exactly as they should.

Hiram continued, "An angel of the Lord appeared to them, and the glory of the Lord shone around them, and they were terrified."

Cee Cee Schaefer, the eldest of the elementary school children and least likely to forget her lines, moved on stage. Her eye-popping silver robe decked with battery-operated lights should have come with a Sunglasses Required warning. No wonder the shepherds all covered their eyes.

"Do not be afraid," she intoned, in a high clear voice. "I bring you good news that will cause great joy for all the people. Today in the town of David a Savior has been born to you; he is the Messiah, the Lord. This will be a sign to you: You will find a baby wrapped in cloths and lying in a manger." She extended a glittering arm toward the stable as Hiram took over.

"Suddenly a great company of the heavenly host appeared with the angel, praising God and saying, 'Glory to God in the highest heaven, and on earth peace to those on whom his favor rests.' When the angels had left them and gone into heaven, the shepherds said to one another, 'Let's go to Bethlehem and see this thing that has happened, which the Lord has told us about.' So they hurried off and found Mary and Joseph, and the baby, who was lying in the manger."

Two of the shepherds picked up their sheep and headed for the stable. The third, Jacob, noticed his dad filming him, grinned, and waved. Maddie pasted on a smile and pointed at the stable, but inwardly cringed. There was always one. But why did it have to be hers?

Handing him his sheep, Mrs. Parks nudged him to move. Finally, all three shepherds were where they should be, kneeling in awe before Jesus.

Brad's arm slipped around her waist, in a consoling hug. Though she tried to focus on Hiram's voice as he finished the Scripture reading, all her awareness centered on Brad. On his strong warm arm holding her securely, offering so much comfort.

And more than comfort.

They exchanged a glance. Love shone in his eyes. Real. True. Deep. A forever kind of love.

The same kind of love she felt for him.

CHAPTER TEN

BRAD THANKED GOD with every fiber of his being for the precious truth glowing in Maddie's eyes. She *did* love him. Her body repeated the message, in the way she leaned against him, surrendering to his support.

His arm tightened around her. If they weren't where they were, surrounded by all her neighbors, he'd kiss her. The yearning grew so strong, he might just kiss her anyway and let Sunset Point think what it liked.

Jacob interrupted with a tug on his jeans and an excited, "Did you see me, Daddy? Did you?"

Somehow, he'd completely missed the end of the play.

"Sure did. I've got you on video, too." He pushed the replay button on his phone and showed it to Jacob. "See? You did great." Releasing Maddie, he scooped his son up in his free arm. Maddie smiled and rested a hand on Jacob's shoulder. As Brad held her close again, they formed a circle.

A family.

Something he'd never felt before, either growing up or in their marriage.

Emotion swelled in his chest, knotting his throat. So this was what she'd wanted from him, what she'd yearned for and not found.

For the first time, he started to understand what she'd meant when she tried to explain why she divorced him. They'd shared the same bed. They'd been physically intimate. But the amazing blessing of this emotional connection and overwhelming tenderness — this — had been missing.

"I want to sing." Jacob wriggled to be put down.

"We'll be singing in a minute," Maddie reassured him.

Brad lowered the boy to the floor, breaking the physical circle they'd formed. But the circle of their love remained, bright and real as an eighteen-karat wedding band. It always would.

As if he'd heard Jacob, Hiram announced, "Tonight's carols are old favorites. 'While Shepherds Watched Their Flocks', 'Hark the Herald Angels Sing', and 'Silent Night'. As always, we'll sing all the verses. So if you don't know them, be sure to take one of the sheets circulating through the room with the words."

Brad took one each for himself and Maddie and passed the last sheet on to the disheveled older man beside them.

"Me too," Jacob protested as the singing began. Brad handed the boy his page, but chuckled when he held it upside down. As Jacob piped, "While shepherds washed their socks at night," he decided they'd better do some practice before next year's carol singing.

He needed to share Maddie's sheet after the first verse. Maddie hardly glanced at it, singing with her whole heart in a clear true voice.

The group worked their way through the traditional carols, ending with "Silent Night". He glanced at Maddie. Joy transformed her. Unexpected salt stung his eyes as he glimpsed the radiant light of love the carol spoke of reflected in her face.

She'd never looked lovelier.

The song ended. After a still moment, a hum of chatter began. Hiram raised a hand. "Before we share our food, let's take time to pray." Once the room quieted, he began, "Heavenly Father, we thank You for blessing us with this time of food and fellowship tonight. Thank You for the greatest gift of all, Your Son, Jesus, whose sacrifice allowed us to be forgiven our sins and to come into right relationship with You."

Hiram paused. His deep tones echoed not just within the room, but in Brad's heart.

"We ask Your blessing on all here tonight, as well as on those who can't be with us. I especially ask Your loving hand to rest upon Pat, Susanna, their daughter, the little baby about to be born, and their other grandchildren.

"We thank You for all who've served their country, both now and in the past, and ask Your special protection on them. At this season of peace, bring peace to our hearts and to this broken world. Teach us to forgive as we have been forgiven by You. Heal our broken places and our broken relationships. Guide us in Your ways, help us to seek Your wisdom rather than the wisdom of this world, and above all, help us to love as You have loved us. In Jesus' name we pray, amen."

"Amen!" resounded around the café.

"Amen," Maddie whispered.

"Can I go play with the other kids now?" Jacob's bright face peered up at them both. He restlessly stepped from one foot to the other as the room filled with noise again.

Maddie nodded. "Just stay where I can see you. Okay?"

He ran to the other children messing around on the stage. Looked like he'd realized his daddy wasn't going anywhere.

Yet.

Knowing he'd leave in nine days sank Brad's heart. But he had no choice.

The man next to them hacked out a cough and grinned a broken-toothed grin. "You have a fine-looking boy there, Miss Maddie. And this feller, he's your husband? Haven't seen him here before." His voice creaked, sounding rusty from lack of use like the hinges of an old gate.

"Thanks, Joe. I think Jacob is pretty special, too." Her gentle smile lit her lovely eyes. "Yes, I married Brad. You haven't met him sooner because this is his first Christmas here. He lives in Los Angeles."

"Cities!" Joe hoicked as if to spit, then thankfully held

back.

"Huckleberry Lake is beautiful, but L.A. is where my work is." Brad shrugged in apology. He was beginning to wish it wasn't, but wishing didn't alter the facts.

The bearded man poked a grimy finger at Brad's chest. "You heard Hiram. Love is our work here. Only love. Remember that." Hunching his shoulder as if he was done with Brad, he twisted away. "I'll go speak to him now."

Maddie reached out but didn't quite touch him. "Joe, please don't leave without seeing me first for your share of the leftovers."

"What's the story there?" Brad asked, low-toned, as Joe stomped across to Hiram.

An ocean of sadness washed over her face. "Poor Joe. Pop told me they grew up close friends. Pop, Hiram, and Joe. Then Joe went to Vietnam, came back… changed. He was one of the people Hiram meant when he spoke of those who'd served. Veterans' wounds don't always show."

Brad nodded.

"He moved to a shack way up in the hills. Once or twice a year he gets a yearning for human company and hikes or snowshoes in. He always comes for the carols. But the rest of the year, anyone who goes too near his cabin is met with a shotgun. When Gran and Pop ran the store, they sent him home with plenty of food. I'll do the same." She grinned. "Which reminds me, people are hungry. Time to uncover the food. Come fill a plate each for you and our little shepherd."

Brad glanced around and laughed. Jacob and the other shepherds raced their sheep across the stage. "Who would have guessed sheep would be more fun than pie?"

"Watch how long the sheep last when we start serving." Maddie chuckled.

As she crossed the room to the food service area, folk stopped her, wanting to talk. As she smiled, laughed and checked in with her gran, he couldn't miss seeing how well loved and embedded in this community she was. No wonder she hadn't been happy in the city. It took a lifetime to grow roots like this.

Was asking her to leave this behind and offering only himself in return a fair trade?

Once, in his confidence and pride, he'd believed so. Now, he wasn't sure.

After taking a plate of treats to Jacob, he squatted on the floor beside his son, listening to the boy's happy chatter. When Jacob wanted to race sheep again, Brad circulated the room, aiming to listen more than talk. Everyone asked about him and Maddie. He answered honestly. She lived here, his work was in L.A., and how they'd work it out, they didn't know.

But surprisingly, unlike business social events, this one wasn't any chore. He found despite their differences, they had plenty else to talk about. He kept a watch on Jacob, too, so Maddie didn't have to. She still did, of course. More than once, their glances collided. The connection jolted him with warmth, sweeter than her gran's sugar-sprinkled pie.

Leaving her post at the counter, Mrs. Parks marched up and took his empty plate. "So, did you enjoy sampling our huckleberry specialties? You won't find huckleberries like ours anywhere else."

"I did enjoy them." He smiled cautiously, wary of what might come next. Her forthright manner and the determined glint in her eyes suggested she had an agenda. "I haven't eaten huckleberries for years, since I was last here at the lake. I'd forgotten how much better they are than blueberries, how complex and deep the flavor is."

"Yes." Her decisive nod shook her wattled throat. "The huckleberry knows where it belongs. You can try to transplant them, but they won't set down roots anywhere except where the Lord planted them, in the soil and conditions He intended them to grow in. They might last a few years at best, but away from their rightful place, they shrivel and die. You think about that."

She strode off again, clearly having said all she wanted to say. He'd expected a lecture about the sanctity of marriage or a man's responsibilities to his wife, not a discussion of horticulture.

Except she hadn't been talking about huckleberries. She'd meant Maddie.

He saw what he hadn't when they'd married and he'd uprooted her. Like the wild mountain huckleberries, Maddie needed to grow in her own soil to develop into all she could be. Taking her away from here would be wrong, in so many ways.

But he couldn't avoid the reality. This was vacation. His life lay elsewhere.

Despair sagged his shoulders and weighted his breath. Dented the confidence he'd felt that if God wanted them together, He'd show them the way. Every minute he spent here reinforced how much he loved Maddie.

And reinforced the challenges keeping them apart.

All he could do was quit worrying about the future, surrender to making the most of this time together, and pray God really *did* have a plan.

Hiram's deep tones boomed above the buzzing voices. "Everyone, thanks for attending. It's time to think about collecting the dish you brought, along with your box of shared leftovers, saying goodnight, and making your way home. Safe travels, and may you all have a blessed and joyous Christmas."

The evening began to wind down as people left. Old Joe first, carrying a huge bag of provisions Maddie put together for him. Then the families and couples filtered away. Jacob ran up to Brad, face puckered as he held up his sheep, displaying a dangling leg.

"We'll fix your sheep tomorrow," he promised, praying he could figure out how as he picked Jacob up. His son's tired head lolled against his shoulder. Love for the boy filled him, fierce and strong.

Maddie hurried over and ruffled Jacob's hair. "Way past your bedtime, Peanut." She smiled at Brad. "I might be hours more here, cleaning up. Would you take him home and put him to bed?"

"Gladly. Then I'll come back to help. I don't want to leave you working here by yourself or walking home late." The thought of those reports waiting in his email for review tweaked at him. He pushed the guilty twinge away. He could pull an all-nighter to get them done if he had to. Maddie and Jacob were more important.

She laughed. "Okay. I'd appreciate your help. Though I'd be safe walking home. The bears should all be hibernating now. I wonder when Gran and Hiram plan to leave?" She gazed past his shoulder and smiled.

The older pair stood behind him.

"We're going right about now," Hiram said, grinning. "I can take Jacob from you, if you want." He reached out to take the drowsy boy.

"No! Stay with Daddy," Jacob protested sleepily, clinging with his arms and legs like a monkey.

Brad checked with Maddie. This had to be her decision.

"If you're okay to carry him home later, I'm sure Susanna won't mind me borrowing a quilt and pillow from a spare bed to make him a nest." She hugged her gran. "You go home, and don't wait up for us. You look a little tired."

"Don't stay too late." Liz patted Maddie's cheek. "Remember what I used to do. Clean up the food mess, and then close the doors. What doesn't get done tonight will still be here tomorrow. Moving the chairs and tables back can wait till spring, if needed."

Surveying the chaotic room, Maddie sighed, and then straightened her shoulders. "Wise advice, Gran."

When they left, Maddie hurried off to the living quarters, returning with bedding in her arms. Claire and Mrs. Parks had dismantled the props and rolled up the artificial grass, leaving only the brown cardboard that served as the stable roof.

Maddie dropped the bedding onto it. "Perfect." Spreading the folded quilts, she made an improvised bed.

Brad knelt and snuggled Jacob in, untangling himself without waking the boy.

"We could probably drop a stack of plates, and he'd sleep through it." Gratitude warmed Maddie's smile. "Thanks for staying."

A busy hour later, the four of them had scraped nearly two hundred plates, loaded the commercial dishwasher over and over, wiped down the tables and counter, and mopped the floor. Last time Brad did KP like this was scout camp when he was a kid.

Maddie planted her hands on her hips, scanned the café, and nodded. "Great work, team! Time to go home."

They *were* a team. As he and Maddie walked home through the stillness of the snowy night, blazing with stars, he carried Jacob, and Maddie tucked a hand in his arm. Again, he felt that sense of belonging, of family. What he'd thought was love when they married was no more than attraction, insubstantial as candy floss.

This new sweet tenderness he felt had God-given depth. The solid bedrock of commitment he'd been too immature and self-absorbed to give before.

But he still couldn't see how they'd make it work.

CHAPTER ELEVEN

Christmas Eve

FOR ONCE, EARLY MORNING SUNLIGHT seeping through her curtains woke Maddie, not Jacob bouncing on her bed before dawn. His voice filtered through her closed bedroom door. He was somewhere near, chattering away. Still drowsy, she stretched like a cat.

Then a bunch of realizations smacked her like a barrage of wet snowballs. She bolted straight up in bed and swung her legs over the edge.

One — Brad was here.

Two — she had to open the store by ten a.m., finish clearing up from last night, and pray for Ruth and the baby.

Three — it was Christmas Eve, so there were presents to wrap, baking to do, and meals to prep for tonight and tomorrow.

Four — she'd slept in. *Seriously* slept in. She had under an hour to get up, dress, check on Gran, give Jacob breakfast, hustle him into his clothes, and make it to the store by opening time.

Help me, Lord! How will I get it all done?

Grabbing her robe, she rushed to Jacob's room then stopped in the doorway. Jacob busily tried to convince Brad, standing with his back to the door, that he really *was* allowed to wear his Superman pajamas all day and didn't need to change.

She failed to hold back a snort. Brad turned his head and

smiled at her. Okay, she admitted it, her heart flipped over. Tightening her robe to cover her ratty, old, paint-splattered yoga pants, she wished she'd thought to wear prettier PJs. In his T-shirt and sweatpants, with his hair all mussed, he looked every bit as adorable as his son.

"Nice try, Peanut, but if you want to come to the store, you need to get up and get dressed now. And you need to brush your teeth."

He pouted and didn't move. Too much sugar and excitement last night. "Is Daddy coming?"

"Sure thing." Brad's enthusiasm rang a little forced, and he stifled a yawn. Normally, he woke with a perkiness she needed two or three cups of coffee to achieve.

"How late were you working on those reports?" Once they tucked Jacob into bed with Trunkie last night, she'd peeked in on Gran, and then flopped straight into bed after a two-minute shower. Clearly, he hadn't.

"Only three a.m." He smiled as if it were nothing. "The problem wasn't as complex as my boss thought."

Three a.m.

Remorse chewed at her. How many of those nights he'd come home so late when they were married had he actually been working? All of them?

Brad hadn't been the only one working overtime. Her imagination had, too. Add late nights and working weekends to his expensive gifts, so much like guilt offerings, and it hadn't taken a big stretch to come up with some crazy explanations.

Mostly involving another woman. And all completely wrong.

She pasted on a grin. "You don't need to come to the store today, if you have more work to do."

"No, it's fine." He tickled Jacob on the tummy. "Come on, up you get. You heard what your mom said. Clean your teeth then get dressed."

Jacob bounced out of bed, giggling.

With Brad's help, it took far less time than usual to get Jacob ready, pack a bag of toys and books to amuse him at the store, and chase him downstairs for breakfast. Gran was already waiting for them, with fresh coffee and the streusel-topped muffins Claire made. They'd turned out great.

But better than breakfast was the sight of Gran's bright smile. No sign of whatever troubled her last night. Even so, leaving her alone half the day worried Maddie.

"Will you be okay while we're out?" She rinsed Jacob's favorite plastic juice mug at the sink, inhaling the soft fragrance from Brad's vase of sweet peas as she did. Mug tucked in her bag, they were ready to leave. "We should be home before two."

"Don't fuss, child. I'll be fine." Gran lifted her eyes heavenward. "Nancy is coming over soon. We'll wrap presents together. I'm sure Hiram will drop by, too."

"Okay. But please, if you go outdoors, take your phone with you." Gran really *did* look fine. But Maddie hoped the older woman understood she wasn't just fussing. Basic safety precautions were important.

Gran nodded. "We agreed. I'd rather a cell phone than that button thing you wanted me to wear."

Now it was Maddie's turn to roll her eyes. Gran flatly refused the emergency help alert the occupational therapist recommended. But she couldn't baby the older woman. All she could do was pray. Laughing, she hugged Gran and kissed her cheek. "I trust you. We'd better get moving."

The lake treated them to a perfect winter morning as she walked to the store with Brad and Jacob. A light fresh snowfall dusted glitter on everything. Just enough to be pretty and fun, not enough to be a slog to walk on. The snowplow hadn't been through, so the overnight fall lay crisp on the road and sidewalk. She paused at the corner to look out across the lake to the pine-covered hills and thank God for all this beauty. Huckleberry Lake could be a Christmas card. Calm and bright, like the carol said.

She loved this place so much.

The splat of a snowball on her back interrupted her musing.

Jacob giggled as Brad patted together another ball and handed it to him. She ducked, scooped up two handfuls of snow, and flung them wildly. Battle was on. As they ran down the street, she chased them, pelting them with snow. Breathless and laughing, they all collapsed on the store steps.

Just when she thought she was safe, Jacob smacked her with the snowball he'd held onto.

"Truce," she cried, raising her hands.

He jumped on top of her, and they rolled in the snow like puppies.

When she finally stood up, snow beaded his red fleece cap and mitts and crusted his woolen coat. Hers, too. Chuckling, Brad stepped close, and gently brushed the snow from her hair and cheeks. As she gazed into his warm laughter-filled eyes, love for him expanded her chest. The thought of going back to the city with him chilled her worse than the snow, but she'd miss him badly when he left. And so would Jacob.

If she were free to leave Sunset Point, would she be willing to go with him?

She simply didn't know the honest answer.

The morning in the store passed quickly. Most of the town dropped by. Picking up their turkey orders, buying last-minute supplies and gifts for Christmas, asking after Ruth, and wanting to get another look at Brad.

He and Jacob stayed busy with what Jacob importantly declared was "boy stuff", moving the furniture back to its usual place in the café. Keeping a straight face, she agreed. When Ryan ambled in just before noon, ready to help, they'd almost finished. All that remained for him was to show Brad how to work the bear-proof catch on the dumpster, so they could cart out the trash.

She worried that she'd heard nothing yet about Ruth and the baby. No reply to her email or text.

Finally, just when she was on the verge of texting again, an email arrived from Pat.

Baby Carol Noelle born at 4:22 a.m., weighing 1 pound 8 1/2 oz.

There's an 80% chance she'll make it. They anticipate at least a two- to three-month hospital stay. Pictures attached. Ruth is tired, but recovering. Thankfully, her blood pressure is better. Susanna will stay in Spokane with her, and I'll stay in Coeur d'Alene with the other kids for as long as Ruth needs us. It's a big ask, but would you keep working there? We'll pay you the profits the store takes while you're in charge, and you can use the living quarters like it's your own home.

Maddie swallowed tears and slumped onto the stool behind the counter. She'd been so blessed to have a healthy child. The photos of an impossibly small baby, attached to so many wires and tubes... her tiny face and skinny body barely visible, would break any mother's heart. The only normal baby thing about her was her little pink knitted hat.

Oh, Lord, please, hold Baby Carol in Your hands. Keep her safe through the long journey ahead. Comfort Ruth and her family.

Without hesitating, she emailed back, telling Pat of course, she'd stay on here. Not for whatever money she'd earn, but to help them. Knowing the store was taken care of would be one less worry.

Somehow, they'd manage. Though she might need to ask Jacob and Gran to move into the living quarters here, so she could keep an eye on them while she worked. That minor inconvenience was nothing compared to what that family would be going through. Gazing at the pictures of Baby Carol again, she couldn't restrain her sniffles, and her throat burned.

Brad hurried from the café, where he'd been playing a noisy game with Jacob. "What's wrong?"

"I can't find a tissue." She stopped searching her purse to point at the computer screen.

"No need to cry over a lost tissue." He handed her one from his pocket. "It's clean."

"Thank you," she sniffed.

He leaned past her to the screen and gulped. "Oh." His hand rested on her shoulder, and she leaned against him. "Now I see what upset you. Do they think she'll make it?"

"It will be a long haul. But she has a chance." Closing her

eyes for a second, she prayed for Ruth and the baby again. Then she pulled away from the comfort Brad offered, to meet his eyes. "I told Pat I'd stay and manage the store." Apology infused her voice.

Brad said nothing. But the hand on her shoulder stiffened, and his jaw tensed. She'd disappointed him.

"I couldn't leave Sunset Point, anyway. There's Gran to think about. But I had to help." Why she felt she should apologize, defend her decision, she wasn't sure. This changed nothing.

"Of course, you must. It's the right thing to do. I wouldn't expect you to choose differently." But his smile didn't quite meet his eyes.

"Dad-dee. Come back. It's your turn," Jacob called.

Brad resumed the game, but his laughter didn't ring quite as true.

At least they only needed to keep the store open till one today. Early closing on Christmas Eve. She printed a sign saying where to reach her and stuck it on the door. Just in case anyone had a genuine emergency, like running out of stove gas halfway through cooking their turkey.

When they got home, rustles and giggles drifted from the kitchen. By the time she'd hung up her coat, pulled off her boots, and walked down the hall, Gran, Hiram, and Nancy all wore blandly innocent expressions. A litter of wrapping paper, sticky tape, and ribbons covered the table in front of them, and a stack of brightly wrapped presents towered on one chair.

She grinned at the conspirators. "So are you finished or do you need us to go away for a bit longer?"

"Give us five more minutes." Gran's eyes twinkled. "And shut the door behind you."

Maddie laughed. So she'd been right. Someone's gift, possibly hers, had been hastily hidden.

Thankfully, first Nancy then Hiram left soon after, so they didn't keep her out of the kitchen long. Time to start preparing the festive food. Ever since she was a little girl, they'd had a special meal on Christmas Eve, and opened one present each.

She baked a fresh batch of sugar cookies. Then she and Gran sat companionably peeling vegetables. After frosting the cookies, she put a few on a plate for the guys and carried them to the living room, where Brad was supposed to be entertaining Jacob. They'd been suspiciously quiet. When she saw why, suppressing her chuckles shook her so hard she nearly tipped the cookies off the plate.

Brad lay stretched out on the couch, Jacob nestled beside him, both sleeping. Their relaxed steady breathing could almost be called snoring. Tenderness pierced her as she stood watching them.

If only it could be like this all the time.

Brad's eyes flickered open, and he smiled drowsily. So much meaning and connection flowed between them, it almost hurt.

"Shhh. Go back to sleep."

His eyelids drifted shut again. Quietly placing the plate on the low coffee table, she tiptoed away.

In the kitchen, Gran turned off the carols they'd listened to, and an unusually serious expression smoothed her face. "Shut the door, child."

Maddie did, then flopped into a seat and stared at her. "What's wrong?"

Gran's smile hinted at uncertainty. "Nothing's wrong. At least, I hope you don't think so." She lifted the large flat envelope resting in her lap and pushed it across the table. "I wanted to give you your Christmas present now, rather than do it with everyone else around."

Mystified, Maddie opened the envelope and slid free the title deeds to the house. She tried to speak, but no sound emerged.

"I want you to have this house." Gran twisted her wedding ring on her finger. "I know you don't have any deep attachment to this place. I don't either. The store will always be our real home. But I'll make the arrangements after Christmas to transfer the cottage to your name. You can live here, sell it, rent it out, or keep it as a holiday home. It's a gift, to do with as you wish."

Maddie gaped at her. "But… what about you?"

Gran ducked her head, and bright color tinged her cheeks. "This is the part I'm not entirely sure you'll like. I know how close you and your pop were. But the thing is…" She raised her head, and her words tumbled over each other. "The thing is, I'm not getting any younger, and these mini-strokes have made me realize I don't have a lot of time to waste. Hiram and I are getting married. We'll live in his house."

"Married?" Maddie's brain seemed to have gone on strike. How could she not have seen this coming?

"Married." All uncertainty gone, Gran gave a firm nod. "We've always been good friends while your pop and Hiram's wife were alive. But since Lucille died this year, our feelings have deepened. I wanted to wait until you were settled again, rather than leave you and Jacob on your own. But then I realized you might not feel free to remarry because of worry over me. So I hope this" — she patted the deeds — "sets us both free to be with the men we love."

"I'm pleased for you." Maddie managed a smile. "I truly am. He's such a good man. Pop wouldn't mind one bit, and neither do I. It's just… I never guessed." Shaking her head, she laughed. "So you felt responsible for me, and I felt responsible for you. What a pair we are!" She hurried around the table and gave the older woman a warm hug. "I'm sure you'll be very happy."

Gran gazed up at her, a hopeful smile curving her face. "And I hope you'll be happy, too. You *will* marry Brad again, won't you?"

Maddie loosed a low breath. "I don't know, Gran. I just don't know."

Even when Pat and Susanna returned to the store, could she leave the lake and the life she loved? Or would the pressures of living in the city and Brad's endless work hours shrivel her love for him, as they had before?

CHAPTER TWELVE

LATER THAT EVENING, after a huge festive meal, Brad looked around the dining table. At Maddie, laughing as she straightened Jacob's paper hat, fallen over his eyes. At Liz and Hiram, giggling over a silly joke from their Christmas cracker like a pair of teenagers.

Liz glanced at him and smiled. "I hope you don't mind two Christmases. My family is Norwegian, so our big celebration was Christmas Eve. When Pete and I married, he wanted to keep his family traditions on Christmas Day. So we did both."

Brad grinned. "Having two celebrations is an unmissable treat."

When they'd been married, he'd never understood the fuss Maddie wanted to make about Christmas. Growing up, his dad was too busy and his mother too gone on martinis to care, though he hadn't figured that out till he was older. They'd dutifully exchanged gifts on Christmas morning, followed by Mom drinking steadily over lunch at her favorite restaurant. Then Dad rushed off to his office to provide emergency liposuction to any starlets worried they'd gained half a pound.

Then once Dad traded Mom in for a succession of younger wives, better ads for his business, Brad became the redheaded stepchild as their kids took center stage.

Bitterness chewed at him. He didn't want to get stuck in blame, but some role models he'd had to prepare him for marriage and fatherhood.

Since he'd seen how Maddie's family did Christmas Eve, he

understood a little more. Saying grace wasn't a rote thing here, but a genuine expression of thanks to God. The candle, up high and safely out of Jacob's reach, a way to remember the light of the world. A true faith, as well as love, shone around the table. And then there were the fun, unusual traditions, like the Christmas crackers.

No wonder she didn't want to leave.

Jacob waved the one remaining Christmas cracker at him. "Pull it with me, Daddy. You haven't got a paper hat." The boy used both hands to hold the end of the cardboard tube and scrunched his face up ready for the bang. As it popped, a silver-colored ring fell onto the table, with a plastic "diamond" that would weigh at least a carat if it was real.

He handed it to Jacob. "You won."

Excited, Jacob passed it to Maddie. "Look, Mommy! A diamond ring. Please wear it. You don't have one."

Maddie smiled indulgently and squeezed the child-sized ring onto her little finger before making a show of admiring it. "It's beautiful. Thank you." She dropped a kiss on Jacob's head.

Her eyes met Brad's. Was she thinking the same thing? That she'd had a diamond ring, and she'd FedExed it back to him, along with her wedding ring.

How naïve they'd been, that summer evening at the boathouse. He'd asked her to marry him two weeks after they'd met, offering his great-grandmother's engagement ring. Their hopes and dreams and crazy-in-love emotions blinded them to all their differences and the challenges of making a marriage work.

"Have another cookie." Liz held out a plate of the beautifully decorated cookies Maddie made earlier.

He raised his hands. "They're delicious. But I can't eat anything more." Clutching his belly, he sat back and groaned theatrically. "I'll need hours in the gym back in the city to work off all the good food you and Maddie have fed me."

"I'll have one, Gran." Jacob reached for a cookie shaped like a snowflake. A chipmunk grin bunched his round cheeks.

"Thank you, Mommy, for making these."

She beamed. "No trouble. I love baking."

Regret tightened Brad's smile. The apartment had only a tiny kitchen, too small to do much more than reheat take-out and make coffee. They'd agreed, five years there, and then they could afford a house. She'd stuck to the deal and never complained. It wasn't till he saw her in the kitchen here he realized how much she must have missed it.

Mom had hated cooking. On the housekeeper's day off, she'd insisted on eating out. He'd assumed Maddie would want the same, thought he was doing the right thing by getting take-out or going to a restaurant rather than asking her to cook.

If by some miracle she moved back to the city, they'd need to talk about what they both truly wanted. Really talk. No more assumptions. He could buy them a house in the suburbs now, with a family kitchen like this cottage.

Though that "if" was a big one. With her gran's health issues and minding the store keeping her here, the best-case scenario was a long wait for her to come to him. The worst, that she wouldn't ever leave the lake. He'd seen how she belonged here.

In that case, he'd need to work out how to visit more often, and convince Maddie to come to him more often, too. Jacob deserved better than a once-a-season dad.

"Let's go to the living room," Maddie said, smiling. "The washing up can wait."

The Christmas lights flickered so brightly on the ceiling-high tree, they had no need of any other lights. Jacob's eyes widened. "More presents!"

Maddie must have sneaked the gifts around the tree while he and Jacob weren't looking. She chuckled, but raised a warning hand. "Only one tonight. The rest tomorrow."

"Ohhhh!" He stared at the parcels in blue cartoon paper, obviously his, reaching first for one, then another, and hesitating. Too much choice.

"I still have one more to bring down. Maybe you should wait till you see it before you decide?" Maddie grinned. Whatever she'd kept back must be good.

"I need to bring mine down, too." Brad stood.

"I'll help you." Jacob ran past him to the first step then stopped, looking back to him for permission, eyes alight.

Brad glanced at Maddie, holding back his automatic, "Sure," till he spotted her tiny nod.

Jacob insisted on carrying Brad's bag of gifts, though it was almost as big as he was. Seeing his son's head held high in pride over helping as he dragged it along, Brad couldn't refuse, though he stiffened as Jacob bumped it down the stairs. Everything was well packed. Nothing should break.

He hoped.

Maddie peeped around the edge of her door to ensure Jacob had gone before hauling out a gift almost as tall as her, and as wide.

"You look like Jacob did, carrying my bag." Chuckling, he hurried to lift one end, careful not to tear the snowflake-patterned paper. "Good thing we really *aren't* competing. Trunkie takes second place in the super-sized gift department."

The wide grin lighting her face held as much mischief as Jacob's. "I wish I could claim I planned it that way, but I decided on this present for him before Thanksgiving." Then her expression stilled, became intent. "I want to tell you how much I appreciate you being here. Having you with him for the holidays means so much to Jacob."

"I'm glad to be here, with you both." Her approval warmed him, glowing like a flame. Though he could wish she was glad for herself, not just for Jacob. "Later, once he's in bed, could we talk?"

Nodding, she glanced away, but he'd glimpsed her blue eyes widening. Surely, she must guess what he hoped to ask her. The best Christmas gift would be seeing a real diamond on her ring finger, not just the glitter of the plastic one from the cracker on her pinky. Her wearing her engagement ring again.

A voice piped up from downstairs. "Mommy, Daddy, come on! We can't open any presents till you get here."

Maddie laughed. "We're coming, Mr. Impatient."

Now wasn't the time to get deep and meaningful. Instead, they wrestled the awkward package around the bend in the stairs. He was almost as eager as Jacob to see what hid under the wrappings.

Jacob waited for them. Wide-eyed and open-mouthed, he stared. "Is that for me?" Wonder rang in his voice and lit his astonished face.

"It is." Maddie paused as she reached the hallway and smiled. "But you don't have to open it tonight. It can wait till tomorrow if you want."

Brad could guess their son's answer.

"This one, this one, this one!" Jacob jumped and punched his little fists in the air.

"Okay, but let's get it into the living room first, so Gran and Hiram can watch, too." Maddie moved to lift it, but Brad stopped her.

"Let me."

No argument. She stepped back and gestured for him to enter the room first.

He laid the gift on the floor, and then edged around it to reach a seat.

Hiram chuckled as Liz clutched her hands to her chest theatrically. "Oh my, what a huge present! Could that be for me?"

"Sorry, Gran. It's for me." All serious, Jacob rushed to her side and patted her knee, looking up at her. "I'll let you play with it, promise. But I don't know what it is yet."

Laughter shook Maddie's shoulders and bounced her glowing ponytail. "You will in a minute. Go for it, Peanut. It's okay to rip the paper."

Gleeful, Jacob didn't hold back. Swiftly tearing off the wrapping, he revealed a traditional wooden sled on runners. Wordless for once, he just stared at it.

Brad did, too. He'd only seen sleds like that in movies or on Christmas cards and certainly never used one. Something else to add to the list of things he'd be depriving his son of if he asked them to move to the city.

Though L.A. offered the ocean and the zoo and a choice of schools. More kids his age to play with. Chicago offered plenty, too. He had to remind himself — it wasn't all one-sided. The move would give Jacob and Maddie as much as it took away.

As if concerned Jacob's silence meant he didn't like the gift, Maddie burst into explanation. "You're old enough this year to sled on your own, instead of being towed in the pull sled. You can ride and steer this by yourself." She showed him how the foot bar worked.

"Thank you, Mommy. I love it." Jacob threw his arms around her, and then jumped on the sled, moving the steering bar with his feet and pulling on the red rope handle like he was reining in a horse. "When can I use it?"

Maddie smiled. "Tomorrow. Every day, if the weather is right, and there's someone to go out with you. The hill behind the house is a safe starter slope. But you need to wear your helmet and always have a grown-up with you. Break those rules, and the sled gets locked away."

He nodded. "Gran can use it, 'cuz I promised."

"Thank you." Liz ruffled his hair. "I've ridden that sled many, many times. It was mine as a girl. I gave it to Maddie's father, and then it passed to Maddie when she was about your age. And now she's given it to you."

More Calder family history to weigh heavy on Brad. Another reminder of what he couldn't offer. He could write his family traditions in a text message and still have characters to spare. "Make money. Succeed. Look good." Not a lot else.

Jacob jumped off the sled and hugged her. "Thank you, Gran." Then he turned to Brad. "Will you come with me, Daddy? We could ride it together."

"Of course." Though he'd need to get Maddie or someone else to give him a crash course — hopefully not involving any actual crashes — before he showed Jacob his ignorance of sledding and put the boy at risk.

"Every day? Promise?" Jacob persisted.

"Every day for the rest of this year, I promise." That wasn't an exaggeration. He was here till the New Year. "Then I have to go back to work in the city. Too far away to go sledding with you." A knife twisted in his heart at the thought of leaving.

But he had to. For them. The next big promotion was so close he could almost taste the sweetness of success. The pay raise meant a bigger monthly child support check for Maddie. And he'd save the rest for that house in the suburbs.

If he'd blown his chances with his boss by taking this time off, he'd just try twice as hard when the next opportunity came along. He'd vowed to his dad he'd make it to the top in hospital management, and he meant it.

Jacob pouted a little. "Poor Daddy. That doesn't sound like fun."

No. It wasn't. Working hard to achieve and to provide for them was necessary, but not fun.

Thankfully, Maddie distracted Jacob before the pout progressed to anything more. "Gran's turn to open a gift." She peeked at Brad, a plea in her gaze. "Perhaps Jacob could give her yours, Brad?"

Eager to help, Jacob dragged over the bag with Brad's gifts. "Here they are."

"Thank you." Brad smiled appreciation at his son, and then smiled over his head at Maddie, too. She'd done a great job teaching the boy. He selected a square box from the bag and handed it to Jacob. "Liz, I hope you'll get a chuckle when you see it." Jacob carried it two handed and presented it to her like a king bearing gold, frankincense, or myrrh.

Liz shook the palm-sized box. "Hmm. It's light, and it makes no sound."

"It's not supposed to." Brad grinned. So it hadn't broken on its bumpy ride down the stairs.

She tugged off the ribbon and started on the wrapping. Then his cell phone rang in his coat pocket, out in the hall.

He grimaced. The irritating ring couldn't be ignored. He

should have switched it off. "Sorry, that's my phone. Open your present. I'll tell whoever it is to have a happy Christmas and call back next week."

The caller display suggested it might not be that easy. His boss. Still in the office, on Christmas Eve.

What was it about "vacation" the corporation didn't understand?

Three little words. Time. Off. Work. They weren't in the business dictionary.

"Merry Christmas, Harry!" He kept his tone cheerful, though he could see another late-night report needing an urgent assessment coming his way.

"Brad. The promotion is yours. We need you back in the office bright and early on the twenty-sixth when the big guns from the head office arrive."

No preliminaries. No congratulations. No acknowledgment Christmas was different from any other day. Harry may as well have replied "Bah humbug."

He'd imagined this day, and the champagne-cork-popping exultation. Instead, the promotion weighed on him like a lead straitjacket.

"Is there any alternative? I promised my son I'd be here till New Year's Day." Brad knew the answer before the words left his mouth.

"Your kid won't remember. Promises like that are made to be broken. There's only room for people who are committed at this level. It's make or break time, Brad. Fumble the ball now, and that's it. You only get one chance to play in the major league." The stream of clichés ended.

Brad's stomach roiled. It wasn't a clear-cut choice. Not Maddie, or the promotion. He could turn it down, and he still wouldn't have her. All refusing would do was make him a two-time loser.

Sure, she still cared for him. But he saw in ways he'd never recognized just how strongly her life tied to this place. He'd fantasized a house in the 'burbs, but like the wild mountain huckleberry, she wouldn't thrive anywhere but here.

He couldn't ask her to leave.

And he couldn't give up his one shot at the top, either.

"I'll be there," he said.

There'd be an afternoon flight. He'd get Christmas morning here, even take Jacob out sledding, the way he'd promised. Then, he'd say goodbye.

CHAPTER THIRTEEN

AS SHE TURNED OFF the kitchen tap and swished the suds in the sink, Maddie wondered how long it would take Brad to open up about whatever was wrong. They'd had so little practice at that. Maybe he didn't trust her enough yet to open up to her at all.

When Gran volunteered them to wash up while she and Hiram bathed Jacob and put him to bed, her intent to give them some private time together had been clear. Just in case Maddie missed the hint, Gran's grin and wink as she clicked the kitchen door firmly behind them made it all too obvious.

But Gran clearly hadn't picked up on Brad's undercurrent of tension. This wouldn't be the warm friendly one-to-one she envisaged.

Oh, he'd laughed and chatted like usual. Hung the Hummel ornament of a boy riding a sled he'd given Gran high on the tree, after everyone oohed and ahhed over the coincidence. Said all the right things about Gran's gift for him, a glossy coffee-table book of photographs of the lake. Admired Jacob's gift for her, a bracelet of chunky clay beads Claire helped him make in Sunday school.

But a hollow echo reverberated through Brad's laughter, and it never quite warmed his eyes.

Taking a deep breath to gather strength, she knew she had to ask. In the past, she would have stayed silent, said nothing, but that hadn't helped either of them. "Brad, what's bothering you? You've been different since you came back from taking that call."

The smile stretching his lips was so obviously fake, she wished he hadn't tried. His shoulders stiffened, and he glanced away.

So she'd been right. Whatever he replied wouldn't be anything she'd want to hear.

"It was my boss, Harry. He offered me the promotion I've been working toward." He didn't attempt to inject any enthusiasm into his tone. So different from the king-of-the-world triumph he'd shown with his other promotions.

"Did you accept it?" Caution edged her carefully neutral words. She couldn't dare to dream his flat disappointed response meant he'd reined back his ambition to reach the top. Finally realized there was more to life than work.

"Yes." His slight hesitation and downward gaze, refusing to meet her eyes, hinted he hadn't told her all he needed to say.

Her dreams they might rebuild a life together shattered with that single word.

Every promotion he'd taken had meant less time at home. This one wouldn't be any different. The corporate culture in healthcare saw sixty-hour weeks as the starting point. Anything less was considered part-time. The fact his boss worked late on Christmas Eve proved it.

How could she uproot Jacob and follow Brad where his career led, when he'd never be away from the office?

Good thing she hadn't let herself hope too much.

Pretending she didn't care, she picked up a baking dish. "And?"

He swallowed audibly. "I'm sorry, Maddie. I have to be in L.A. to meet with the guys from head office. I'll need to leave tomorrow."

"Tomorrow? But it's Christmas Day!" Loss and hurt racked her, tightening like a vise on her chest.

Then a hot torrent of rage from some dark place deep inside flooded her, the Red Sea crashing back just when it seemed there was a safe way through. Swallowing hard, she battled to force it back down. The baking dish slammed into the sink, splashing water down her front. Her fingers curled so tightly that even through rubber gloves her nails pressed into her palms.

Suppressing the urge to whack the tray over Brad's head instead of into the water took every ounce of willpower she possessed.

Please, Lord, stop me saying or doing anything I'll regret. I know I'm being selfish. My reaction is out of proportion. I shouldn't want to hold Brad back when he's worked so hard for this and his job is so important to him. But there's something about him going so soon I just can't bear.

A sharp intake of air hissed past her gritted teeth as she scrubbed desperately at the dish. She didn't dare to speak. Maybe the physical activity would burn off her fury. Or maybe not. The way she felt, she'd scrub right through the enamel first.

What a fool she'd been to begin to trust him, to believe he'd changed. When she'd known all along it wouldn't work, she shouldn't feel so betrayed he'd chosen work over family again.

"There's a late-afternoon flight. I'll still have Christmas morning here, to take Jacob out with his sled, like I promised." His defensive voice sounded as if he wanted to convince himself as much as her.

She thunked the clean dish on the draining rack and reached for the big saucepan. "You promised you'd go out with him every day till the end of the year." Pitching her voice low so Jacob wouldn't hear them argue, she fought to keep her anger out of her words. "You and I know it's only a week away, but a week is like a lifetime to a kid his age. Did you even ask? Did you tell your boss you promised your son and you've hardly seen him?"

"I'll apologize to Jacob and explain. I'll send him another gift to make up for not being here." He picked up the baking dish and began to dry it.

Knowing it was childish, she still longed to snatch it from his hands and tell him not to touch her stuff. Only the plea for her to understand gleaming in his eyes stopped her. Filling her lungs and holding her breath, she struggled to contain her hurt.

It didn't work.

"Gifts won't make up for you leaving. That's what my dad used to do. He'd come home once a year, loaded with exotic presents from whatever country he'd been posted to. Then after a day or two, he'd be gone again. His mission work was always more important than being with his family. I don't want the same for Jacob. He needs *you*, not more toys. Whether he's in the city or here, he needs that."

And what she needed, too. That was all she'd ever wanted from him. And Dad.

The gift of time. Of feeling valued more than work.

Everyone always told her how wonderful her father was, doing such noble work out in the mission field. But that didn't help a little girl who wanted her daddy. And knowing Brad ran a big hospital group wouldn't help Jacob, either.

"I'm doing it for you both. The promotion means a pay raise. I told you, I'll send you a bigger monthly check." He reached out a hand to her, but she couldn't take it.

All her attention focused on scouring a troublesome patch of stuck-on potato. If only the troublesome parts of her life could be scrubbed away so easily. Like a heart that insisted on loving Brad. Even though he valued status and money more than her and Jacob. And assumed a bigger check made up for a husband and father who was never home.

"You earn more than enough already. Where does it stop? Is there some place you'll finally reach where your family starts being worth more than another promotion?"

"You and Jacob *are* worth more."

It didn't feel that way. She shook her head, remembering all other those times he'd let them down. "I hoped you thought so. You coming here, the way you've been with us these couple of days — it's been wonderful. But now you're choosing to go. You're breaking another promise. What are you trying to prove with all these promotions? To who?"

"I'm not trying to prove anything to anyone. I'm trying to

earn a good living, to support my family. Isn't that what a husband should do?" Irritation heated his voice. "I hoped you'd understand. I even hoped you'd be pleased for me."

She abandoned any pretense of washing up. "A husband should be there for his family. Not working his paternity leave. Not leaving on Christmas Day, and coming back who knows when. Will we see you next year? Or not till the year after, because your work is too important to take a vacation from?" Her shoulders sagged as her anger fled, replaced with desolation, a numbing emptiness. "I'm pleased for you, if it's what you truly want most."

"Maddie, I've worked hard for this. I have to go." His voice softened. "I need to support you and Jacob. And you can't ask me to give up the promotion when you don't know whether you'll ever be able to come back to me. I accept you can't leave yet. You have commitments. Your gran, the store. I know they're important to you."

"Gran told me today, she's marrying Hiram."

Now, why had she admitted that? The hope sparking in his eyes showed what a mistake it was. Fear clutched her stomach. Because next, he'd ask her to leave the lake. She'd be forced to decide.

"If all that's holding you here is your promise to mind the store, you could be free in a couple of months, even less. I'm pretty sure you still have feelings for me, just like I still have feelings for you. Am I right?"

She couldn't lie to him. She nodded.

Brad grinned, his old confidence back. "Good. I know living in the apartment was hard for you, especially when Jacob came along so much sooner than we planned. Next time, we'll have a house out in the suburbs, with a yard and a proper kitchen. I can earn enough to buy whatever will make you and Jacob happy."

He didn't understand. He'd never understand. What she wanted from him couldn't be bought. She stared at the sweet peas on the kitchen windowsill, still bright and fresh. She'd hoped they meant something. But it seemed they had no more emotion behind them than his flashy roses did. Jacob's gift of the dime store plastic ring held far more genuine love.

Stripping off her rubber gloves, she slumped into a chair and covered her face with her hands. Her heart ripped, hurt beyond hurting any more.

"I can't, Brad," she whispered past her hands. "A bigger house won't make any difference. It will be like this, all the time. Promises broken, family events missed, Jacob disappointed. Again and again and again. Your job will always come first. Living like that will kill my love for you. And it will break Jacob's heart, like my dad broke mine." Her voice broke, betraying a weakness she couldn't afford.

Lord, make me stronger, for Jacob's sake.

She forced words past the hard lump choking her throat. "Please, just go now. Say goodnight to Jacob. But leave me alone."

CHAPTER FOURTEEN

BRAD STARED AT MADDIE, hunched over the kitchen table. Her hands hid her face. He couldn't see her expression, but obviously, it wasn't happy. Seeing her like this reminded him painfully of his mom. He'd never been able to make her happy, either — no matter how good he was or how hard he worked to get high grades.

He rested a hand on her shoulder. "Maddie, I'm sorry. I *do* need to leave tomorrow. But I'll come back as soon as I can."

Shaking her head, she shrugged off his touch. Her hands dropped, and fire flashed in her eyes. She pushed back from the table as if she couldn't get away from him fast enough. "Go to Jacob. Read him his bedtime story. He deserves you give him that much time, at least. I'll stay down here and finish washing up."

Fury over how unfair it was lit a slow fuse in his belly. He should pray, hand this over to God, but he couldn't. He didn't want to. That low crack about "trying to prove himself". He worked as hard as he did for her and Jacob, not for himself.

Sure, the money and success weren't bad, but that wasn't why he did it. If she didn't recognize that now, she never would.

He couldn't figure her out. What more did she want from him? She asked him to come here, and he came. He paid her far more than the court-mandated child support. He was willing to marry her again, though she'd been the one to instigate the divorce. He'd offered to give up his apartment and let her choose a house.

She admitted she loved him. But clearly, she didn't love him enough to leave her life here or to see he didn't have the choices she did.

It was simple as that.

"I'll spend some time with Jacob, and then reschedule my flight. Goodnight, Maddie." His words emerged abruptly, short with anger. He was done trying to please her. Nothing he did was ever good enough.

By the time he opened the kitchen door, she already had her back stiffly turned to him, head high, spine rigid, clattering dishes in the sink again.

Her choice.

He charged up the stairs to Jacob's room. Fresh from his bath, the boy sat up in bed, arms wrapped around Trunkie, chattering rapid-fire about taking his sled out. At least his son was pleased to see him. Though knowing he'd disappoint Jacob by leaving tomorrow twisted the knife of guilt Maddie planted in his gut.

Liz threw him a hopeful, questioning glance. Poor gal. She'd engineered things perfectly. Making sure Maddie knew about her marriage plans, then giving them time alone together.

What ifs clustered in his mind. If he hadn't had the call about the promotion. If he hadn't decided to accept. If Harry hadn't wanted him back in the office so soon. Would Maddie have said yes, when he asked her to marry him again?

Probably not.

He gave Liz a tiny headshake.

Her lips tightened, and she rolled her eyes. So he wasn't the only one impatient with Maddie. "We'll go downstairs and help finish the washing up." She stooped, kissing Jacob on the forehead. "Lie down now. Daddy will tuck you in tonight. When you wake up in the morning, it will be Christmas."

Left alone with Jacob, Brad wondered whether to confess he had to leave early. Leaving it to tomorrow was surely less likely to upset the boy. And he admitted, easier for him, too. Besides, until he checked the flight times, he had no idea when he'd need to go.

Instead of spoiling Jacob's happy anticipation of Christmas, he sat beside him and listened to his prattle. No need to tell Jacob a bedtime story, Jacob told him one. A long, convoluted tale involving Trunkie, a circus, airplanes, and possibly Santa, though by that stage the boy was so drowsy he mumbled a slew of barely audible words.

Even after Jacob's slow, steady breathing showed he slept, Brad sat there, gazing at his son. A fierce, protective love rose in him. He had to go back to L.A. tomorrow, and then eventually, on to Chicago. No escaping it. But he also needed to work out how to get more time with Jacob. Angry as he was with Maddie, he acknowledged she'd done a great job raising the boy. But Jacob was getting to the age where he needed his father.

Show me how to do this, Lord. How to be a better father to my son.

After switching on the nightlight the way Maddie showed him the night before, he turned off the main light and tiptoed out the door. To pack his bag. And to book the flight that would take him away from his son, as well as Maddie.

Christmas Day

Jacob woke him before dawn, pulling the curtains back then jumping on his bed. "Daddy, Daddy, wake up. It's Christmas! And it's snowing!"

Brad sat up and peered out the window. Far from blizzard conditions, but white flakes swirled down in a continuous stream. "Can we still go sledding?"

Jacob shook his head and pouted. "Mommy says no. Not till the snow stops."

No sledding. And no escaping the truth. He couldn't put off telling the boy he'd be leaving today.

His mood couldn't sink much lower.

Grabbing his phone, he checked the airport website. Flights

all running as scheduled. Disappointment twinged him. No excuse not to leave. Anyway, Harry would only expect him to drive the whole way if the airports were closed.

He dragged in a deep breath and braced himself. "Jacob, I'm sorry. I'll have to miss the sledding this time. I need to go back to the city today. Hopefully, we can do it when I visit next." Even as he said the words, he knew it wouldn't happen. No matter how much he wanted to, he wouldn't get back before the end of winter. The promotion would make it harder than ever to take time off.

Jacob's lip wobbled, and his little face crumpled. "But, Daddy, you promised."

Brad raised his hands and scrubbed his face as his heart clenched. Reaching out to hug the boy, he felt like he'd kicked a sweet trusting puppy. "I know, and I'm sorry. I don't *want* to go. I *have* to."

He glanced over Jacob's head, to see Maddie standing in the doorway. Even in yoga pants and an old sweatshirt, her hair bundled into a messy braid, her beauty stirred him. But her twisted lips and headshake showed she'd heard what he said — and didn't agree.

"Let's go downstairs for breakfast now." Her brisk no-nonsense tone, warned him as much as Jacob not to argue or sulk, though her hard gaze warmed and softened when Jacob turned to her. "Come on, Peanut. We have pancakes. And then we'll open the rest of the presents."

"O-kaaay!" Jacob swiveled to face Brad. "Mommy makes the best pancakes."

Brad chuckled, though a touch of hurt shot through him at how fast the promise of pancakes eased his son's distress over him leaving. Thankfully, kids were resilient. Jacob would know he loved him, and was doing his best for him.

If only Maddie could see that, too.

"No need to get dressed first," she told Jacob. "Jammies are fine this morning."

Jacob raced downstairs. As they followed, Maddie spoke,

tightlipped. "I hoped you might have reconsidered, but it appears not. What time are you leaving?"

Why couldn't she understand he had no choice? "The late-afternoon flight is full, so I had to book an earlier departure than I wanted. And because of the snow, I should allow longer for the drive. Before eleven, I think."

She nodded slowly. "Right. Now I know when I need to plan something to distract Jacob. Hiram should arrive about then. At least Christmas Day is filled with diversions. All I care about is making sure Jacob isn't too upset over this."

"I care for that, too. The last thing I want is to upset him."

Her raised eyebrow showed his protest rang hollow. Clearly, she thought he could easily make sure the boy wasn't distressed. But it wasn't so simple.

"Truly, Maddie, I don't. Anyway, wouldn't he be just as upset if I left on New Year's Day as planned? Going sooner won't make much difference." The salve to his aching conscience also happened to be true. Even Maddie would have to admit that.

She didn't reply. Probably a good thing, as they were right outside the closed kitchen door and he could hear Jacob's excited voice.

Liz pulled the door open. "Small change of plans. The living room and the presents instead. I agreed with Jacob that the pancake batter would be all the better for sitting in the bowl another half hour."

Maddie ruffled the boy's hair. "I should have known you'd remember, when I said that last week."

"The 'gredients need more time to mix 'agever. You said." The serious way he repeated it, stumbling over the big words, was so comical Brad had to laugh, too.

No choice but to swallow his anger with Maddie and play happy families, for Jacob's sake. They trooped into the living room where the unopened presents waited under the lit-up tree.

Jacob opened Brad's gift first. "Oh wow." His eyes widened, and his mouth fell open as he examined the child-friendly tablet computer, complete with bright blue rubber bumpers. "Thank you, Daddy. The bigger kids at Sunday school all have these." It only took him a second to switch it on and grin with delight as music played.

Brad reveled in Jacob's appreciation. Trying to decipher Maddie's expression was a little less fun. Surely, she couldn't object.

"It's got kid-safe features already installed," he explained. "It's even got a child's version of the Bible on it."

Her tight, fixed smile didn't alter. "Thank you. I prefer him to read real books, but I guess he needs to be computer literate, too. Don't forget the rest of your presents, Jacob." She nudged the pile in front of the boy, and then turned to hand Brad a small flat parcel. "Merry Christmas."

Driving gloves. Quality, expensive ones. Had she remembered him mentioning all the driving between hospitals he did and how hot the steering wheel was till the aircon kicked in? A thoughtful gift. "Thank you."

She nodded, but her expression stayed tight.

He passed her the present he'd bought in the same Christian bookstore as Jacob's tablet. After trying to remember the sort of things she liked, and asking God to guide him, it seemed perfect at the time.

Now, he wasn't sure. He hadn't imagined such a strained, uneasy gift-giving. The tension almost vibrated between them.

Maddie unwrapped the gift, and then flicked through the pages of the feminine, fabric-covered New Testament in a modern translation. Her eyes rose, meeting his gaze, and she swallowed. "It's beautiful. I—"

The phone rang. Seeming grateful for the interruption, she jumped up to answer it. "Merry Christmas to you, too.... I'm so glad.... No, it makes sense. If you've prayed about it.... Of course I will." Only right at the end did he guess who she must be talking to. "Tell Ruth we'll keep praying for Carol."

She hung up the phone, shaking her head, eyes wide. "That was Susanna. The good news is, the baby is a little fighter. The other news? Well, I don't know if it's good or bad. They've decided to sell the store and stay in Coeur d'Alene to support Ruth. They're contacting a Realtor tomorrow."

Ridiculous hope sparked in his heart. Once Liz married and the store sold, Maddie would be free to leave the lake. Except she never would. Love kept her here.

And she loved this place more than she loved him.

They got through opening the rest of the gifts, and breakfast. Maddie's laughter and appreciation seemed subdued and forced. His, too. Though he tried to act normally, to joke and respond so Jacob wouldn't pick up on anything, the pancakes could have been made with sawdust.

He timed his departure right after Hiram arrived with more gifts. As Maddie said, the older man's presence would divert Jacob. The snow had stopped falling, so the chance of sledding added another distraction.

Still, the boy clung as Brad hugged him, unwilling to let him go. "I'll be back as soon as I can. And we'll talk on the phone, okay?"

Jacob nodded, but sniffed.

Liz enveloped him in a warm embrace. "Don't give up hope," she whispered. "I feel sure the way will open for you two."

Brad didn't want to disillusion her, but he couldn't believe that. Despite winning the promotion, the optimism he'd traveled here with had crashed and burned. He'd truly trusted that God had a plan, that He intended for them to reconcile and remarry.

He'd been wrong.

And he wasn't sure who he was most angry with. Maddie, himself, or God.

Right now, it felt like a three-way tie.

Maddie offered him a dutiful kiss on the cheek, their bodies barely touching. Hiram's hearty handshake held far more warmth. Not difficult. The nearest snowbank held more warmth than Maddie.

As he drove away, he looked back at them in the rearview

mirror. Jacob jumped up and down waving, but Maddie stood still, with one hand raised. Brad glimpsed something in her face, something so lost and desolate it wrenched him and tore his chest.

For a second, the craziest urge to turn the car around and go back to her swept him.

Then he steeled himself and drove on. Going back was pointless. All he'd do was lose his promotion, upset Jacob again, and give Maddie another chance to reject him. Time to harden his heart and forget her.

Once he rounded the corner onto Main Street, they disappeared from view.

He tried to dredge up some enthusiasm for work, and mentally ran through the documents Harry sent him in preparation for the meeting tomorrow. This was it. His chance to play with the big boys at last. He couldn't blow it. He had to know his stuff, impress head office. That was what mattered, not wondering what etched those lines of sadness into Maddie's features as he drove off.

But he couldn't forget her face, and he couldn't forget what she'd asked him last night. What was he trying to prove and to who?

The snow-slick road needed all his concentration, but that question nagged at his mind. Along with a Bible verse that kept niggling his conscience. Something about not being conformed to the world.

He couldn't keep going. He had to stop the car.

The parking lot for the old boathouse was right ahead. Slowing as he approached, he impulsively pulled over. Though this was the worst possible place to stop if he wanted to quit thinking of Maddie, taking five minutes to look up that Bible verse wouldn't make him miss his flight.

Then he'd drive on.

Back to L.A. And then on to Chicago and his new job, even further away. He'd leave his ridiculous hopes of reunion with Maddie far behind.

CHAPTER FIFTEEN

MADDIE TRIED TO FORGET the emptiness she'd felt as Brad left.

It should be easy. She had plenty to keep her busy. Thankfully, Jacob's tears hadn't lasted too long. Hiram stepped in and took him sledding. Gran went too, giggling like a schoolgirl, throwing snowballs at them both.

Normally, she'd be out there with them. But today, Maddie couldn't join in. Numb and cold, she had no joy and no playfulness in her. Not now. Not when Brad had let her down again.

Needing to tidy the house and get lunch started was a good excuse to stay inside, but she and Gran had prepared too well. Once she cleared up the discarded wrapping paper and set the dining table, she ran out of things to do. Giving the turkey an occasional basting wasn't the distraction she needed.

She picked up her gifts and carried them upstairs. Her fingers clenched on the floral linen covers of the pretty New Testament Brad gave her. Rage broke through her icy detachment. She wanted to fling it at the wall. Without love, it was just another book. Nothing but empty words.

He'd chosen to leave. Chosen yet again to put his ambition before his family. She didn't want the things he valued, the fancy meals, the clothes from the right stores, the new car. Those trappings of success weren't enough to give life meaning.

"Trappings" was the right word for them. The desire for them seemed to have trapped Brad.

She wanted a family life, a life of love.

This time, she really didn't think she could forgive Brad. She knew she should. She knew she ought to pray, take this to God.

But she couldn't.

It was too big, too raw, too deep a hurt. Just when she'd started to trust Brad again, to believe he'd changed.

As she threw the Bible onto her bed, the pages caught and crumpled. Muttering a hasty apology to God, she picked it up. She was angry, sure, but not angry enough to think mistreating His Word was a good idea.

Her gaze dropped to a creased page as her fingers smoothed it. She hadn't intended to read. But still, the words seeped in, past her anger and her hurt.

> Live a life that is worthy of the calling He has graciously extended to you. Be humble. Be gentle. Be patient. Tolerate one another in an atmosphere thick with love. Make every effort to preserve the unity the Spirit has already created, with peace binding you together....When you are angry, don't let it carry you into sin. Don't let the sun set with anger in your heart... Banish bitterness, rage and anger... be kind and compassionate. Graciously forgive one another just as God has forgiven you....

Something twisted in her heart as the words spoke directly to her. All the things she'd been refusing to do and refusing to let go of. But until she did, she wouldn't know peace and she wouldn't know love.

Straightening the final few bent pages and closing the Bible, she bent forward, covering her face with her hands.

Help me to forgive Brad, Lord, though he keeps breaking his promises. I try to, truly I do.

Suddenly, she winced, as if God had gently shaken her, with strong but loving hands. That was the problem. She'd been *trying*. Trying to be loving. Trying to be good. Trying to forgive.

She wasn't that good. No one was.

She'd asked the wrong questions. She'd focused on all Brad had done wrong, on the reasons she shouldn't trust him. And on the reasons she felt she shouldn't trust God.

She'd stopped trusting God *really* had a plan and a purpose for her, a long time ago. Maybe even as a little girl, when Dad told her it was God's will he left her behind.

She'd let her anger carry her into sin. Her eyes hadn't been on Him. Or on love.

Only on her bitter anger and resentment.

For the disappointment. For her marriage not being easy and effortless like the sweet, lovely homemaker blogs she read. For the way she'd made sacrifices for Brad. For moving to the city. For all those evenings and weekends alone. For all the "not fairs" in her life. For feeling abandoned, all over again.

Her anger felt so righteous.

And so wrong.

She had to let God change her from within. Only God could heal her angry, hurting heart, walled and barricaded and barred like a fortress. She had to decide, now, whether to let Him in. Tears filled her eyes, and she bit her lip as emotion racked her chest.

God wouldn't force her. This had to be her free will.

She had to open her heart. She had to let go of being right and just *be*. She had to choose to forgive — He would do the rest. Not just forgiving Brad, but forgiving God and forgiving herself, too.

All those broken relationships to heal. And she couldn't do it on her own.

Letting go of the struggle, she surrendered.

Yes, Lord, yes!

The walls dissolved as if they'd never been. In place of the dry arid desert they'd contained, flowers sprang up and blossomed. Joy bubbled in her, a fountain in the middle of the garden of her soul. She could love again. Really, truly, love. She felt it, swelling in her, expanding in her heart and mind. Tears poured down her cheeks, but she smiled, laughed, and lifted her hands to God.

Thank You. Thank You.

So this was what grace meant. A gift, freely given, and all she needed to do was accept it. She didn't need to try harder to earn love. She didn't need to try harder to be the good, loving and forgiving wife she should be. She just needed to be where she was — broken and fallen and hurting — and let God into her heart. He would make her over to be the wife He created her to be.

She'd thought being a good wife was about making sacrifices for her marriage. No. A happy marriage wasn't about quietly and bitterly waiting for her husband to fulfill her dream. It was about being partners. True teamwork. Learning each other's love languages. Sharing the joys and the burdens.

She wasn't perfected yet. No doubt, she'd slip back into feeling she had the right to be angry and into trying to do it on her own. But God would be there, waiting for her to hand it over to Him. Always.

Now she could see and feel how Brad loved her, all the things she'd been too blinded by hurt and need to see before. He'd done the best he could, coming from the family he came from.

That Christmas Day they'd gone to his father's L.A. mansion, Brad's dad hadn't been interested in him or Jacob. He'd only cared about how much money Brad was making, Brad's status in the hospital hierarchy, and showing off the glossy new Lamborghini he'd bought to match his glossy new Italian wife. That was what Brad's father loved. Money, status, flashy cars, and flashy trophy wives.

And now God asked her to choose. What did *she* love? Her life as it was or Brad? Her life as it was or obedience to God and to her marriage vows?

She couldn't shake the feeling He wanted her to step out in faith.

To take a risk for love. To follow Brad.

Grabbing her car keys, she ran downstairs to the kitchen and quickly basted the turkey. She touched a sweet pea blossom in the vase on the windowsill with a gentle finger. And then she hurried out to the hillside, just in time to see Jacob do a perfect sled run down the slope.

"I'm going after Brad," she explained to Gran. "Will you take care of things here for me? I don't know how long I'll be."

No surprise, Gran grinned. "Of course."

Maddie hadn't thought she'd argue with the plan.

As it coasted to a halt, Jacob jumped off the sled and victory punched the air. "I did it!"

"I saw. You did great, kiddo!" She scooped him up. "I need to go talk to your daddy. I'll be home long before your bedtime. Okay, Peanut?"

He flung his arms around her neck, and his hot breath fogged her ear. "Tell Daddy I want him with us all the time."

Maddie squeezed him tighter. "That's my plan. We'll all end up living together again."

How, she wasn't sure. As she started her battered old truck and headed out of town, she acknowledged it might mean moving back to the city. God might ask her to take that step of surrender.

And with God's help, she could do it.

Intent on catching up with Brad somewhere along the road, she almost missed seeing his big black rented SUV parked at the boathouse. She'd driven past before she realized. As she swung around at the next turning point to go back, she prayed.

Please help me, Lord. I don't know what to say to him. I do know it's Your will for this relationship to be healed. Help me to be the woman You intend. Make me humble, patient, loving, kind. Open my heart, make me willing to give and to forgive.

As she parked beside him, Brad ended a phone call and then glanced over. The joy lighting his face was the best Christmas gift ever. Heart pounding, she jumped out of her truck and ran to his vehicle. He swung open the passenger door.

"Maddie." He shook his head in amazement. "Please, get in. It's too cold out there." He reached a hand to her.

Gratefully taking it, she climbed in beside him and braved an uncertain smile. "I'm glad I spotted you. Because you've had less practice driving on snow, I guessed I'd overtake you long before you reached the Interstate. But I wasn't expecting you'd still be in Sunset Point."

His hand tightened on hers. "I'm not going on to Spokane. I was about to drive back to the cottage."

She blinked — not going? He couldn't mean...? Could he? She gaped at him. "But what about your job? The promotion?"

"Leaving you and Jacob behind made me realize some stuff. I've phoned Harry and told him I'm letting the promotion go. Family is more important."

Maddie gulped. "No. Don't do it. I know how much it means to you. Phone him back and say you made a mistake."

He chuckled, a deep warm sound that filled the car. "I can't. I *meant* what I told him."

"You don't have to give it up for me. I'll move to L.A. Or to Chicago. Wherever you go." Releasing his hand to steeple her fingers over her mouth, she loosed a shaky laugh. "After you left, I realized some stuff too. I blamed you that I wasn't happy in the city. But I didn't try to make the best of things there. I expected you to do it all for me. This time, I'll do things differently. I'll find the right church, with a playgroup and a good Sunday school."

Brad shook his head. "What about Jacob? You said he's happier in the country."

"If we're together as a family and Jacob sees I'm happy, he'll be happy. Gran wants to give me her cottage, so we'd still get vacations at the lake. Like you said, it's only a plane and a car ride away."

"You'd give up the life you love and move back to the city? For me?" Such doubt crackled in his voice. Something painful that didn't dare to hope clouded his eyes.

"I love you, Brad. I want to be with you. I believe God intends us to be together. If I have to leave the lake for that to happen, yes, I'll do it." The words she'd hesitated over saying flowed so simply and easily in the end.

Wonder lit up his face, and he reached for her hands again. "Oh, Maddie! That means so much." He smiled, a smile containing a universe of emotion and truth. "I love you, too. I've always loved you, but it's different now. Deeper and more real."

Tears filled her eyes, at his sweet, heartfelt words. Silently, she nodded. Her love was the same. Deeper, richer, truer.

Looking out to her beloved pine-covered hills, she knew leaving would wrench her heart. But she could do it. Not in a haze of romantic, hormone-fueled dreams like last time, expecting he'd give her an instant happily-ever-after. In a more grown-up love, understanding the need to give as well as receive, depending on God to carry her through any trials.

"It might be a while. I need to keep my promise to Pat to look after the store till they find a buyer."

"I don't think they'll take long to find buyers." Brad grinned, looking so like Jacob plotting mischief she couldn't resist grinning back. "You and me. With our savings and what I'd get for the apartment, we'd probably have enough."

She stared at him, covering her open mouth with both hands, shocked beyond speaking.

Her obvious surprise triggered an even wider delighted grin. "I want us to buy the store your great-great-grandfather started, and run it together as a family. I've seen how much being part of the lakeside community means to you, and I can't take you away from that. I want it for myself, too."

"But your job… your apartment… your whole life. You'd leave that behind?"

He shook his head and smiled wryly. "There's a lot of good stuff and a lot of good people in the city. But I've been chasing the wrong dreams. I don't want to be like Harry, in the office instead of with his family at Christmas. Or like Dad, in a perpetual midlife crisis, lusting after younger wives and faster cars."

"I'm so glad you figured it out." Joy and thanksgiving

flowered in her heart. This blessing was so much more than she'd dared to hope for.

He pulled out his cell phone. "As I drove away, a verse kept going through my head. That's why I stopped, to look it up in my Bible app. Can I read it to you?"

She nodded.

"Do not conform to the pattern of this world," he read, in his rich, expressive voice. "But be transformed by the renewing of your mind. Then you will be able to test and approve what God's will is — his good, pleasing and perfect will."

Clicking his phone off, he raised his head, and truth shone in his clear hazel gaze. "I've conformed to the wrong things. My career was meant to prove myself to Dad. I took on his values, but they weren't mine. Or God's. He's asking me to start following *His* will for my life. And to stop pretending to myself."

"God told me something similar, after you left." She lifted her shoulders in a rueful shrug. "That I hadn't been living my life in a way that was worthy of Him."

"Me neither." Brad sucked in a sharp breath then let go. "It's embarrassing to admit, but part of the reason I was away working so much was because being a husband and father scared me. I didn't know how to do it right. I didn't know what to do for Jacob. I didn't know how to make you happy. But I did know how to make money. I felt like a loser at home. At work, I could feel like a success. But I want to learn to be a good husband and father. I really do."

Fresh tears stung her eyes as the painful honesty of his confession struck her. She owed him the same. "Brad, I'm so sorry. We really made a mess of things. But my unhappiness wasn't your fault. I wasn't a good wife to you." She squeezed his hand. "I had a lot of wrong expectations of what married life would be like. I blamed you, and I blamed God, for stuff I needed to take responsibility for. I didn't tell you how I felt. We'll both do things differently next time."

"Next time." Joy sparked his eyes. "That sounds good. Isn't

that the greatest Christmas gift of all? The gift of forgiveness and second chances." Releasing his warm grip on her hand, he leaned over and reached into his bag on the back seat. "I brought another Christmas present with me, but the time wasn't right to give it to you sooner. I hope you'll accept it from me now?"

Mystified, she nodded. "Of course."

He opened his hand, revealing a small blue box. She knew what it contained. Her engagement ring. A lovely oval diamond surrounded by smaller diamonds in an antique setting.

Shame heated her at the memory of mailing it back to him. Believing Brad had broken his commitment to her, she'd broken her commitment, too, and ended their marriage. But God reminded her, forgiving Brad also meant forgiving herself. They'd been blessed with a new start, fresh and clean and forgiven, right with God and right with each other.

Spreading her fingers wide, she held out her left hand. It shook a little, and tears blurred his beloved face as he asked the same question he'd asked her here all those summers before.

"Maddie Calder, will you marry me?"

She gave him the same answer she'd given then. "I'd love to."

He slipped the ring back onto her finger, where it belonged. Leaning closer, she nestled against his chest. His strong arm came around her shoulder, holding her in a warm safe embrace. They sat together, gazing out over the sunlit, snowclad lake, silent and calm and bright. God's peace settled over her like a comforting blanket.

Soon, they'd drive back to the cottage. To Jacob, Gran, and Hiram. To the warmth of a family Christmas. But for now, they could enjoy the sweet gift of this moment, of second chances. Both with God, and in their marriage.

This time, keeping Him at the center, they'd do it differently. They'd live the life of love God intended for them to live.

Together.

THE END

THE ROWDY BAKER'S WILD MOUNTAIN HUCKLEBERRY MUFFINS
©2013 The Rowdy Baker
(Used with permission)

Makes 12 scrumptious muffins!

Ingredients
1¾ cups all-purpose flour
⅓ cup sugar
2½ teaspoon baking powder
¾ teaspoon salt
1 teaspoon grated lemon peel
¾ cup small mountain huckleberries, fresh or frozen, divided. (Do not thaw frozen berries)
1 well-beaten egg
¾ cup milk
⅓ cup oil (I use peanut oil)
½ teaspoon vanilla
2 tablespoons flour (if using frozen berries)

Heat oven to 375 F.

Mix together all ingredients for streusel topping (see below) and set aside.

In a large bowl, combine flour, sugar, baking powder, salt. Sift twice.

Add lemon and ½ cup berries, and toss. If you are using frozen berries, toss them with 2 tablespoons of flour in a small bowl and then add to the dry ingredients. Make a well.

In a medium bowl, combine the egg, milk, oil, and vanilla and mix well. Add all at once to the dry ingredients, folding gently just until the dry ingredients are moistened.

Divide between 12 lined muffin cups. Press remaining berries gently onto tops of muffins and cover with streusel mixture.

Bake for 20-25 minutes, or until a toothpick inserted in the middle of a muffin comes out clean. Cool on a rack.

When cool, drizzle with icing (see below) if desired.

Enjoy!

Streusel Topping:
1/2 cup all-purpose flour
1/2 cup chopped pecans (or walnuts)
1/2 cup brown sugar
4 tablespoons (1/4 cup) butter, melted
1/2 teaspoon cinnamon

Mix together well.

Icing:
3/4 cup powdered sugar
1 tablespoon lemon juice
1/2 teaspoon vanilla. Water if needed to thin.

Mix together well.

BIBLE VERSES & OTHER REFERENCES

Chapter 1
Matthew 19:26 NIV
Jesus looked at them and said, "With man this is impossible, but with God, all things are possible."

Chapter 3
Daniel 9:9 NIV
The Lord our God is merciful and forgiving, even though we have rebelled against him

Chapter 4
Jeremiah 29:11 NIV
For I know the plans I have for you," declares the Lord, "plans to prosper you and not to harm you, plans to give you hope and a future.

Matthew 18:20
For when two or three gather in my name, there am I with them.

Chapter 9
Isaiah 61:3 NIV
Bestow on them a crown of beauty instead of ashes, the oil of joy instead of mourning, and a garment of praise instead of a spirit of despair.

Luke 2:1-20 NIV
In those days Caesar Augustus issued a decree that a census should be taken of the entire Roman world. (This was the first census that took place while Quirinius was governor of Syria. And everyone went to their own town to register.
So Joseph also went up from the town of Nazareth in Galilee to Judea, to Bethlehem the town of David, because he belonged to the house and line of David. He went there to register with Mary, who was pledged to be married to him and was expecting a child. While they were there, the time came for the baby to be

born, and she gave birth to her firstborn, a son. She wrapped him in cloths and placed him in a manger, because there was no guest room available for them.

And there were shepherds living out in the fields nearby, keeping watch over their flocks at night. An angel of the Lord appeared to them, and the glory of the Lord shone around them, and they were terrified. But the angel said to them, "Do not be afraid. I bring you good news that will cause great joy for all the people. Today in the town of David a Savior has been born to you; he is the Messiah, the Lord. This will be a sign to you: You will find a baby wrapped in cloths and lying in a manger."

Suddenly a great company of the heavenly host appeared with the angel, praising God and saying, "Glory to God in the highest heaven, and on earth peace to those on whom his favor rests."

When the angels had left them and gone into heaven, the shepherds said to one another, "Let's go to Bethlehem and see this thing that has happened, which the Lord has told us about."

So they hurried off and found Mary and Joseph, and the baby, who was lying in the manger. When they had seen him, they spread the word concerning what had been told them about this child, and all who heard it were amazed at what the shepherds said to them. But Mary treasured up all these things and pondered them in her heart. The shepherds returned, glorifying and praising God for all the things they had heard and seen, which were just as they had been told.

Chapter 10
SILENT NIGHT LYRICS
Silent night, holy night
All is calm, all is bright
Round yon Virgin Mother and Child
Holy Infant so tender and mild
Sleep in heavenly peace
Sleep in heavenly peace

Silent night, holy night!
Shepherds quake at the sight
Glories stream from heaven afar
Heavenly hosts sing Alleluia!
Christ, the Saviour is born
Christ, the Saviour is born

Silent night, holy night
Son of God, love's pure light
Radiant beams from Thy holy face
With the dawn of redeeming grace
Jesus, Lord, at Thy birth
Jesus, Lord, at Thy birth.

Ephesians 1:7 NIV
In him we have redemption through his blood, the forgiveness of sins, in accordance with the riches of God's grace.

John 13:34 NIV
"A new command I give you: Love one another. As I have loved you, so you must love one another."

Chapter 15
Ephesians 4: 1-3 The Voice
I urge you: Live a life that is worthy of the calling He has graciously extended to you. Be humble. Be gentle. Be patient. Tolerate one another in an atmosphere thick with love. Make every effort to preserve the unity the Spirit has already created, with peace binding you together.

Ephesians 4:26
When you are angry, don't let it carry you into sin. Don't let the sun set with anger in your heart…

Ephesians 4:32
…be kind and compassionate. Graciously forgive one another just as God has forgiven you…

Romans 12:2 NIV

Do not conform to the pattern of this world, but be transformed by the renewing of your mind. Then you will be able to test and approve what God's will is—his good, pleasing and perfect will.

DEDICATION

Love to my dear husband Arthur for our adventure of marriage, where I'm growing in love and learning what commitment means, even in the toughest times.

Thanks to Shannon, crit partner and dear friend, whose insight into relationships is so deep and so true. I value your support so much!

Thank you to my lovely editor Deidre at Brilliant Cut Editing. She's the best! Any grammatical errors and misplaced commas are mine, added after she did her edits.

Thanks to Lorinda, The Rowdy Baker, for her scrumptious recipes and for so graciously permitting me to use her huckleberry muffin recipe. Now, if only I could get some huckleberries…

Thanks most of all to God, for always loving us, always forgiving us, and always being willing to give us second chances, when we ask Him.

And thank you, dear reader, for reading this book. I hope you enjoyed the story and were blessed by it.

Midnight Clear

HUCKLEBERRY LAKE #3

"Stop fighting and know that I am God!"
Psalm 46:10 ERV

DEAR READER,

I found writing this story an intensely moving experience. Every story I write is, of course, but this one was particularly emotional. Not only had I been blessed with new story words after several months of being unable to write because of health problems, the story ended up touching on some deeply personal issues that have affected me directly, both as a woman, and as a nurse/ midwife.

God snuck that one up on me! I didn't discover Claire's hidden past until halfway through writing the story. Although my past is not the same as Claire's, He used this story to move me closer to healing right alongside her. The process reminded me yet again of how important it is to trust God's plan and purpose, and let go our own plans when He guides us in a different direction. No matter how painful or discouraging things seem at the time, He always plans for our highest good, often in surprising ways.

I hope and pray you enjoy Claire and Ryan's story, and that it blesses and uplifts you in the reading as much as I was in the writing process!

PROLOGUE

HER HANDS WRIST-DEEP in soapy water, Jeannie Connor forgot the breakfast dishes for a minute and gazed out the kitchen window at Ryan, working in the yard. She appreciated everything her son did for her. And he did so much. Moving back in when his Dad fell ill, staying to help her since Hank passed on.

A man like Ryan deserved a good wife.

Yet here he was, thirty and still single, when all his friends married years ago. This big old house had housed four generations of Connors with room enough for half a dozen children, though she and Hank were only blessed with the one. She'd gladly deed the place to Ryan, move into a granny annex or a smaller home, if that meant he could raise his family here.

Hank's death this past year, at barely sixty, reminded her of two things. The Lord's goodness, above all else. And how we could never know how much time we have left here in this world.

More than anything, she longed to see Ryan happily married with children of his own.

"It is not good for man to be alone." The pastor quoted that verse at every wedding. And yet here her wonderful son was, still alone. All she could do was pray.

Lord, please find a very special wife for Ryan. You know how much he wants a family of his own and how much I'd love grandchildren. I've even suggested he try internet dating! There are some decent Christian sites, after all.

But I've seen that certain glow in his eyes when Claire Robinson is around. And sometimes, when she thinks no one is looking, I've seen her peek at Ryan with that same glow. So, though she's always feisty and argumentative with him and I can't help wondering if she's hiding some sort of heartbreak, if You could get those two together, that would be just perfect.

CHAPTER ONE

HEAVY BOOTS THUDDED on the schoolroom porch, a sound Claire Robinson recognized all too well in her second winter teaching here. Someone stomping snow off their boots before coming to the door. The likely identity of the "someone" snapped her senses to instant alert.

This wasn't Maddie, the Friday afternoon parent volunteer she'd been expecting.

Ryan Connor. It had to be. No one else thumped the snow off their boots quite the way he did. Her teeth clenched, and her eyes narrowed as she looked up from the dinosaur book she'd been reading with five-year-old Jacob.

Small heads swiveled toward the door as all sixteen of her elementary school students ignored the work she'd set before them and waited to see who'd appear. They'd probably figured those heavy steps weren't Maddie's, just as fast as she had.

Her volunteer parents were always welcome. In the one-room kindergarten to fifth-grade school, with just one computer, Claire appreciated all the help she could get.

Except Ryan's. A distraction she did not need. He wasn't a parent, and he wasn't welcome.

At least, not by her. The kids, of course, all adored Ryan.

His smiling face appeared at the window beside the door,

confirming her guess. His hand circled in a cheery wave. Beneath her heavy braid, the back of her neck prickled as her hackles rose. What was the man doing here?

If he thought he'd help by fixing that award plaque the school just won to the wall, he'd be too late. She'd brought in her electric drill and a screwdriver and had it where she wanted it before the first student arrived this morning.

Ryan meant a bigger problem than an interrupted lesson. With Maddie due here any minute, she'd have to field more knowing grins and matchmaking attempts. This place needed a few more single women. Give the happily-married who wanted everyone paired up two-by-two like Noah's ark someone else to pair him up with.

Being single at thirty-two was *not* a crime.

Her gaze strayed from Ryan's widening grin to the huge evergreen he hauled into view. Huckleberry Lake's Mr. Fix-It — Mr. Know-It-All, more like — had brought her a Christmas tree.

A tree she didn't need or want.

As the kids started giggling and clapping, a loud huff escaped her. Trust Ryan to ruin her afternoon. She bristled, prickly as the pine needles.

Forgetting their work and the smattering of classroom discipline she usually enforced, the excited kids jumped up and ran to the window, giggling and chattering as they peered out at the tree.

"Wow, look at that. It's got to be bigger than the biggest dinosaur. Ryan's brought us the biggest Christmas tree *ever*!" Wide-eyed Jacob breathed the words. Unlike most of the class, he hadn't moved from his seat. But the book they'd been reading may as well be closed for all the attention he paid it.

Looked like she'd have to forget classroom discipline for the rest of the afternoon, too. No matter how much she longed to tell Ryan to take his tree and —

She chopped off the rest of that thought. Hardly a good example for the kids to see their teacher explode, over a Christmas tree of all things. Especially when she taught many of them in Sunday school, too.

Time to clamp the lid down hard on the simmering pot of her temper and wait till she was alone to let loose. She clapped her hands loudly to get the kids' attention. "Back to your places, everyone. I'll go see what Ryan wants."

As if it wasn't obvious.

With more than a few backward glances and pouts, the children wandered to their seats. Only the most industrious even glanced at their worksheets.

Pasting on a smile, for the kids' sakes, not Ryan's, she took her time strolling to the door leading to the cloakroom and porch. Bringing the tree was his idea. Leaving him to stand out there in the cold a little longer wouldn't hurt.

Everyone else in town loved Ryan. Always ready to extend a hand to anyone in need. Often doing handyman jobs for no charge, though that was how he made his living. Not waiting till asked, but stepping forward to offer.

Sure, some people needed and valued his assistance. The older widowed women used to having a man do certain tasks for them. Not her. Strong, independent, and capable of looking after herself just fine. She'd learned how to get by on her own. No need for *any* husband and especially not him.

The man irritated her every time they met. Every. Single.

Time.

When he was around, she proved the old line about redheads and temper far more often than she liked. She just couldn't help it. She'd had her prickles out with him from Day One.

After dragging on her thick padded coat and pulling up the hood, she braced herself, stepped out onto the porch, and closed the door behind her. The least heat that escaped the building, the better. The school's creaky old furnace didn't need more strain. If it broke down, she'd have to call on him to repair it.

Strong and independent was one thing, attempting to fix ancient furnaces something else again.

The icy air hit like walking into a freezer. It might be her second December here in Idaho, but this Texas girl still hadn't acclimatized. Ryan's bright smile didn't warm her one bit.

No way. Couldn't possibly.

Some people might call him handsome, with his dark-chestnut hair, designer stubble, and those laugh lines crinkling the corner of his clear, brown eyes. Left her cold.

Some people might admire his community spirit, the way he always pitched in. Not her. She called him a pesky interruption who didn't know when to butt out.

Some people in Sunset Point didn't welcome his helpfulness. Okay, so they could be counted on one hand.

Honesty compelled her to admit, counted on one finger.

"What are you doing here with that?" Keeping her voice low so her sharp-eared students wouldn't overhear, she gestured to the tree. "I'm trying to teach a class."

Impossible to detect any hint that her lack of welcome dented his annoying cheerfulness. "I was out in the woods today getting a few trees for the folk who can't cut their own, and I saw this beauty. Just right for the school. The bigger the better for the children, right?"

Gritting her teeth, she prayed for patience. Shame God never answered.

"Not really. I've rearranged the classroom this year to make room for the computer workstation, and there won't be nearly enough space for a tree that size. Besides, I can find and cut my own tree for the school. I had it all planned for this weekend. I didn't want their schoolwork disrupted until the final week of the term."

"I know you're capable of doing it yourself. And I figured you'd do it when you were ready." His smile faltered, and he audibly swallowed. "I guess… it just felt wrong not to do it, especially when I spotted the perfect tree. Dad and I brought a tree to the school for Mrs. Parks every year, right from before I started kindergarten here."

Claire closed her eyes and cringed inside. Sure, make her feel an insensitive rat for being angry over his gift of a tree. Only pushing her hands deeper into her coat's fleece-lined pockets stopped her from acting on her instinctive urge to lay a comforting hand on his arm.

Her gloveless hands truly were cold, after all. It wasn't an excuse. Not really.

But even with Ryan, she couldn't ignore the raw grief shadowing his eyes and the knowledge she'd unintentionally made his pain worse.

Though she struggled to find any useful words.

All she knew was what didn't help. Plenty of experience there.

When she'd battled with her own losses, most people mouthed meaningless platitudes. Having something so big invalidated with pat, easy answers just made her angrier. And then sent her looking to move somewhere no one knew her or knew what happened to her.

Avoiding the subject suited her best. Way best. She shoved her unwanted memories of the accident back into their mental closet and slammed the door shut. Her urge to touch Ryan could go in there, too.

But she still needed to speak, to acknowledge his hurt.

"I'm so sorry, Ryan. You must miss your dad a lot. This time of year can be difficult when you've lost someone close to you."

He loosed a heavy breath. "Yep. I'm praying for Mom to get through the holidays okay. Her first Christmas as a widow will hit her hard. Thanksgiving was tough enough, but she and Dad always tried to make Christmas extra special." Then he shook himself, shaking off his grief like a dog shaking off water. "We'll be fine. Just need to lean on God's support harder than usual for a while."

Claire just nodded. She sure hoped God offered them more support than she'd felt her first Christmas after the accident.

Maybe Jeannie and Ryan had stronger faith.

Or maybe it was only her God had on ignore.

"I'm sorry I misjudged in bringing you this." He hefted the enormous tree and moved to haul it off the porch. "I'm sure to find someone else to take it if you don't want it."

"Too late now." Her lips twisted in a humorless smile as she raised a hand to stop him. "Want it or not, do you really think I can let you take it away now that the kids have seen it? I'll have a classroom rebellion on my hands."

A glance behind her showed exactly what she expected. Her students clustered at the window, staring out at the porch. All waiting for her to let him bring the tree in. At least they remembered the rules enough to scurry back to their seats as soon as they realized she could see them just as well as they saw her and Ryan.

He chuckled. "You just might. Okay, lesson learned, teacher. I should have waited and asked, not turned up with the tree. I'm sorry."

Her smile this time felt far more genuine. Was she really such a sucker for his contrite grin, complete with dimple? Surely not.

Still, she shrugged. "Well, whether for this tree or one I brought in myself, I'd planned on losing a day or two of class decorating the tree with the kids. May as well start now instead of Monday."

She swung the door open, ready for him to carry the tree in. Good manners insisted she should step forward and help him, but she stood back. If he insisted on bringing a tree this size to the school, he should be the one to deal with it. Besides, the door might swing shut on him if she let it go. That was her excuse, and she'd stick to it.

"Making decorations for the tree and classroom might help keep them out of the worst of their holiday-induced mischief," he offered as he lifted the tree past her. "Unless kids have changed since I was at school."

Claire snorted and shut the door. "I doubt they've changed that much. The killer combo of sugar overload and excitement can turn even well-behaved students into holy terrors."

"Well, since messing with your plans today was my fault, I'd better volunteer to stay and help with them." Why did he have to be so nice, so sincere? Why did he have to love kids just as much as she did, even the difficult ones, and want a huge family of his own?

If he was a kid-hating jerk, things would be so much easier.

With both doors closed, the tiny cloakroom suddenly felt a whole lot smaller. Not even enough space to take their coats off, now. As she edged past him to the inner door, something tightened her chest and caught her breath in her throat.

The sap-rich scent of the huge pine. Had to be that. Not Ryan. Maybe she'd developed a pine allergy. Stranger things had happened.

But when she couldn't avoid brushing her arm against his while reaching for the door, no ignoring facts. The minimal contact with him made her tingle, not the pine needles.

Same as always. That annoying, uncontrollable reaction she seemed unable to suppress.

The reason she avoided Ryan. Made excuses whenever she could — not often enough — to get out of being paired up with him at community events. And never, ever touched him unless absolutely necessary. She blew out a long irritated breath.

God, if You're listening, will You please take this stupid attraction thing away? I am not letting myself fall for Ryan Connor. Absolutely, positively, one-hundred percent not!

CHAPTER TWO

RYAN TENSED AS CLAIRE sidled past him then paused with one hand on the door to the classroom.

"Just a minute. I need to think about this." A frown furrowed her smooth forehead. Her green eyes, almost the same deep color as the pine, narrowed as she eyed the tree. Wondering where the tree should go? Or whether *he* should go?

Nodding, he forced himself to focus on the pine he'd propped against the wall, instead of remembering the brush of her long braid against his bare wrist as she'd turned. Or the touch of her arm on his as she'd reached past him to the door.

Hiding how he felt about her became more difficult every time they met. So much harder to keep acting like she meant nothing more to him than any of the other women here, and pretending he only paired up with her at events needing a partner because he had no more choice about it than she did. As the only two singles older than high-school age and younger than middle-aged in Sunset Point, their choices were simple — stay home or partner with each other.

Seeing they organized half the community events, and were close friends with the organizers of the other half, neither one of them had too much option of sitting out.

They'd sat together at dinners, danced together at weddings, and smiled for the cameras as they did. And in between, she'd sniped at him. For at least six months, he'd wanted to ask her on a real date. But if he was fool enough to ask her, she'd probably tell him she'd rather date a grizzly.

Claire's thoughtful frown lifted, and she nodded. Looked as if she'd reached a decision on whatever made her hesitate at the classroom door.

"Leave the tree where it is for now, will you? I need to get the class started on some activities before we try finding where in the room it will best fit. I don't want them underfoot until that tree is safe and secure." She lifted her chin, eyes brimming with challenge. "At least, I assume you *are* going to set it up for me, not dump that monster here and run? I'm not even convinced your 'perfect tree' will fit into the stand."

Typical attitude. He didn't expect her to be any different. The strength of Claire's allure had a flip side. No one else had such an ability to rile him.

Still, a touch of anger sparked. Her snarky retort was one thing, but did she really imagine he'd leave her to struggle with managing a class full of mischievous kids *and* manhandling a tree two feet taller than her? A little good-guy credit would be nice.

"The tree will fit. And of course, I planned to stay and set it up for you. Just tell me where the tree stand is and where you want the 'monster' to go." Somehow, he kept his voice level, stopped irritation from seeping into his tone.

It wasn't easy.

"Thanks." Her single word almost sounded as if she meant it. Almost.

She opened the door, and he followed her into the classroom.

A lot of changes since he'd gone to school here. A lot of changes in the past fifteen months, too, since Claire replaced Mrs. Parks. She had the same strict, no-nonsense manner as the stern woman who'd taught two generations of Sunset Point children their ABCs and right from wrong. As long as he could remember, Mrs. Parks had been gray-haired, bony, and more than a little terrifying. She still was.

Though Claire was adorably petite, red-haired, and slender

yet with feminine curves in all the places he tried not to let his gaze linger on, her bossiness and snark left him little doubt that at times she put the fear of God into this new generation of students, too.

Some of the kids pretended to be busy with their work, but most peered past him, trying to see the tree through the window in the cloakroom door. Goggle-eyed as if they'd never seen a pine before. Not likely, when most of them grew up here, and densely forested mountains surrounded the lake on all sides.

Probably, if Claire hadn't had her eye on them, they'd be clustering around him, begging for piggyback rides or for him to show them the tree.

Claire clapped her hands to get her students' attention. "You can put away the work I gave you to do this afternoon."

None of the kids wasted even a second pretending regret. A relieved sigh echoed around the room.

Claire eyed them, shaking her head a little. "Don't think that because this term ends next Friday you'll get to skip it. We'll come back to those worksheets on Monday."

Ignoring the muted groans, she assumed a sunny smile. "As you all saw, Ryan's been kind enough to provide our class Christmas tree. And it's such a wonderfully *big* tree, too. That means I'll need your help. While Ryan and I set it in its stand, I want you all to make paper chains and ornaments to decorate it. I have everything you need ready, so you can start that now."

She did? He blinked.

Claire's bright announcement and the confident way she directed two of the older students to go to the supply closet and fetch the boxes labeled Christmas Craft made it appear as if she'd known all along he'd bring the tree today. Planned for it.

But she couldn't possibly have known. He hadn't himself till he saw this tree, so perfect for the school he couldn't ignore it.

Clearly, she believed in planning and preparation. And clearly, she cared too much for the kids to disappoint them by insisting he take the tree away or letting them guess her initial words to him on the porch had been less than friendly.

She'd given him a brief glimpse of her softer side when he mentioned Dad. The sweet, caring, and *very* appealing woman who shone out of her tough exterior now and then.

Most of the time, Claire stayed pricklier than a porcupine, stubborner than a mule, and opinionated to boot. Unwilling to accept help from anyone, especially him. Never missing a chance to needle him.

Even so, she'd come to mean far more than he imagined possible when they first met. Far more than any other woman he'd known had ever meant.

And she obviously didn't feel the same for him.

He had a habit of choosing the wrong women. The ones who saw him as nothing more than a nice guy and a friend.

Until she gave signs she returned his feelings, he'd keep on making sure she didn't guess. And he'd keep praying no other single guys or single women the right age moved to Sunset Point. Then they'd still be each other's only option when a local event needed everyone partnered up.

A guy needed all the chances he could get when he fell for a woman like Claire.

The kids she'd sent to the supply closet finally emerged, proudly hauling boxes nearly as big as they were — boxes wrapped in bright Christmas paper as if they were gifts. That soon dragged the children's attention away from his tree.

Claire smiled at the pair, a high-wattage beam warm enough to melt the thick ice already coating the lake. "Thank you, Adam and Sally. Well done! Want to open the boxes and see what's inside?"

"Yes, Ms. Robinson!" The two fifth-grade kids chorused at once.

Remembering her manners, Sally rushed to add, "Please."

Ryan suppressed a chuckle. A ten-year-old saying no to opening a huge gift-wrapped box seemed unlikely any time. But at Christmas, surely impossible.

As the excited kids each untied the ribbon holding their box closed and opened the paper-covered flaps, Claire grinned. Of course, the contents of the boxes were no surprise to her.

"Oh, wow." The boy's eyes widened as he stared into the box. "It's lots of presents. Enough so there's one for everyone."

"That's right, Adam. It's exactly what they are. You can see each smaller box has a name on it. Would you and Sally pass them out, please?"

As the pair began scurrying around the room delivering boxes, Claire raised a warning finger to the other children. "And, class, I don't want anyone to open their box until they're all given out and Sally and Adam are back in their seats. I mean it."

Those last, sterner words, and an even sterner glance, were aimed at Christopher Mullins. One of the first to receive a gift box, he'd already tugged at the ribbon. Her piercing glare made him pull his hands back like the box stung him.

Ryan's eyes probably opened as wide as the children's did as box after box, all brightly wrapped and carefully ribbon tied like the bigger boxes, appeared. Mrs. Parks never did anything like this when he was at school. This took being prepared to a whole new level, especially when he'd surprised Claire by bringing the tree.

She was probably the sort of Girl Scout who earned every badge and was *always* prepared.

"Okay, *now* you can open your boxes," she announced to the excited class.

The giggling kids untied the ribbons and peeked into the boxes, barely glancing up when someone stomped snow off their boots out on the porch.

"Want me to get that?" Ryan asked.

Claire shook her head. "I'll go — if you're okay to watch the class for a few seconds. I'm expecting Maddie. While we set up the tree, she can keep the class busy and hopefully stop them from sticking too much glitter on themselves and each other. I'll just give her advance warning there's been a change of plan." She rolled her eyes. "Though I'm pretty sure your truck outside and the monster tree taking up the entire cloakroom will clue her in."

He grinned. "Guess it might."

As she hurried to the door, he saw why she'd been concerned about glitter. Now he was, too. The kids better not start sticking it anywhere before Claire came back.

Each box contained all they needed to create their own tree decorations. Pre-cut strips of colored paper. Pages of outline stars and angels, simple enough that even the youngest student could manage them. A stable and a manger, sheep and shepherds, all ready to color in. Blunt-ended scissors, safe for little fingers. Glue sticks. And glitter. *Lots* of glitter.

She'd invested a load of time and care to put these boxes together. So much effort, simply to create a few fun hours for her class.

Seeing Claire at work lifted his respect for her an extra notch. Outside of school, she could be impulsive. Even a little flaky at times, in her stubborn insistence she could manage everything herself from home repairs on the old fixer-upper she'd bought to cutting a Christmas tree.

Here, he saw a different Claire. Calm, organized, with attention to detail, and in complete control. Even staying in control of things she'd had no control over, like his arrival bearing an unexpected Christmas tree.

She bustled back into the classroom, glanced around, and gave a quick decisive nod. Thankfully, the kids had held back from glitter incidents so far. No need for her to target him with the look she'd aimed at Christopher.

Unlike Chris, he probably would have laughed.

Now heavily pregnant, Maddie entered the room more slowly. No mistaking the wink and the knowing glance she threw at him. She and her husband, Brad, knew exactly how he felt about Claire. Never missed a chance to push them together.

Looked like the tree did that job for him, today.

Seeing Maddie and Claire standing side-by-side, he wondered once again how he could have imagined for a minute he still had a thing for the then-single Maddie, after Claire arrived in town.

"Mrs. Hughes will help you with whatever you want to make

to decorate the tree while we get it set up," Claire announced to the class before turning to Maddie. "Thank you so much for helping out with this."

"Happy to." Maddie beamed. "You know how much I love Christmas. This will be far more fun than reading and math."

"I hope you still think that in an hour's time." Claire rolled her eyes again, such a characteristic expression he was hard put not to laugh. "I can't help thinking loose glitter was a bad idea. Worth shelling out for glitter glue next year. I won't be going any further than the cloakroom or the supply closet, so if you need help, just holler."

"I'll manage here fine. You two just get on with whatever you need to do together." Maddie's laughing tone and her emphasis on "together" couldn't be more obvious. At least she hadn't winked this time.

Could be, his matchmaking friends were more of a hindrance than a help.

Claire turned her gaze onto him, making his stomach flip over like he was a school kid with his first crush. "Okay, now we tackle the monster."

"Where do you want me to move it to?" His voice cracked a little, and he cleared his throat.

"Nowhere, yet." She rummaged in her desk drawer then pulled out a tape measure and a calculator. "First thing I want to do is to measure it. I'm not letting you bring it in here until I know it's not too big for the tree stand. If it won't fit, you'll need to cut the tree back till it *will* fit."

Without waiting for him to reply, she hurried to the door. Though the kids were making enough noise as they created their decorations not to hear, he wouldn't argue with her in front of her students.

Out in the cloakroom, he shook his head at her and huffed. "It will fit. I already told you that. I've cut the tree for the school often enough with Dad to know how big is too big."

"I want to check, anyway." She bent to wrap the tape measure around the trunk.

As she slowly rewound the tape measure, he couldn't help wondering if God was doing him a favor making sure Claire didn't return his feelings. Of all the pigheaded, annoying, exasperating women for him to fall for, she was surely the worst.

CHAPTER THREE

CLAIRE STRAIGHTENED AND TOOK HER TIME rewinding the big tape measure. She'd already worked out the answer, near enough. And it wasn't the one she wanted.

Ryan was right. The tree, now christened The Monster, *would* fit the tree stand. Much as she hated to admit it.

He stood beside her, almost but not quite touching in the limited space his ridiculously large tree left in the cloakroom. Arms folded across his broad chest and a told-you-so smirk curving his lips. Waiting for her to concede.

"Well?"

Purely to aggravate him, and to delay having to back down, she ignored his question and punched the trunk circumference into her calculator. Divided by 3.141. And came up with a number a little smaller than what she'd already figured by taking a shortcut — simply dividing the measurement by three.

Her mind got busy designing age-appropriate Christmas-tree-themed math worksheets for the older kids to do next week. Learning *and* Christmas, the perfect combination. Then Ryan interrupted her impromptu lesson planning.

"Well?" His smug smile widened as he asked again, doing that crinkling thing with the creases around his eyes and flashing his dimple. She could slap her foolish self for melting every time he did that.

What she wouldn't give to wipe the smile from his annoyingly handsome face. The urge to tell him his tree wouldn't fit and he'd need to take it away swept her, the unsaid words sweet as candy canes in her mouth.

Sadly, she couldn't say them.

First, it would massively disappoint the class, and she wouldn't do that. Not even for such an excellent cause as taking Ryan down a peg or two.

Two, she'd spoken first and had to ask forgiveness later too many times in her life, especially since the accident. A couple of times she probably should have asked forgiveness but hadn't still niggled at her.

Maybe this Christmas, she should call Mom and Dad, not just send them a Facebook message. If only they wouldn't insist on asking how she was, with their concerned, caring expressions and concerned, caring voices making all the reasons she wasn't fine impossible to ignore.

Sending a Facebook message was far easier to handle.

Anyway, she didn't want to think about that. Back to her list. Three? Well, it was Christmas. If she couldn't behave right during the holiday season, what hope did she have for the rest of the year?

Maybe it was time to call a truce with Ryan. Purely temporary. Come December 26, his tree would go out in the trash, along with any cease-fire.

She'd start the truce right now. Just for the sake of the students. No other reason.

Peeking at him under her lashes, she laughed and held her hands up in surrender. Just on this one point, nothing else.

"Okay. You know you got me. The Monster *will* fit the stand. Are you really going to insist on making me say out loud 'you were right'?"

He guffawed. Good thing the kids were making plenty of noise, so Maddie shouldn't hear his laugh. Claire hadn't missed the wink and the conspiratorial glances her so-called friend threw Ryan. Yet again, she was being set up with him. If it got much more obvious, she might have to tell Maddie the truth. Once she knew, she'd stop the matchmaking.

The only good thing was that Ryan didn't seem especially interested. Nothing more than his usual nice-guy manner. The way he was with everyone else in town.

That thought really should *not* disappoint her.

"I won't make you say it again." Ryan grinned his triumph. "After all, you did just say it. But if only you knew how much I want to make you repeat it. Hearing you say those words again would be so sweet. You. Were. Right." He dragged it out, savoring each syllable.

"Don't go thinking you'll hear me say it again in a hurry. If ever." Her lips twitched. May as well admit how tempted she'd been. "Anyway, I can guess how sweet. Exactly as sweet as being able to tell you your tree was too big would have been for me."

"The school's tree stand is older than I am. I know what size it is. Unless you've bought a new one?"

She shook her head. "No new tree stand." Serve him right if she *had* bought a new one. Except she hadn't. Something for next year's wish list, in case he pulled the same stunt again.

"So, no surprise it will fit. Dad taught me years ago how to find the biggest tree to work with that stand." Grinning his triumph, he made a circle with his strong fingers, using both hands. "One with a trunk about so big. What a coincidence. Exactly the size of this tree's trunk."

"I'll take your word for it." If he expected her to measure the diameter of that tanned and calloused circle, he'd have a long wait.

Ryan's hands lowered to his sides.

"That's just looking at the trunk. And okay, you *are* right about that." Before he got any more mileage from her admission, she spread her arms wide to assess the tree's width, careful not to touch him in the process.

He pressed back against the door as if he wanted her touching him even less than she wanted to touch him. Suited her fine. She didn't need her feelings stirred up any more than necessary.

Lifting her head, she pushed the wayward strands escaping her braid behind her ears and eyed his tree critically. "The tree really *is* too big. Just not too big to fit the tree stand. I already measured it earlier in the week, same as I measured the space available in the classroom, so I knew what tree to pick when I went looking tomorrow. What a pity I never got the chance to choose my own." No need to keep the acidic edge from her voice.

A chuckle was *not* the right response to her tone and her hint of a glare. "Don't worry. I won't do it next year, promise. You can snowshoe into the woods, cut your own tree, and haul it here yourself if you want. Most of the bears should be hibernating by then."

Hmm. Didn't sound quite so appealing put that way. Not that she'd say so. "That's what I want. Anyway, a bear hungry enough to try to eat me would get indigestion."

Ryan knew that she knew the bears around here weren't actually likely to eat anyone. They preferred berries, plant roots, and insects. She'd learned the bear safety rules fast. If a bear attacked a human, it was simply protecting their territory.

He laughed. "I'm sure that thought will comfort you greatly if you meet one."

"It will." Snorting, she rolled her eyes again — something she did way too often around him. "Worth the risk of meeting a bear to get the tree I wanted for the class. I would have chosen a far smaller one. I'll need to rearrange some furniture to get The Monster to fit the space I planned to use."

"Not 'I'. We. Seeing you have some extra muscle here, use it." He tapped his chest.

Thankfully, he didn't go as far as flexing his biceps, the way some guys would have done. One thing she couldn't help admiring about Ryan — he didn't show off. Though he *did* hide some impressive muscles behind his red plaid shirt. Not easy dragging her thoughts from those pesky memories of him in his swimming trunks at the Lake Festival last summer, helping inexperienced visitors go canoeing.

If only she could hit Delete on those images and erase them from her mind permanently.

Along with a whole bunch of other stuff she'd rather not remember. All the reasons she needed to ignore whatever she felt for Ryan. The stuff that pushed her into leaving Texas and coming all the way up here. Huckleberry Lake, Idaho. Next stop, Canada.

If the bears didn't eat you first.

He stood smiling, waiting for her answer. Better and wiser to say no and send him away. Try to manage on her own. But though she was all for doing everything she could for herself, by herself, trying to maneuver a tree this size into place and fix it in the stand when he'd offered to help would be just plain nuts.

Still, she couldn't just cave and say yes, either. "Don't you have somewhere else to be? Other trees to deliver?"

"Neither Mrs. Parks or Nancy Johannsen will mind if I'm a little later taking them their trees. I'll be helping those ladies move the furniture and set their trees in their tree stands, too." His mischievous grin and the way he watched for her reaction suggested he knew she wouldn't like him adding that "too".

She didn't. Nancy had to be at least eighty. And though "only" in her early seventies, as Mrs. Parks liked to say, recovering from a recent hip replacement surely would have slowed her down from her usual vigor. Neither woman was in fit shape to get her own tree.

Claire's lips twisted. "Thanks for the comparison."

"What, you don't like being compared to women who are feisty and independent, yet wise enough to know when to accept help?" His guileless expression didn't fool her for a nanosecond

The man *was* trying to provoke her.

If she rolled her eyes at him one more time, they might just roll right out of their sockets. But she refused to answer his rhetorical question.

Aggravating, frustrating, irritating man! He deserved for her to make him move every stick of furniture in the classroom. That would teach him.

Of course, to get his ridiculously oversized tree in place, they might *have* to. Totally disrupting for the students, as if their learning today hadn't been disrupted enough.

"We can't do it now. The best way to manage this is to do it while the classroom is empty, the way I planned. Pointless trying to rearrange the room and set up the tree with a class in progress. But no one will be able to get their outdoor gear on with The Monster in the way." She threw the tree and Ryan a disparaging glance, though she'd rather aim a kick at them both.

Wasn't the poor defenseless tree's fault it was stuck here blocking the cloakroom.

It would be hard enough getting the kids to accept being unable to add their decorations to the tree till Monday, let alone sending them home without it even being in the classroom. They'd be so disappointed.

And she really couldn't do anything to prevent that, apart from find the right words to explain why.

He gave no sign he noticed the narrow-eyed look she threw him. "If you want, I can lug the tree outside for now and come back after three o'clock to reorganize the furniture. Should give me plenty of time to deliver and set up the other two trees. What do you think?"

Placid as the lake on a windless summer's day, he needed a lot to ruffle his calm. Unlike her. Today's personal weather forecast threatened squalls and thunderstorms. Maybe she should issue PMS warnings, the way the National Weather Service issued storm warnings.

Pesky hormones. Even more annoying now that they were completely pointless.

"Thanks. That'll be fine. It's kind of you." Her muttered words hardly sounded grateful. Because it wasn't really fine, and PMS-ing or not, she didn't plan to spend any more time with Ryan than she had to.

He just smiled, staying as calm as he always was. "Okay. So that's our plan."

Yes, okay, he *was* kind, giving up his time to rearrange a bunch of pint-sized desks and chairs. That part of what she said wasn't total fiction. And she couldn't pretend not to be aware he seemed to find excuses to spend more time with her whenever he could.

What might have thrilled her if things were different, now just fueled her resolve to keep him at arm's length.

When things *weren't* different, knowing he might want to be more than friends and sparring partners just made it worse. Being around him stirred up feelings she wanted to ignore. Reminded her too much why she was exactly the wrong girl for a guy like him, a guy who longed for kids of his own.

Once they had the furniture moved and the tree in the right place, she'd do her darnedest to go back to her standard operating procedure. Avoiding Ryan as much as she possibly could. Keeping the memories at bay and her unruly emotions under better control.

Not easy to avoid *anyone* in a community of fewer than two hundred people. Some might say impossible. Especially when they were more or less neighbors. And when even her best friend and her best friend's husband seemed determined to matchmake them.

But she had to try.

She'd manage it. Somehow. For his sake and her own. She wasn't the right girl for him.

And the man was far too disturbing to her peace of mind.

CHAPTER FOUR

SETTING UP THE TREES for Mrs. Parks and Nancy Johannsen was a snap compared to helping Claire arrange things at the school. The toughest challenge Ryan found with the two older ladies was evading Nancy's insistence he stay for another cup of coffee and a few more of her homemade pepparkakor.

As he'd already eaten more than a few of her addictively delicious spice cookies, and past experience warned if he sat down, Nancy would keep him there chatting for hours, his arrangement to help Claire at the school was a blessing.

Though after an hour of shuffling furniture around the classroom three times over and trying the tree in three different locations, he'd gone well past starting to doubt that. Next year, he really might leave her to haul in her own puny tree. He could've split several tons of firewood in the time satisfying her requirements took.

If her requirements actually *were* satisfied.

As she walked around the classroom assessing the tree from every angle, Claire turned to face him. "Sorry to keep you waiting."

"It's okay." It was. He didn't have anywhere better to be. Though it didn't sound too much like a genuine apology. More a pretense at politeness she felt she ought to do.

Then she smiled, a wide bright smile he wished would light up her face more often. "I really am grateful for your patience with all this. I'm not being difficult. I just want things how I want them."

"You're not being difficult," he repeated her words and quirked an eyebrow. "O. Kay. Millions might disagree, but I'll go along with your little fantasy." She should guess from his light tone he was joking.

She laughed. "You're not supposed to say that! You're supposed to say, 'No, Claire, of course, you aren't being difficult. I've loved moving The Monster and every chair and desk in the room so many times.' That's the correct answer."

"'No, Claire, of course, you aren't being difficult. I've loved moving The Monster and every chair and desk in the room so many times.'" Like before, he mimicked her words and tone.

Their gazes met and clung in a moment of shared amusement that flipped something in his chest head over heels.

Then she glanced away fast, spinning around so her back was toward him. "Won't be much longer. I just need to check a few things." Her voice lost its laughter and became brisk and businesslike.

Relaxing against her desk, he waited for her to make up her mind about the latest setup. She stood in front of him, hair shifting softly on her shoulders as she tipped her head side to side.

Sometime between him leaving to deliver the other trees and him returning, she'd loosened her hair from its braid. It suited her, even more than her usual style, making her look even prettier. Though he suspected Maddie had more to do with that than Claire had. Her hands-on-hips stance in front of him drew his attention unavoidably to the way her cute dress and leggings revealed rather than hid her curves.

Quickly, he forced his gaze to the brightly colored artwork pinned up all around the room.

Wasn't easy to look away. Wasn't as much help as he'd hoped, either.

Staring at the students' paintings raised thoughts almost as unwelcome. When would he have kids of his own to go to school here?

He trusted God, of course. But waiting so long when all his buddies were married with kids of their own wasn't easy. Mom surprised him by suggesting he try internet dating and sent him links she'd found to Christian sites full of happy-ever-after success stories.

Trouble was, he didn't want just any woman to be the mother of his children. He wanted Claire.

The way things were looking, he'd have a long wait.

Though she joked and bantered, he sensed a keep-your-distance chill beneath her fiery surface. With him, but not anyone else. The rest of the townfolk, she hugged every time she met them.

Maybe her being different with him was a good sign? No way to know for sure.

He knew the response he'd get if he suggested a date. Best to avoid being too obvious about his feelings till he saw definite signs of a thaw.

It seemed about as likely as the frozen lake thawing for Christmas.

No matter how unlikely, he let himself hope. Today wasn't the first time in the past year he'd caught her looking at him and then turning away fast when she realized he'd noticed. In those split-second connections, he couldn't help wondering if she really *did* feel as antagonistic toward him as she appeared.

Then, just like it had today, her freezer-burn chill soon popped up again, leaving him guessing. Only Claire and the Lord knew what was really in her heart.

Whether I marry and have kids is in Your hands, Lord. Just like how Claire feels for me. Please, though, bless me with more patience while I wait. Either way, whether she thaws toward me or not, I'm going to need it.

Claire still stood assessing the room. His suspicions grew by the minute. More than making sure the setup worked safely and well for her students motivated her. She'd deliberately chosen to keep him waiting.

Perfect way to pay him back for messing with her plans and ensure he didn't make the same mistake again.

It worked, though it also raised an urge to laugh as he wondered what her next move would be. As if this were a game of checkers, move and countermove. A man could never be bored with a woman like Claire.

Though he'd definitely need to pray at least once a day for a double helping of not only patience, but forbearance and most of the other fruits of the Spirit, too.

As if she sensed his gaze had switched back to her, she swiveled toward him. A hint of laughter lifted her mobile lips and lit her eyes. Maybe, finally, the classroom was arranged just how she wanted it, and the tree positioned just where she wanted it. Or maybe she'd just dreamed up some new way to get him to rearrange the room.

Insisting he shuffle everything a fourth time would surely be taking things too far, even for Claire.

Though if she asked, he'd do it and even smile as he did. No matter that it might make him look like a pushover. Refusing or showing irritation would mean Claire won this round.

"Okay, if you're wondering if I'll ask you to move it all again, you'll be pleased to hear, I think this time it should work as it is."

"Really?" He raised his eyebrows in doubt. "You're *sure* nothing needs switching around?"

Her smirk told him his guess had been right. "Nope. You've had enough punishment for one day. I'm hoping you learned your lesson already."

"What lesson would that be?" He didn't attempt to keep the edge from his voice.

"A simple one — no more offering me help I don't need."

"Don't we all need help sometimes? We're all different parts of the same body, no man is an island, all that stuff?"

"No man is an island, but that doesn't mean a woman can't be," she quipped, her wide grin suggesting that if this was a game of checkers, she'd just taken his King.

Lips tightened, he shook his head and imitated her eye roll. No need to say more. Quick enough on the uptake, she'd get the message.

Her smile faded. Hands clasped in front of her, head tilted to one side, her cute gesture of apology appealed so strongly he couldn't even pretend to stay angry with her.

"Joking aside, I know it might look a lot like I made you move it all so many times for fun, but honestly, I didn't. The other two places we tried the tree didn't seem safe enough. Now it's far enough away from all the different workstations the kids use. And I'm hoping The Monster is now secure enough in the corner so even if someone climbed on it, it wouldn't topple over."

So she hadn't done it deliberately? Doubts still lingered. But he wasn't complaining. More time with Claire, even if spent shuffling furniture, was no hardship.

"Best to be prepared for all possibilities. Especially when some of the Sunset Point kids are on the..." He paused, searching for the best word. "Uh, adventurous side."

"Definitely." She snorted. "Or high-spirited, another word parents like to use to describe it. My first-aid certificate is up to date, but that's knowledge I hope never to need to use." She studied the tree again. "Maybe I should screw some sort of fastener into the wall and tie the tree to it? That would make extra sure they couldn't pull it over."

As far as he knew, Mrs. Parks hadn't bothered with that, in all the years he'd delivered the tree with Dad. He couldn't decide if Claire was simply more careful, or if the kids were less afraid of her than the formidable older teacher.

"Sounds a wise precaution. I can do it tomorrow if you'd like." He carefully scrubbed any suggestion of eagerness to see her again from his voice. "I have some big, solid eyebolts in my workshop. They'd be perfect for the job."

Shifting her attention back to him, she shook her head, dusting off her hands as if the job was already done. "I can manage. You know I'm happy to do my own DIY. That small task is well within my abilities. I won't need to ask for any more help from you."

Probably true. Over the summer and most fall weekends, she'd done a pretty good job working on her old fixer-upper house, taking on repairs most women wouldn't think of tackling on their own. Repairs many men wouldn't attempt, either.

And good thing, or he'd be out of business.

He didn't try to argue with her. Just hunched one shoulder to show he wasn't bothered, either way. "Okay. Your choice. If you change your mind, you know where to find me."

Did disappointment dim the spark in her eyes, just for a moment? As if she *wanted* him to argue. He stifled a chuckle. Her contrary nature always kept him guessing.

"I won't change my mind." Her voice rang firm, without a trace of doubt. Then she nodded toward the door. "C'mon, school's out for the day, for us and not just the kids. It'll soon be dark and likely snowing again, too. Time to lock up and leave."

Class dismissed. With a smile, but definitely dismissed. So typically Claire.

In the cloakroom, he pulled on his coat, hat, and gloves, then stood waiting while she struggled into her coat and snow boots. With the boots wrestled into place at last, she stood. "Sorry to take so long. Us Texans don't get a lot of practice with all this cold-weather gear, you know."

"Take your time. Like I said, I'm not in a rush to get anywhere else. You've adapted better than most newcomers to the winters here at the lake. For a Southerner, that is." He added heavy emphasis to the last sentence, letting the words curl off his tongue with mock condescension. Just enough to needle her ever so slightly.

She huffed and rolled her eyes again but didn't reply.

Her guess there'd be more snow to follow the earlier fall turned out accurate. As they stepped off the schoolroom porch, occasional fat flakes floated around them. Dense clouds hung low over the mountains, their dull gray hiding the peaks and the usual alpenglow.

"Heavier falls overnight, for sure," he predicted.

"So I'll get plenty more cold-weather practice this winter." She peered around, puzzlement wrinkling her forehead. "Where's your truck?"

"I left it at home after I delivered the last tree." He shrugged. "I had to go right past home anyway, and no point using gas driving here when I can easily walk."

So his attitude was downright un-American. He liked to walk. Maybe he hadn't been too unhappy with the thought of walking Claire home, either. If he'd driven here, she would surely have refused a ride the short distance to her house.

Since his tree kept her late at the school, he had a responsibility to make sure she made it safely indoors before the snow started falling in earnest. That was all.

Or pretty much all. He wouldn't try pretending he didn't have an ulterior motive, too.

"Okay." Unusual for Claire not to make an issue of it. It would have made no sense if she had, but that didn't always stop her. "I guess that means we're headed the same way, then."

She stomped off through the few inches of snow that had fallen earlier, since anyone last cleared it. He fell into step beside her.

Her determined pace limited small talk and carried them to her house in under a minute.

A glance at her woodshed showed plenty of logs, but only a couple of baskets worth of split firewood. He eyed Claire, wondering whether to offer.

"Thank you, but no." Her firm words showed she'd noted his glance. "You know I can split my own."

No point arguing, though his exasperated huff should give her the message he wanted to. "Okay. Up to you."

A fluffy tabby cat, barely half-grown and wearing a blue collar, emerged from Claire's porch and meowed.

"Hello, Mr. Mehitabel," she practically purred to the cat. Pity, she didn't talk to people like that — or maybe she did, just not him.

He'd heard a cat turned up on her doorstep a few weeks back, and she decided to keep it when no one else admitted ownership. Installed her own cat door, of course.

Since he lived just over the back fence, he'd heard her doing it.

"Ryan, do you know anything about cats?"

Her sudden question surprised him. She wasn't someone who ever asked for advice.

"I'm no expert, but Mom's always had a cat or two. You've probably seen her current furbaby, Sacha, out in the yard. Why?"

She blew out a long breath. "I know *nothing* about cats or dogs. We never had pets growing up. The nearest vet is twenty miles away. And the internet wasn't much help. A zillion sites, and all saying different things."

"If you want to make that a zillion and one different opinions, ask away." He smiled.

"I'm wondering why he's always so hungry and if it's okay to let him eat as much as he wants." Her forehead creased as she studied the cat. "I figured once he was with me a week or so, he'd stop eating so much. But he still wants way more than what the cat food instructions say. It's hard to see if he's gained any weight, because of all that fur. I don't want to overfeed him. But he meows so pitifully if I don't."

"I guess, with abandoned pets, it might take a while for them to trust they have a good home now?" He wasn't quite sure though. Best not to mess up the one time Claire willingly asked for help. "Want me to ask Mom?"

The cat stretched delicately and padded across the snow to them, rubbing against their legs. Ryan bent to pet the friendly creature, then skimmed a gentle hand along its thickly furred belly.

Straightening, he turned to Claire. "Uh, I hate to be the one to break it to you, but I'm pretty sure this cat isn't a he. And though it's unusual for this time of year, she has plans to present you with proof."

Unmistakable pain flashed across her face, so fast he almost missed it.

The eye roll and huff he'd expected soon replaced that hurting, crumpled expression. Maybe he'd imagined it, along with the way she'd seemed to sag in on herself for a moment. The hand he'd automatically extended to support her dropped back to his side.

"I assumed he — I mean, she — was a boy because of the blue collar. She had it on when she turned up on my porch." Her hands rose to cover her ears. "I don't think I want to hear the reason she's so hungry."

A chuckle escaped him. "So I won't say it. I'm sure you know the facts of life and can figure it out for yourself."

"Thanks for that vote of confidence." Droll sarcasm heightened her slight Texas drawl. "Though it could be misplaced. I've had this cat three weeks, and I didn't realize it intends to thank me with some unexpected Christmas gifts."

"That's how it goes. Find one stray cat, get six kittens free."

"Six?" The horrified word shot from her as her eyebrows winged up to her hair. She waved her hand as if shooing him away. "Go home, Ryan. I don't need any more of your 'help', whether it's landing me with the monster tree or telling me my cat's expecting."

Laughing, he went.

So he had no clue how Claire really felt for him? God knew. And he trusted the Lord planned for his good, no matter what. That was enough for now. It had to be.

CHAPTER FIVE

AFTER A WHIRLWIND final week of school, Claire breathed a huge sigh of relief as she opened her front door on Friday afternoon. Ten minutes later, she sat slumped on her sofa, feet up. Mrs. Mehitabel purred on her lap, a fire blazed in the woodstove, and she sipped from a steaming mug of hot chocolate.

At last, she could let herself relax.

For a short time, anyway.

Her To Do list remained endless. As soon as she crossed one item off, she added two more to the end. The few weeks with no school during the Christmas break just meant she'd be busy with other stuff. This weekend was no exception.

Visiting Mrs. Parks to check how she was recovering from her hip replacement, deliver a few groceries, and invite her over for Christmas lunch.

Making sure the props for the nativity play survived storage in the barn. With Mrs. Parks out of action, she'd need to set up on her own this year.

Then getting to work laying new hardwood flooring in the small spare room. Best to practice there before tackling the far bigger main bedroom.

And no getting away from the need to split more firewood if she wanted to keep enjoying the treat of a real fire.

Maybe she should have let Ryan split some for her instead of refusing his unspoken offer last week. He had a mechanic splitter after all, while she used the old-fashioned method — lifting and swinging a heavy maul. A word she hadn't even known meant a type of ax before moving here.

Whatever she called it, it was sheer hard work. Ryan could split the wood in a fraction of the time.

"No way! You forget that idea, right now."

Her emphatic words startled the cat into jumping from her lap. Quickly, Claire leaned forward to stroke and reassure the tabby. No mistaking that there were kittens on their way. Even she would have figured it out by now, despite the cat's long fur. "Sorry, Mrs. M. I didn't mean to scare you. You can sit on my lap a little longer."

The cat didn't listen, taking up station in front of the woodstove and sitting mesmerized by the flames dancing behind the thick glass panel in the door.

Claire wrapped both hands around her mug and took a soothing sip. The warm, milky chocolate strengthened her enough to list the many reasons *not* to accept Ryan's help.

As if a pregnant cat and a pregnant best friend weren't enough reminders.

One: the exercise of splitting wood was good for her. Thanks to that, all the walking she did here, and fixing up the house, she ate more than she ever had yet still toned up and even lost a few pounds. Plus, she'd developed muscles she never knew she had back in Austin. She hadn't missed the gym one bit.

Two: he had a business to run. She couldn't take advantage of his generous nature by letting him work for her for free. Everyone in Sunset Point knew buying this old house and slowly renovating it more or less cleared out her bank account. Her meager teacher's salary was public record.

Almost certainly, Ryan wouldn't permit her to pay him to work on her house or in her yard or would quote a ridiculously low amount. The only folk he charged full price were the summer people whose holiday homes he maintained.

Three: she *could* do it herself, unlike some of the town's older widows he routinely helped.

Four: her vow never to depend on anyone else again. To become self-sufficient and independent enough to do everything she needed on her own. Like the pioneer women had to. She wouldn't let herself think about what sparked that vow.

And five: more time with Ryan than absolutely necessary was a *very* bad idea. Those hours of verbal sparring with him last Friday over his Christmas tree addled her brain. She'd enjoyed his company a little too much.

Okay, a *lot* too much. She needed to stop thinking about the man, right now.

A large gulp drained her mug, and she set it on the coffee table.

Time to go visit Mrs. Parks before it got too dark and she got too comfortable to want to go out in the cold again. Besides, if she left running the errand much later, Brad and Maddie would have closed the store. Though they'd gladly open it up again for her to purchase the items Mrs. Parks wanted, she wouldn't ask. They deserved their rest, too. Especially Maddie.

Getting back into her cold-weather gear took her almost as long as walking to the store. The bright lights shining through the big glass doors showed she'd made it in time. Brad, out on the wide porch putting things away for the night, waved as she passed.

She waved back.

Something she loved about Sunset Point — the real sense of community. Of course, that had its drawbacks, like being unable to avoid anyone she didn't particularly want to see.

And there she was back thinking about Ryan again.

Her hurried entrance into the store set the bell above the door jangling. No sign of Maddie.

"I'll be right there." Maddie's voice sounded from the storeroom.

"Don't hurry. I'll let you know when I'm done." After picking up a basket, Claire began to assemble the items she needed to deliver. It didn't take long to locate everything Mrs.

Parks requested.

Maddie plodded from the storeroom, way more noticeably expecting than Mrs. Mehitabel. "Hey, here's my bestie."

Putting the basket down, Claire gave her friend a gentle hug. Normally, she'd go out of her way to sidestep being around pregnant women. Such a good friend was impossible to sidestep.

Despite the baby on the way and the far-too-obvious matchmaking, she still loved Mads.

Though pulling the scrunchie from her braid last Friday and refusing to give it back was seriously pushing their friendship. Not to mention, wasted effort. Ryan seeing her with her hair loose couldn't make any difference.

"How did your OB visit go? I hope he gave you the reprieve you wanted."

Maddie beamed. "Yep. He agreed to delay the C-section till the twenty-seventh. I can have my Christmas at home. And I'll be here for the carol singing too."

"Yes!" Claire victory punched the air. "Awesome, Mads. I'm so glad your doctor didn't stick to his insistence the baby should be born next week."

"I'm glad, too!" Maddie almost glowed.

Overjoyed though she was for her friend, Claire couldn't stop an ache gripping her heart hard enough to squeeze the blood from it. Fear for her friend and the baby, that they might not make it through safely. Along with the aching certainty she'd never be where Maddie was — married, secure in her husband's love, and soon to add a much-wanted second child to her family.

Yet again, she longed to demand God tell her why, but she didn't bother trying. No reason He'd answer this time when He never had before.

Dragging her thoughts away from pointless self-pity, she focused on Maddie.

"I want to make our first Christmas back together as a family something special for Brad and Jacob. That would be tough to do if the baby and I were stuck in the hospital, and they were in a motel room."

"It would. So it's fab the doctor has given you that chance."

"Dr. Romero worries over things that will never happen." Maddie shook her head. "Like me suddenly going into labor before Christmas. If he *really* thought that, he wouldn't have laughed when I told him I wanted to try for a normal delivery this time. I guess going two weeks overdue with Jacob, having to be induced, laboring twenty-four hours, and then having an emergency C-section because I got nowhere kinda rules that out."

"At least with the planned C-section, you won't need to go through that this time. Phew! But can Susanna and Pat still come to mind the store? You know I'll gladly help out if needed."

"Though they'll be sorry to miss the carol singing, after Christmas works out better for them. God's perfect timing, as always." Sure in her faith, Maddie spoke with confidence.

Claire wasn't so sure. Not the least bit sure. But she wouldn't say so to her friend. Instead, she'd fuss over her. "You need to rest way more than you do. Why not let me mind Jacob next week."

"I'll see how things go. Liz offered, of course, but she forgets she's his great-grandmother, not his grandmother. She really isn't well enough. Besides, Jacob will be thrilled to visit with you, because of Mrs. Mehitabel." She chuckled. "I warn you — he's already staked a claim on one of the kittens."

"He's welcome. One less for me to find a home for. Unless I become Sunset Point's very own crazy cat lady and keep them all." The idea did have a certain appeal. Claire lifted her basket of groceries onto the counter. "I'd better pay for these and get over to visit Mrs. Parks."

Laughing, Maddie began to add up her purchases. "Somehow, I can't see you as an old spinster cat lady. But hey, if that's what you want, go for it."

"I might!" Claire paid, picked up her shopping, and left the store. Out on the street, the cold air bit through even her thickest coat. Thankfully, she didn't need to walk far.

Despite doctor's orders to use crutches, Mrs. Parks took less time than Claire expected to answer the doorbell. Even managed to hold back Toto, her little bitzer dog, with the tip of one crutch, while he yapped wildly.

Her surprise at how sprightly the older woman appeared must have shown.

"I know I'm convalescing, but I see no reason to dillydally. Simply get on with things, that's what I say. I know not everyone agrees with me." A somewhat scornful lift of the retired teacher's chin suggested she had little time for anyone who didn't.

Claire managed a noncommittal, "Hmmm."

Not wise to get in an argument with Mrs. Parks.

And she knew better than to try to pet the dog. Last time she tried, Toto bared his teeth and growled at her. Normally folk said owners become like their dogs. This seemed more a dog becoming like its owner.

Mrs. Parks ushered her into an immaculately tidy living room and invited her to sit on the hard couch. The small and sparsely decorated Christmas tree Ryan delivered stood in one corner, far more the size Claire wanted for the school.

"Here are your groceries." She proffered the bag. "Would you like me to put them away for you?"

"No need. I can manage," the older woman snapped the words out. "Once I'm allowed to drive again, I won't need to trouble anyone for help."

Mrs. Parks seemed even more brisk and bracing than usual, making Claire hesitate over the wisdom of inviting her to Christmas lunch. But with Christmas less than two weeks away and the rest of the Parks family off visiting other relatives, she shouldn't leave asking too much longer. "I wanted to ask what your plans are for Christmas Day. You're welcome to come to my house for lunch. I'll drive you both ways, of course."

No answer but a frown.

"Of course, you may already have plans," Claire rushed into

speech. "I just thought, with Richard and Jan away...? Didn't you spend Christmas with them last year?

"Them being away makes absolutely no difference to my plans. Just because we bear the same last name doesn't mean we live in each other's pockets." Mrs. Parks's voice sharpened. "Younger folks won't want an old third-cousin-by-marriage hanging around like the Ghost of Christmas Past. My husband died long before Richard was born. Besides, I don't make a fuss about Christmas. Never have, never will. We should give thanks every day for our Lord's birth, not restrict it to one day a year."

Well and truly told, Claire blinked and shook her head a little, then pasted on a smile. "I guess we all should thank God more often." Not that she could. Not after what happened.

"And what about you? Why aren't you going to your parents again, as you did last year?"

Claire almost jerked back as, like Toto when she'd tried to pet him, Mrs. Parks went on the attack after an attempted kindness.

She *hadn't* gone to her parents last year. She'd given in to Mom's nagging to go home and been relieved when flight cancellations meant she spent Christmas in the airport hotel, and could drive back to Sunset Point the next day. Though she really did miss her family, avoiding them was far easier.

Allowed her to also avoid talking about the past or having to think how different things could have been if Rose had lived. She'd be five this year, excited over Christmas trees and presents.

Pushing that thought away, Claire had an honest excuse handy for Mrs. Parks. "They'll be at my sister's this year. She doesn't have space to entertain a crowd in her dining room." She stood. "Sorry to rush off so soon, but I really do need to go. I'm very busy."

"Busy is the best way to be. Thank you for getting these." Mrs. Parks indicated the shopping bag beside her chair, then picked up her purse and fumbled in it. "I must pay you, of course."

"Please don't worry about it." Claire smiled. "You can

consider it my Christmas gift to you."

"Most definitely not. I don't need charity. If you won't let me pay, I can't possibly accept them." Mrs. Parks poked a twenty-dollar bill toward her. "Here, take this. Or take the groceries away."

"But they didn't cost that much."

"In that case, you can consider the difference recompense for your time." Ignoring her protests, the older widow stayed adamant.

No point arguing. She could be stubborn, but in Mrs. Parks, she'd met her match. Rather than take the bread, milk, and other essentials away, Claire reluctantly tucked the cash into her coat pocket.

Back home, the mention of the Ghost of Christmas Past still haunted her. She had ghosts, too. Bittersweet memories of Christmases with her family and with Karl. Today, a new ghost joined the painfully familiar old ones.

The Ghost of Christmas Future.

Would she go through the years ahead like Mrs. Parks, becoming more and more alone and bitter?

Not something Claire wanted to consider. Better to think about anything but that.

Well, anything apart from Ryan.

And all she'd lost in the accident.

She put a casserole in the oven, then busied herself upstairs, laying out the hardwood flooring in the spare bedroom. According to the instructions, the wood needed to adjust to the room conditions before she began cutting and placing it.

Only one problem. The room overlooked her backyard, as well as all the way into the adjoining yard of the house Ryan shared with his mom, directly behind hers. Their outdoor lighting gave her no chance to ignore Ryan, busy carrying tools from his truck into his workshop.

And there she was, back thinking of him again, the way she'd done all week. Worse, feeling uncomfortably like a stalker, covertly watching him.

Somehow, she'd made it through the final week of school without bumping into him, though it took some ducking and diving to avoid him.

This Sunday, it wouldn't be so easy. Pastor Roberts would be in town, and the schoolroom would become a church for the morning. She'd *have* to see Ryan there. Summer or winter, he never missed attending.

To make things worse, if he asked, she'd have to admit the annoying man had been right about everything he'd said.

The children loved the huge classroom tree, far more than they would have appreciated the smaller one she'd planned. And a quick phone call to the vet in Sandpoint confirmed her cat most likely was pregnant, but as long as Mrs. Mehitabel seemed well, Claire didn't need to drive through the snow with her for a face-to-face consultation.

He'd simply better not ask.

At least it was her turn to take Sunday school this week. Hiding out with the kids in the tiny log cabin beside the school, once the original schoolhouse and now the library, would surely help her avoid him.

She turned her back to the window. And to Ryan.

And in the meantime, she'd simply better stop thinking about him.

CHAPTER SIX

RYAN USUALLY ENJOYED splitting firewood. Unlike much of his other work, where attention to detail could make the difference between a house staying up or falling down, feeding logs into the hydraulic splitter was a no-brainer. He could slip into an easy rhythm — bend, lift log, drop into splitter, repeat — and let his mind wander.

Normally, his only problem with it was the noise. Hand tools worked better for just about every woodworking task. Made the user slow down, think about what he was doing. But he'd never split enough firewood the old-fashioned way.

Besides, today he had a reason for wanting the noise.

Claire Robinson.

He'd heard her at work in her house, the Mitchells' old place, all morning. Using a circular saw, by the sound of it. A huge distraction.

He couldn't help but be concerned for her. Not that he'd make the mistake of letting her guess so again. He'd offered help and advice before and been sent away with his tail between his legs.

No doubt, she'd call him sexist for worrying more about her than he would over a man doing DIY. He still *did* worry. Not so much because she was a woman.

Because she was Claire.

When she first moved in, he'd seen her cutting replacement clapboards for her porch and offered to help her. She'd insisted he shouldn't assume she was incapable of using power tools. That any woman who could safely use a blender or a food processor could just as capably use a circular saw. Probably they could. But she wasn't just any woman.

Sure, he admired her gutsy attitude and willingness to tackle big jobs. But admiring it didn't stop him from offering help. Didn't stop him from wanting to make the work easier for her. Or stop him wanting to spend more time with her, either.

And there was the problem. Today, a bigger issue than the splitter noise was where the mindless task let his thoughts wander. Claire, Claire, and more Claire.

Had she really sent him so nuts over her he imagined she was calling his name?

Surely not.

Yet somehow, even through his earmuffs, even over the splitter, he kept hearing it, over and over.

"Ryan."

"Ryan."

"Ryan!"

He pulled up his earmuffs with one hand and switched off the splitter with the other.

"Ryan Connor, so help me, if you don't hear this time I'll have to jump out this window!"

That frustrated yell was *not* his imagination.

He spun 180 degrees and looked up. She'd opened the sash window in one of her upstairs rooms as far as it would go and sat on the sill, jeans-clad legs dangling. No sign of smoke or any other danger. But for Claire to ask him for help, something must be *really* wrong.

Lord, please don't let it be anything serious.

No sign of smoke, and she didn't sound injured, but still, no harm praying. "I hear you. On my way," he shouted back.

Stripping off his work gloves and dropping them, he ran to the fence dividing the two properties, vaulted it, and raced to stand below the window. By the time he got there, her head and shoulders poked out of the window instead of her legs.

Either anger or embarrassment flushed her cheeks. Knowing Claire, probably a mix of both. He'd never known anyone so reluctant to accept help.

"Am I ever glad you heard me. I've been shouting for ages. Everyone else must be either out or indoors. And my cellphone's in the other room so I couldn't call anyone. I really thought I'd have to jump."

Estimating the distance from the window to the ground, he shook his head. "Good thing you didn't. It's plenty far enough to break bones."

Her lip curled. "Tell me something I don't already know. I kinda figured that one out myself."

"Gratitude!" Shaking his head again, he rolled his eyes right back. "So, what's the problem? Or do you plan on letting down your hair and having me climb the side of the house?"

As expected, an eye roll met that comment. "I can't get the door to open, so I'm stuck in here. I've been here hours. I really need to get out now." Her pretty face scrunched up. "Like, *really* now."

Somehow, he managed not to chuckle when he guessed what made the situation so urgent. "I'll go get a ladder. But I'll be a few minutes. It won't go over the fence as easily as I did. I'll need to take the long way around."

"Please, hurry."

He did.

As soon as he propped the extension ladder against the wall, she appeared at the window. The relief in her expression was almost comical. But she still had to get safely out of the window and down to the ground.

"I'll hold the ladder steady for you. Take it slowly. Make sure you have a solid footing before you let go of the windowsill. Getting out an upstairs window is way harder than it looks in the movies."

Claire clambered out feet first in an awkward maneuver, fumbling for the rungs while lying tummy down across the windowsill. He called directions up to her, silently praying as he did.

The thought of her lying on the ground, injured and in pain, racked him.

Once she had both feet on the ladder and slithered out of the window, he could breathe again.

As soon as she reached the ground, she dashed toward her kitchen door, throwing a hasty "Thank you," as she went. Headed straight for the washroom, if his guess was correct.

"Mind if I go upstairs to see what the problem is?" he called after her.

"Do what you want. But forget getting in through the door. You'll have to use the ladder, too." Her usual defensiveness vanished as fast as she did.

While she did whatever she needed to do so urgently, he climbed the ladder and did his own awkward move, tumbling head first into the room. Being here gave him the chance to assess the issue with the door before Claire came back and told him she didn't need or want his help and advice.

New oak floorboards. And a door that only opened a couple of inches before sticking.

Laughter or saying "told you so" would be unkind. Still, he truly did long to laugh. Or to say "told you so".

A rattle on the ladder behind him alerted him of Claire's return. He swung around to help her a little too late. She'd already nosedived through the open window, and then waved away the hand he reached out to get her back on her feet. "I can manage."

Typical Claire.

"Nice flooring," he said as she dusted herself off. "You did a good job, especially for a first-timer. Shame about the door. When you're laying any flooring, it's best not to forget it." So he didn't quite resist the "told you so", after all.

Huffing, she glared. "I *didn't* forget the door. I knew there could be problems because the new boards are thicker than what was here before. So I tested it with the board closest to the door before I started to put them down. The door swung right over it, no sign of sticking. I don't know why there's a problem."

"It happens. You need to do it in a few places, not only at the doorsill. The floors and door jambs in older houses are rarely straight or level." He pulled the door open as far as it would go again, careful not to force it and damage her new floorboards. "Nope. No way to get at the hinges now. That's why it's best to take the door off its hinges first then rehang it once the floor's done. Doors often need a little taken off the lower edge."

She loosed a long sigh. "Okay, I won't argue with you. All I know about laying flooring is from the internet and the instruction leaflet that came with the wood." Then, unexpectedly, she grinned. "As long as you realize I really do *want* to argue."

He chuckled. By now, he should know to expect the unexpected with Claire. "Noted. Your self-control is truly admirable."

"I wish." One small but capable hand indicated the boards causing the trouble. "So, what now? Is the only way to fix it pulling up these boards so the door can be opened?"

"'Fraid so. I could try knocking out the pins holding the hinges together, but then you'll need new hinges. If we lift the boards carefully, you'll be able to reuse them once the door is adjusted."

For a change, Claire didn't argue his "we" and didn't insist she could do it herself. Had to rank as a miracle. Or as first time for everything.

And he prayed it wouldn't be the last time.

Claire didn't know why she let Ryan stay. Far more sensible simply to thank him for the loan of his ladder and then insist he go back to his firewood while she sorted out the problem herself.

She'd been too distracted to stop and tell him no when he'd asked permission, but she didn't have that excuse when she climbed back up the ladder to her spare room, like Rapunzel in reverse.

Instead, she let him fetch the tools he'd need. Let him lift the floorboards she'd so painstakingly cut and nailed down. Then picked at a hangnail while he unscrewed the door.

Standing by while someone else did work she wanted to be able to do for herself was *not* her style. So, what was she doing leaning against the wall, unable to drag her gaze from the play of muscles in his forearms as he rhythmically planed the excess timber from the door's lower edge?

And she had to admit the truth. Fascinated by Ryan himself, not just a skilled carpenter at work. Good thing she had the wall to lean on because her knees were now more than a little wobbly.

Plaid shirts with rolled up sleeves should be illegal for guys with work-honed muscles like his. *Especially* when the muscles belonged to such a wonderful guy.

Whoa! Stop that thought right there!

This meant nothing. Just the killer combination of admiring his forearms, and misbehaving hormones that apparently hadn't read the forget-having-babies memo. Her pesky biological clock reminded her far too often that she'd passed thirty and her time to have children was running out. Why couldn't her body realize she'd already missed that particular boat?

Anyway this crazy tangle of emotions she didn't want to feel for him couldn't *possibly* mean more. No matter what it was, she fully intended to ignore it.

Even though Ryan Connor had to be the kindest, most levelheaded, most giving man she'd ever known. Everyone in Sunset Point loved Ryan, for good reason. He could be her Mr. Right, if only she wasn't so completely his Ms. Wrong.

With an effort, she forced herself to ignore his forearms.

Ignore all his other qualities, too.

And her unwanted thoughts.

No matter how many good reasons she had to admire him, anything more than some banter was *not* going to happen. No matter how deep down, she ached for the kind of care Ryan offered to give her. No matter how many times she'd longed just to sit quietly together, with his arms wrapped around her while they sipped hot chocolate and watched TV, the way she had with Karl.

Guilt twanged painfully at even admitting such disloyal thoughts. No one could replace Karl. Her marriage vows meant staying faithful to him for however long they both lived, and she had. Now he was gone, he wouldn't mind her marrying someone else. She knew that.

Trouble was, knowing that didn't make her the right woman for Ryan.

Nothing could.

Instead of the way the muscles shifted under the tanned skin of his arms as he bent to his task, she focused on the wood shavings curling in front of the metal blade and the tang of cedar rising from the cut timber.

A chance to learn from a real craftsman. Focus on that, not on him.

Easy to see why he preferred working the slow way with traditional hand tools rather than power tools. More control.

Watching him work, she'd even consider getting rid of the noisy dust-producing modern devices she'd been so proud to teach herself to use. Maybe she should learn how to work wood the old-fashioned way. Ryan would probably gladly give her lessons if she asked him.

Her attempt at distracting herself hadn't lasted long. Here she was, right back to thinking of him again.

And not just thinking. Fantasizing.

Wondering what it would be like to have him teach her how to use that plane, his arms around her, his strong hands on hers as he guided her in getting just the right touch to shape the cedar or oak how she wanted.

Her silly daydream still heated her cheeks when he set aside the plane, ran his fingertips along the edge he'd smoothed, looked up, and smiled.

His slow, sweet, heart-thumping smile should be illegal, too.

She rushed into speech. "Thank you. Enough gone to let it open over the new flooring now?"

"Should be. I'll rehang the door. Then all that's needed is simply to put your floorboards back in place to test it. *All* the floorboards, not just one. And without nailing them down."

She rolled her eyes at his obvious statement. "I'd already figured that."

Once the door was in place, she'd make sure he left. The only blessing here was that he couldn't possibly guess what she'd been thinking.

She hoped.

Because once again her mind had filled with happy-ever-after dreams she shouldn't dream about any man. And especially not Ryan. Not when she knew how much he longed for a loving wife and a houseful of kids.

Letting herself fall for him when she'd never be what he wanted made no sense.

No good for her or for him.

Unlike Rapunzel, this particular fairy tale had no chance of a happy ending. And the sooner she forgot hoping for anything different the better.

CHAPTER SEVEN

Arriving extra early at the schoolroom, to set up for church on Sunday morning, Claire turned up the thermostat, pulled out her smartphone, and clicked through to the Sunset Point Facebook page to double check who she'd be working with today.

Her name on the volunteer roster, as expected.

With Ryan? When she checked a couple of weeks ago, surely it had been his mom, Jeannie, down to help?

Not Ryan, the last person she wanted to work alongside today, so soon after having to accept his help yesterday. Thankfully, no one was around to hear her groan.

This *totally* messed with her plan. It should have been perfect. Get here early, clear the path of snow, fix the room up, and then escape to the library. A space barely big enough to hold two adults and the Sunday school kids.

And now she'd be stuck in there with Ryan.

Shaking her head, Claire huffed. Everyone knew how much Jeannie wanted grandchildren. But if that prompted her to play at matchmaking, along with Brad and Maddie, she'd be disappointed.

Ridiculous as it seemed, Claire couldn't help wondering if God was in on this crazy matchmaking thing, as well.

He hadn't helped her last night, as she lay awake churning over this unwanted attraction to Ryan and all the reasons she shouldn't hope he felt the same for her. Admitting that maybe, just maybe, what she felt might be more than out-of-control hormones. Praying her feelings for him would simply go away.

They hadn't.

Lord, if You're trying to push us together, too, I'm telling You now, it won't work.

Will. Not. Happen.

So why mess me around this way? Please, wouldn't just stopping me from falling for Ryan be so much easier?

No reply. Not surprising. She hadn't really expected one.

Keeping on praying when all her prayers went unanswered felt more and more pointless. Just like her pesky hormones. Maybe she should simply stop, as if prayer was nothing more than a bad habit she needed to break.

Why keep bothering God, if He even listened at all? Save herself the disappointment.

She needed Jesus for her salvation, no denying it. But in the five years since the accident, five years of unanswered prayers, she should have learned that for everything else she'd do better managing on her own.

So she'd manage this on her own, too. Be polite, even cordial with Ryan in front of the kids. And keep well clear of anything liable to stir up other feelings.

Right. A new plan. Easy peasy. She could do this.

And seeing it was him and not his mom down to help, she'd let *him* shovel the snow from the path and salt the steps.

Time to get busy. She started stacking the kid-sized classroom chairs and pushing the desks up against the wall, to make room for the rows of bigger chairs.

Of course, Ryan was the next to arrive. And he looked better than ever in cord trousers and a soft denim-blue sweater. The warm glow brightening his eyes suggested he might have feelings for her, too. More than merely being his usual nice-guy self.

Just what she didn't need.

Gritting her teeth, she fought down her instinctive surge of joy. This could be harder than she thought. If only she could close her eyes and click her heels together to make it all disappear.

"Hi, Claire. Mom suggested I should come help out today instead of her, seeing so much snow fell last night and there's so much furniture to move." His smile held a hint of mischief. "After all, I had that practice rearranging pint-sized chairs and tables with the tree."

She rolled her eyes at that, pinned on a chirpy smile, and waved toward The Monster. "As you can see, it's still here. Thanks for offering to help today."

Saccharine sweet, the words left a bitter taste in her mouth. Who was she trying to kid? Ryan, God, or herself?

He grinned as he studied the tree. "The kids did a great job decorating it."

His response suggested he had no idea how much she longed to avoid him. Good. She did *not* want him guessing how she felt. Or how much she struggled to stop feeling it.

"Yes, and they had so much of it to decorate." Her usual snark colored her voice. Better not be too sticky sweet, or Ryan might wonder why.

That earned her a chuckle. "How's your door? Still opening

okay?"

"It's fine, thanks."

"Great." He smiled, that gorgeous eye-crinkling smile that melted her every time. "If you find it starts sticking again, just let me know. Sometimes it happens after a bit. I'll be happy to plane a bit more off it for you."

She nodded. That wasn't the same as lying, which she'd be doing if she said yes.

If the door stuck again, it would have to *stay* stuck.

"I hope you would let me know." He raised one brow and eyed her.

So, her nod hadn't fooled him.

"Uh-huh." She rushed into falsely bright speech. "So, for the kids in Sunday school today, I'd planned rehearsals for the Nativity. Talk them through the original story again, make a few props to replace the ones that didn't survive a year out with the spiders in my barn, and practice any parts they're having problems with. I have a big red box with what we'll need in the supply room, ready to go."

"Sounds good." He glanced around the room. "I'll get on with the setting up. And just ask when you want me to carry that box to the library for you."

She lifted her chin. "I can manage it on my own."

Unoffendable as always, he simply nodded. "Yep, I'm sure you can. But why do it yourself when you don't have to?"

Because letting him look after her would be nice, but another bad habit. One she needed to stop before it started. Not fair of her to encourage Ryan in any way.

Of course, she couldn't tell him that. She shrugged and turned his question back at him. "Why let you do it for me when I can do it myself?"

"Because we're both down on the list to set up this morning, that's why. We could keep going around in circles like this all day. If you want to be stubborn and independent, it's up to you. You almost deserve to be the one to go out in the cold to clear the path. But because I'm a nice guy, I'll do it." He laughed, and walked away.

That job would keep him out of the room for a while. And other folk would get here soon. Able to breathe again, she continued moving chairs. Ryan's voice sounding from outside alerted her to the first arrival. Phew. No chance of time alone with him now.

Beaming, Jeannie hurried into the room and hugged her. "I'm so glad I caught you on your own, Claire, before anyone else got here. Perfect timing while Ryan is outside salting the steps." A sparkle in the older woman's eyes confirmed her suspicion.

Jeannie was in on the matchmaking, too. No wonder it felt like *she* was the one being set up, not the classroom.

Eyes scrunched shut, Claire returned the hug. She liked the older woman, really she did, despite what she, Brad, and Maddie were up to. They had no way to know the truth — she would never produce the grandbabies Jeannie made no secret of wanting. It wasn't his mother's fault she couldn't possibly be the wife Ryan deserved.

"I want to ask you about Christmas." Jeannie's warm smile looked so much like Ryan's it almost hurt. "Maddie told me you're not going home to your family this year. I'd love for you to join us for lunch."

Well, at least she wasn't kept waiting long to discover what

Jeannie had planned. But she wished Mrs. Parks hadn't turned down Christmas lunch at her house, so she had a good excuse to refuse the invitation.

"It's very kind of you to ask, but—"

"Please, do say yes. Ryan will take this first Christmas without his dad particularly hard, I know. I'm hoping having someone else with us will help us get through the holidays easier." Jeannie lowered her voice for the last couple of sentences, clearly not wanting her son to walk back in the room and overhear.

Way to ladle on the pressure and make her feel a complete rat for refusing.

She had no idea how Christmas after losing a parent would feel, though she could imagine. Christmas as a widow, she knew far more about than she'd ever hoped to know. It fueled her decision to move right away where no one knew what happened and she wouldn't need to discuss her losses with anyone ever again.

"I...uh..."

She stacked a couple more chairs while she struggled to find a gracious way to say no. Her search for the right words failed dismally.

Despite the uncomfortable echoes of Mrs. Parks refusing her Christmas invite, she really couldn't spend Christmas with Ryan and his mom. Getting through today would be challenge enough.

Jeannie loosed a small sigh. "It's okay. I won't push you for an answer. But I wanted you to know you're most welcome to join us. I always cook too much, so turning up on the day will be fine."

Somehow, Claire managed a smile, though it was more with

relief to have time to think of a good excuse than gratitude over the offer. "Thank you. I appreciate it. I truly do." She rested a hand on the older woman's arm.

Jeannie would make some lucky woman a wonderful mother-in-law. But that woman wouldn't be her.

If only she knew how to *un*-feel these feelings she didn't want. Not only about Ryan. About everything she'd moved here to get away from.

As if thinking of him made him appear, Ryan strolled in, followed by the Schaefers. The Mullins family arrived right after. The swirl of noisy greetings and conversation left no room for any private chat.

Plus, all the people arriving made it easy to keep as far away as she could from Ryan as he carried a stack of adult-sized chairs from the supply room and placed them in rows. Shame she stayed aware of him, even across the room and with her back turned.

Instead of escaping to the library as soon as possible, she now planned to stay in the schoolroom as long as she could. With the Sunday school kids already arriving and the final preparations for the Nativity play to keep them busy, she could easily make sure she and Ryan had no time to talk privately together.

If she hadn't imagined that glow in his eyes, at least she had no need to worry about him being pushy or trying to get her alone. Even if he *did* want them to become more than verbal sparring partners, he wasn't a pushy kind of guy.

Just, if she made sure they always had other people around, less chance of her drifting into thoughts she didn't want to think or discussing topics she didn't want to talk about.

Maybe even a chance to control her unruly feelings for him.

Brad, Maddie, and Jacob walked into the room, along with Maddie's grandmother, Liz, and Liz's husband, Hiram. Brad kept a protective arm wrapped around Maddie. They really were the perfect couple. Hard to imagine they'd divorced and lived apart for over a year.

A pang of envy hit her. She was happy for them, of course she was, though seeing them together reminded her of all she'd lost. At least the newlyweds, Samantha and Daniel, wouldn't be here today. They'd left to have Christmas with Sam's folks.

One perfect couple near her age was more than enough.

She studied her friend. Maddie looked more tired than usual. As she stood chatting with Sarah Schaefer and Liz, she rubbed her lower back.

Claire waved to them, then threaded through the quickly filling room. "Are you okay? I saw you rubbing your back."

So her anxious question made her sound like an old mother hen fussing over her chicks.

Maddie smiled. "I should have guessed that wouldn't escape your eagle eye. I'm doing fine. It's only practice contractions. They kept me awake last night. My OB said they're nothing to worry about, normal for thirty-six weeks."

All seriousness, Jacob stared up at Claire. "Ms. Robinson, did you know Mommy has a baby in her tummy? She and Daddy are going to give me a baby brother or sister for my Christmas present."

She tensed and struggled to smile.

Maddie ruffled her son's fine blond hair. "I think Ms. Robinson already knows, Peanut. And you'll still find some other presents waiting for you on Christmas Day."

Unwelcome pain swept Claire. She and Karl should have been wrapping presents and then hiding them from inquisitive little eyes, like she knew Maddie and Brad had been doing for Jacob.

Stiffening, she pushed that thought away. Time to get her emotions under better control.

Perhaps she should have stayed substitute teaching. Kept moving from school to school without forming deep friendships or letting anyone get too close. Deciding to settle here and allowing herself to get involved with people began to feel like an uncomfortable mistake. The only blessing was that no one here knew about Karl and Rose.

And that's the way she intended to keep it.

Somehow she summoned a grin. "Wow, Jacob. Presents *and* a new baby. This will be a very special Christmas for you."

Much as she loved Maddie and Jacob, she had to get away from them before the memories crushed her.

Away from all the other happy families, too.

She clapped her hands and raised her voice to announce to the room in general. "Pastor Roberts is due to arrive any minute. Time for everyone twelve and under to come with me for Sunday school."

And Ryan, as well. No escaping Ryan.

Though she knew she should, a big part of her didn't want to escape him at all.

This was all his fault. If he wasn't so annoyingly appealing and so frustratingly nice, none of her memories and feelings would have been stirred up. She could have kept them all safely buried where they belonged.

Could be, she'd hit up against something too big to DIY.

CHAPTER EIGHT

RYAN ALMOST CHUCKLED at the way Claire so obviously chose to stomp along the opposite side of the street from him, ignoring him as if he wasn't there. She'd been the same at church on Sunday. Her avoidance was so comical, it couldn't possibly offend him.

Besides, only one place she could be headed at this time on this particular Wednesday afternoon. The store, to help set up for the annual Sunset Point carol singing and Nativity play.

Same place as him.

After getting it so wrong with Maddie last year, he figured he wasn't the sharpest judge of whether a woman was just being polite, hated his guts, or if she was truly interested in him as more than a neighbor or friend. But even an ordinary Joe like him couldn't mistake Claire's attitude.

She seemed to go out of her way to try to rile him.

Everything redheads were reputed to be, with bells on. Half the time, she acted more or less polite, with a side of snark. The other half, she acted like she didn't want to be on the same planet as him, let alone in the same room.

Problem was, he couldn't be sure which half was acting and which half was real.

He hadn't been stupid enough to try to come up with a

reason to see her since Sunday. Not quite true. He'd come up with dozens of reasons, none of which she would have accepted. He had plenty of easy excuses to stop in at her place like he would with the other neighbors. Help fill her woodshed, make sure that door stayed unstuck, check on how her adopted cat was doing, for starters.

The clamor of her bashing away at her unsplit logs on Monday warned him off the first one. Not wanting to make a fool of himself again over a woman with zero interest in him warned him off the other two.

Trouble with falling for someone — it made being normal and neighborly almost impossible.

They both arrived at the store at once, and he stepped back to let her go ahead of him.

"Thanks." The single word, muttered without as much as a glance his way, proved he wasn't quite invisible.

After thumping the snow off his boots, he followed her through the double swing doors and into the warmth. As he pulled off his hat and coat, he glanced around. The doors leading to the café were still closed. Maddie leaned on the counter, wilted as a week-old salad, but attempted a welcoming smile. No sign of Brad.

"What's wrong, Mads? You look exhausted. You should be resting, not minding the store." Concern sweetened Claire's voice like sugar in coffee.

Maddie sighed. "I wish I could, but there's so much to do. I'm way behind where I wanted to be with setting up for the carols. I hardly slept last night with the practice contractions and the baby kicking so much. Then an hour ago, Brad had a phone call — his dad's in the hospital after a heart attack. He's on his way to the airport now." Tears filled her eyes, probably not the first she'd cried today.

Ryan whistled out a long, low breath and prayed for Brad's safety. Good thing he'd planned to come early to help his buddy set up. Doubly good that Claire had the same idea.

While she wrapped a comforting arm around her friend, Claire's forehead furrowed. "Oh, I'm so sorry. Terrible timing."

"Yep." Maddie attempted a watery smile. "Jacob's upset Brad won't be here to see him play a shepherd again. I had to promise I'd film him and email it to his daddy straight away to stop his crying."

Jacob gave Ryan something practical he could offer to help. "Where is Jacob now? Mom would be happy to sit with him if you need it."

"Thanks, Ryan, but he's fine for now. Liz and Hiram love having him visit. Problem is, an active five-year-old is more than two eighty-somethings can handle. Thankfully, Hiram's son is visiting, so I could let them take Jacob for the afternoon. Liz minded him for me last Christmas, but she's so much frailer now than she was then."

"So if they need a break, just call Mom, okay?"

"I will." Maddie nodded. "And thank you."

"Make sure you do." Hopefully, she would. He rubbed his chin. "It's almost like a replay of last year's carol night when Susanna and Pat had to race off to Coeur d'Alene, leaving you and Brad to set up."

"Except this time I'm not able to do nearly as much as I could last year." Resting a hand on her baby bump, Maddie sighed again, her lips drooping. "I so wanted to make this Christmas special. Our first since we remarried, and Jacob's last as an only child."

"We'll manage. You know Ryan and I will both do whatever we can to help." Claire's glance warned him he had better.

Shaking his head at her for even *thinking* such doubts, he jumped in to reassure Maddie. "Gladly. And I can help out in the store till Brad comes back. I know this is a busy time of year. Not just the carols tonight, but you have the turkeys and all the other Christmas supplies arriving soon. Since all the firewood and Christmas trees are delivered, the only work I'll have to deal with are emergency callouts. If I get one, then maybe Claire will cover for me here?"

"Of course. No problem helping in the store *or* with Jacob. After tonight, once the Nativity play is done, that's it for me till the new school term begins." Claire eyed him almost pugnaciously as if they were competing for who'd chalk up the most good-neighbor points.

He held back a chuckle. Wrong to laugh when Maddie's plans collapsed like a poorly built house. But Claire's attitude promised the next few days could be interesting. He couldn't hold back a tiny spark of hope. Even as he prayed for Brad's father to make a quick recovery, he wouldn't complain one bit about the opportunity to spend more time with Claire.

Maddie stood straighter, and her eyes brightened. "Thanks so much. I'm blessed to have friends like you two. I won't say no to your help. Brad will be home by Christmas Eve. And we'll all fly back to L.A. in February so his family can meet the new baby."

"I'm praying that's so." Ryan threw Claire a challenging glance. Maybe she'd decide she wanted to start a praying contest, too. "And that the outcome for Brad's father is as good as the outcome finally turned out for Pat and Susanna's grandbaby." He gestured to the wall behind Maddie.

As she turned to study the corkboard covered with photos of tiny Carol Noelle, he considered the pictures. The baby had grown up a lot since her birth last Christmas as a scarily tiny preemie.

He added an extra prayer — never to go through such an ordeal with a child of his own.

"She's doing fine now, according to Susanna's last email." Maddie's smile widened, looking a whole lot more genuine than her previous attempts. She patted her belly. "I'm so glad Peanut Number Two here has made it this far with no problems. God willing, it should be plain sailing now."

Pain contorted Claire's face for a moment, before she masked it. "I sure hope so," she said. Suddenly all action, she hurried across the room to open the big double doors separating the café area from the store. Her lips quirked to one side as she surveyed the space. "You know, Mads, we could move the entire event to the school. That would make things so much easier for you. I can go home and bring my car down to move the props I left here."

Not taking as much as a moment to ponder Claire's suggestion, Maddie flattened her hands on the old timber countertop and shook her head emphatically. "I know it would be easier, and thanks for offering. But having the carol singing and Nativity here is part of my history. And it's part of Sunset Point's history, too. If my great-grandparents could manage it in the Depression years, I can manage it now." She grinned. "With your help, of course."

Claire rolled her eyes. "I guessed you'd say that."

He had, too. Maddie didn't give in easy, any more than Claire did. Or his mom. Life at the lake seemed to attract headstrong, stubborn women.

A wise man, a man like Dad had been, knew when to stand firm with a woman like that and when to back down. He hoped he'd learned that lesson, too. "Okay, we'll get moving setting up here."

"Not you." Claire raised a warning hand before Maddie took more than a single step forward. "You sit down. If I catch you trying to lift or carry anything, you'll discover my Ms. Bossyboots side."

Maddie snorted. "Discover? It's at least a year too late for that."

He didn't bother holding back his chuckle this time. Same for him, too.

"Rats. You weren't supposed to suss my true nature so soon." Smiling wider, Claire gurgled with laughter. "In that case, you know I mean it. If you want to supervise us, you can sit in the café while we work. But lift one finger…" She waggled her own finger in the air and narrowed her eyes in mock menace.

He loved seeing Claire like this, naturally warm and compassionate with her friend. So much more to her than her vivid unconventional beauty. Okay, and she *was* bossy with it. But in a good way. A caring way.

Her bossiness didn't matter. That he'd imagined himself so in love with Maddie he'd hardly noticed the new teacher during her first months here seemed unbelievable to him now. What a fool he'd been.

And now, though he'd come to his senses months before, it seemed he was the only one Claire reserved her refrigerator treatment for. He could only pray that just as he'd had a change of heart, she would too.

Despite her attitude, they worked smoothly together and rearranged the room faster than he expected. The chairs, plus some extra from the back storeroom, formed a circle facing the makeshift stage, nothing more than a sheet of artificial grass Claire spread on the floor. The café tables edged to one end of the room extended the small service counter for tonight's potluck supper.

When he returned from carrying the latest delivery of Christmas foodstuffs into the store's walk-in cooler, he found Claire struggling to set up the lightweight gazebo that in past years formed the Nativity stable.

He hurried across to hand her the piece of rigid plastic tubing she couldn't quite reach without letting the part-constructed structure collapse. Then he supported the tubes she'd already connected while she slid the one he'd passed her into place.

So unlike Claire not to fight his offer of help. In any other situation, she'd be insisting she could do it. His surprise must have been obvious because she rushed into explanations.

"Yes, occasionally I *do* accept help. I know that revelation must shock you." She glanced up at the ceiling again, and her lips twisted in self-mockery. "I've never had to do this part on my own. Last year, Mrs. Parks took charge, and I was her assistant while she showed me what to do. This year, it's just me."

"And me," he added gently, praying he wasn't about to say too much. "I'm always willing to be there for you."

Their gazes met and clung for a long moment that dragged all the air from his lungs and left his last words hoarse and breathless. Her lovely eyes widened, and her lips parted. Though they weren't touching, not even the slightest brush of their fingertips, their connection felt solid and tangible. As real as if he took hold of her hands or embraced her.

He didn't try. She'd run a mile if he did.

"Thank you, Ryan. You're a true friend." She rested a hand on his arm. Then laughing shakily, she tore her gaze away from his and pulled her hand away. "But don't go thinking this means I'll willingly accept help next time. Treat it as a once-only. I doubt it will happen again."

"I won't expect it." He smiled and chuckled, as he guessed she'd intended him to. "Back to your normal 'I can manage' after tonight."

For a moment, he'd seen the Claire he loved most of all. This precious glimpse of the soft, vulnerable Claire, peeking out from behind her snark and attitude, formed enough of a blessing for today.

He just wished he knew what made her feel she needed to act tough, do life all on her own, no help from anyone. Had someone let her down? Or had she lost someone close to her?

Sureness grew in him, as real and certain as God's love. In the Lord's good time, he'd know. And when she told him, that would be the key to healing whatever hurt her so badly.

CHAPTER NINE

CLAIRE EYED MADDIE, cheerfully singing along with the Christmas carols on the sound system as she straightened the Christmas display in the store window.

Where did the woman get her energy from? And could she have some, please? While Claire felt limp as a washed-out dishcloth thanks to the Christmas Eve rush, her friend flitted happily from one task to another, cleaning and tidying and ringing up the till.

When Maddie crashed, as she surely would, it would *not* be pretty.

Marching over to the window, Claire snatched up the tree ornament Maddie bent to reach and shook her head reprovingly. "Leave that, Mads. Please go rest. I'll sort the mess out. We're almost due to close the store, anyway. When it reopens, Christmas will have been and gone."

Maddie pretended to grimace. "I love you dearly, bestie, but no need to fuss over me. I'm fine." Then contradicting her words, her breath caught, and she rested a hand on her belly. A minute passed before she spoke again. "Oh my, that one was a doozy. But I *am* fine. Truly."

She might claim to be fine, but Claire's concern for her didn't let up. Unease tightened her chest and cramped her tummy.

Maddie's contractions were getting more frequent. And stronger. "Do you think you should call your OB again?"

"Nah." Her friend laughed. "I know what he'd say. Practice contractions. I had them when I saw him last week. And I had them for weeks and weeks with Jacob. Three times, I got all excited thinking this was it, real labor at last. But when I went to the hospital, they just said no progress and sent me home again. Then I went so far overdue, I had to be induced. And then they made me have the C-section."

All Claire could do was nod. Maddie had way more experience with this than she did. Experience with a happier ending than hers. Maybe the hospital would have sent *her* home, too, if she and Karl had made it there in one piece. "Okay. You know your body best. But I wish you'd rest and let me tidy up. I still can't help worrying about you."

Maddie snorted and pointed to the mess. "You should worry more about how you'll stop your classroom from looking like this next year when Matthew Mullins starts kindergarten."

Righting the big glitter-covered reindeer lying on its side, Claire managed to summon a grin. "Easy. I'll make sure there are no reindeer in the classroom. And I won't be distracted by Christmas shopping, like Becky was, or by helping other customers, like I was."

She'd been kept running since she arrived right after lunch, fetching turkeys and other preordered food from the walk-in fridge, so she hadn't been able to stop the kids from destroying Maddie's display. Matthew's mom hadn't even noticed her four-year-old galloping the reindeer up and down the window, kicking up the fake snow as he went, and eighteen-month-old Charlotte busily pulling ornaments off the tree.

"True. And maybe you're the teensiest bit better at the gentle art of disciplining kids."

Claire shrugged, fighting off yet again the thought of how unfair it was she'd never have children of her own . "It's easier when they're other people's children. And it *is* part of my job. I'm sure being a mom is just as challenging as teaching."

Not that she knew. Not that she would ever know.

Spending such big chunks of her time with Maddie over the past few days raised memories she didn't want to revisit, gave her nightmares about things she never wanted to think about again. Things that woke her sweating and trembling. Soon she'd get them pushed down hard and bottled up again.

It's just, she knew too well what could go wrong, even at thirty-six weeks when the baby was no longer considered a preemie. So, of course, she fussed over Maddie.

Which reminded her… "Now, about that rest." Gently but firmly, she steered her friend to the staircase and pointed upstairs. "I can manage down here. Go, now." She used her best classroom discipline voice.

Maddie just laughed. "Yes, Ms. Robinson." She perfectly mimicked the singsong tones the kids used.

At least she went upstairs. Though knowing Maddie, probably not to rest. Chances were, she'd start baking a pie, then remember more presents for Jacob she needed to wrap and find a mobile for the baby's bedroom she simply *had* to hang.

Lord, I really hope You hear my prayer just this once. Keep Maddie and her baby safe. Don't let anything go wrong. Please?

She might not have stopped praying yet, but that didn't mean she'd waste a second waiting for an answer. Getting the mess cleared up so Maddie didn't do it herself when she came back down gave her a far more practical way to help. The last ornament clipped into place on the tree as heavy steps thudded on the wide porch.

Ryan? Her misbehaving heart jumped in her chest.

No, no, no! She did *not* want that joyful little skip of anticipation at the thought of seeing him when he brought Jacob back. His mom loved minding kids when any parent needed some time out. She'd like nothing better than for Ryan to give her grandchildren of her own to fuss over.

Claire skated away from that uncomfortable thought, fast.

Anyway, it wasn't him. When she glanced up, Leroy Schaefer's bulky form filled the doorframe. As he ambled into the store, the bell over his head jangling, she gave him a wave.

"Hi, Leroy! I'll go fetch your order now." After doing this for hours, she knew the routine.

She breathed a sigh of relief as she dumped the last of the Christmas turkeys into the oversized carrier Leroy held. With four children plus other family there for the holidays, he'd ordered one that won the prize for the largest. Even Leroy oofed when he hefted the bag.

"Hope Sarah can fit this in the oven!" The big man grinned. "Now, say, what are you and Maddie doing tomorrow? You're more than welcome to join us, young Jacob, too. Always room for more guests at our table."

"Thank you, you're kind to ask." Claire managed a smile. Like everyone in Sunset Point, he meant well and his neighborly spirit was real. "Brad called earlier. He's on his way home, though he won't arrive till late tonight. I'll stay with Maddie until he gets here. Tomorrow, they'll be with Liz and Hiram all day."

"Good to hear Brad could get away so they could have Christmas together. That's an answer to prayer, I'm sure."

Somehow, she restrained a doubtful snort. Answers had been in short supply for her. Seemed she was somehow outside the favored circle of believers God heard.

Thankfully, Leroy didn't appear to notice she hadn't mentioned what her plans were. Now was probably not the moment to declare she wanted nothing more than a day alone tomorrow with nothing to do. No fancy dinner to cook and no dishes to wash.

Picking up the carrier, Leroy headed home. Once the stomp of his boots on the porch faded away, Claire sagged across the counter. How such a small community could keep a store so busy, she didn't know.

Everyone had visited today, so maybe she could close the store a little early. She plodded to the doors and peered through the thick glass. Despite the softly falling snow making the frozen lake and its mountain backdrop look like a scene from a corny greeting card, peace and goodwill or joy to the world were nowhere near appearing on her wish list.

More like getting a good night's sleep and hitting the erase button on parts of her brain.

Much as she wanted to turn the open sign over to closed, she'd better not. No knowing who might need some more wrapping paper. Or an extra can of cranberry sauce. Though she had zero Christmas spirit, she'd hate to ruin anyone else's day by closing too soon.

A firm tread on the porch alerted her to put on her happy face as if she didn't have a care in the world.

This time, it *was* Ryan, laughing with Jacob as he brushed

snow from the boy's coat before opening the door. From the amount of snow, Jacob hadn't simply been walking home as it fell, he'd been rolling in it, too. His upturned face glowed. If they were strangers and she didn't know better, she'd assume they were father and son.

Regret stabbed through her, painful and sharp-edged with rage.

Why, God? Why put a man like Ryan in my life when I'm so wrong for him? It's so unfair. What did I do to deserve what happened? Up until then, I did everything right. Went to church, prayed, read my Bible, waited till after marriage for anything more than kissing. I never once doubted. I still do all that. But now, I have plenty of doubts. Maybe, more doubts than faith.

As usual, God didn't reply. He hadn't when she'd complained to Him before. Hadn't when she'd begged Him for His help. So she didn't expect Him to now, either. Maybe He wasn't even there at all, just a made-up story, like babies coming from the cabbage patch. A bolt of lightning striking her down would be better than being ignored.

Swallowing her anger, pretending everything was fine and dandy, as she'd done so many times since the accident, she straightened and assumed a cheery grin before Ryan pushed the door open.

Jacob ran into the store, speed and volume turned to high. "Hi, Ms. Robinson. Mommy, I'm hoo—ome. Where are you? I've got loads to tell you!"

"Up here, Peanut." Maddie's voice floated down the stairs, a little frayed around the edges.

"Ryan showed me how to play the bestest game. It's called Animal Snap. He even gave me the cards to play with. I'll teach it to you — then you can play too." He charged up the stairs, talking all the way.

Ryan quirked an eyebrow and chuckled. "Maddie's in for a treat."

Oddly shy with him these last few days, and careful not to show any sign of how she really felt, Claire fiddled with the candy display to avoid meeting his intent tawny gaze.

"Yep, she is." No need to restrain her snort now. "She'll *love* you for teaching him that game. The only thing better would be giving the kid a drum set for Christmas."

He grinned. "How did you guess what I have for him? I figured it's a gift that keeps on giving."

"Wow, so thoughtful!" He had to be joking. She hoped. Her eye roll should tell him what she thought of that. "She'd hand it straight back to you. Such a wonderful gift should be kept at your place for whenever you or your mom have him visit."

"Hmm, on second thoughts…"

"Right. They're often wise." She glanced at the big clock on the wall. Maddie better have rested while she could. If not, she'd lost her chance for sure. Something about her friend's reply to Jacob escalated the unease tugging at Claire all day.

"Want me to mind the shop for you?" As if she'd spoken out loud, Ryan offered exactly what she wanted.

"Please. It's not quite time to close up yet, but I'd like to go check on Maddie." Worrying over nothing. This was simply to reassure herself, not because she actually thought anything was wrong.

If she kept repeating that, maybe she'd believe it.

"Sure, no problem. I'll stay as long as you like and help close up, too." So easygoing. Nothing was ever a problem for Ryan.

If she really answered honestly, her answer would be, "Stay a lifetime."

Best to give the not-quite-honest answer, instead. "Just long enough to make sure she's okay. Thanks."

The less time she spent in his presence, the easier it was to keep her distance. To ensure they never as much as accidentally brushed fingertips. No matter what everyone else in Sunset Point seemed to think, she wasn't the woman Ryan deserved.

If only her heart and her hormones didn't react quite so enthusiastically to him. Another cosmic joke God played on her.

Before she'd taken two steps, a deep guttural moan echoed from upstairs. A sound she recognized from all the birthing videos she'd watched in Lamaze.

"Is Maddie okay?" Concern sharpened Ryan's voice.

Throat tight with terror, Claire froze for a split second before common sense kicked in. "Lock up now, then come upstairs to look after Jacob. Call the hospital. Tell them Maddie's baby isn't waiting, and she's booked for a C-section next week. She needs an ambulance."

Without waiting for his response, she took the stairs two at a time. She could trust he'd do whatever was needed. The question was, could she?

In the bathroom, Maddie stood in a puddle of clear fluid, shaking her head, surprise and disbelief clouding her eyes. "I thought I needed to go to the bathroom. But I think my waters broke."

"Guess those aren't just practice contractions. Ryan's calling for an ambulance." Claire smiled, pretending a breezy confidence she didn't feel. Fear shuddered through her.

So much could go wrong. Prenatal classes and a first-aid

certificate weren't enough preparation to help her friend. Especially a friend who might not be able to deliver naturally. There'd have to be a good reason her OB didn't want her to try for a VBAC.

Then Maddie again loosed that primal, instinctive groan as the next contraction hit, breathing fast and hard. "Oh, oh, oh. The baby's coming. I can feel it."

"It's okay. You're doing fine." Soothing reassurance Claire hoped was true, even as her heart pounded louder than her words.

With only the smallest break, another contraction came. And another. This baby *really* wasn't waiting. The ambulance would take an hour to get here. They'd be too late.

Claire grabbed a clean towel ready to catch the baby who might arrive in the next few contractions.

Fear gripped her, driving her to pray like she hadn't prayed since that night five years ago.

Please, Lord, help me here. I don't know what to do, and I really can't manage this one on my own. I couldn't bear another baby dying. Or another best friend. Don't let Brad or Maddie have to go through what You let happen to me. Please?

CHAPTER TEN

Ryan wasted no time slamming the door sign to closed, clicking the lock, and then dialing 911 on his cellphone. Maybe better to make the call down here, so he didn't upset Jacob with talk of an ambulance.

He'd never been around a birth, but he'd seen enough TV shows to guess the frequent grunts and groans coming from upstairs meant Maddie's baby wasn't likely to stay put till Brad got back. And maybe, wouldn't wait for the ambulance to arrive, either.

Deliberately slowing his breathing, he took a second to pray as he waited for the emergency services to pick up. Far more useful than panicking.

Lord, protect both mom and baby. And please, guide me in what to do, because I really have no idea!

Of course, he didn't know the answers to the questions the dispatcher asked him, apart from Maddie's name, age, and address. And of course, the woman on the phone also assumed he was the baby's father.

"It's okay. Just relax, Dad. Take your time. It's unlikely to be an emergency. Most babies take longer to arrive than you think."

"I'm not the father. Just a friend of the family. I don't know exactly when the baby is due, but she's booked to go into the hospital for a C-section next week. And I don't know how long she's been in labor. Not long, I guess. I think maybe it just got started. But it sounds like she's in strong labor." His string of words rushed out fast. Somehow, he didn't think they had as much time as the dispatcher thought.

"Okay. Her being booked for a C-section does change things. Why not hand the phone over to the mom-to-be and let me talk to her." Again that calm, artificially soothing voice. It made him want to grab the woman and shake her. Get her to send an ambulance, now.

"I'll take the phone to her." He galloped upstairs and stopped beside Jacob, sat cross-legged outside the closed bathroom door. Resting a comforting hand on the boy's head, he hesitantly knocked on the door. Making calls and doing practical stuff was one thing, but he really didn't need to see what was going on in there. Jacob probably shouldn't, either.

Anxiety contorting his small face, Jacob jumped to his feet. "Is Mommy okay? I'm scared."

Ryan picked the boy up and gave what he hoped was a reassuring smile, though, truth be told, he was scared, too. "She'll be fine, L'il'un. Looks like your Christmas baby could be arriving sooner than expected."

"Could I speak to the patient, please?" The dispatcher rasped from his cellphone, a lot less patient and soothing this time.

He knocked again on the door. "The ambulance dispatcher wants to talk to Maddie."

"They'll have to wait." Claire's response rose, clipped and sharp with tension.

He passed that on to the dispatcher, a little more politely.

"She's in the bathroom. The friend with her says she can't talk now. I'll—"

The mother of all groans from the bathroom stilled his words. As a series of loud sobbing breaths followed, he closed his eyes and prayed, incoherent and wordless.

Claire's voice sounded faintly. "Please, God. Please, God." What she asked Him for, Ryan couldn't guess.

Trembling and sniffling, Jacob clung harder. "Mommy?"

"It's okay. God's looking after your mommy. And so is Ms. Robinson." He hugged the boy, hoping his attempts at reassurance worked better than the dispatcher's had on him.

In the silence, the air around them seemed to thicken, shimmering with the sense of something miraculous about to happen. He held his breath. After an endless moment, a newborn baby's first cries rang out.

Relief and joy surged through him, leaving him limp against the wall. He blinked back tears.

Thank You, Lord, thank You!

Hugging Jacob closer, he grinned at the kid. "That's your new baby brother or sister."

"Wow." Wide-eyed, Jacob breathed the word.

Ryan lifted his cellphone. "You hear all that?"

"I sure did." The dispatcher chuckled. "Sounds like she won't be needing that C-section next week. I've dispatched a vehicle. Now I need you to pass the phone to whoever is helping the mom, so I can provide guidance on what to do next."

He knocked again on the door, even more softly this time, and lowered his voice. "The ambulance is on its way, but the dispatcher wants to talk to you, Claire. Give some advice on what you should do."

Claire opened the door just enough to peek out. An emotion he couldn't name darkened her tear-filled eyes. It almost looked like sadness, but that made no sense. Smile wobbling at the edges, she reached for the phone.

He restrained an instinctive grimace. She'd probably wiped her hand, but a few streaks of blood still clung. Having babies was clearly a messy business.

"Good. Because my first-aid certificate is zero prep for this. Just one moment." This to the dispatcher, not him. Claire switched her focus to the boy he held. "Jacob, congratulations. You have a little brother."

"Can I see him now? And Mommy?" Jacob bounced in his arms, clearly anxious to get down and see his new sibling.

"Not yet, Peanut." He couldn't see Maddie, but her shaky voice mingled joy, triumph, and exhaustion. "I'll bring him out soon so you can meet him. Stay with Ryan for now."

"Okay." The boy's lower lip quivered, but he didn't argue.

"Can I do anything to help?" Ryan had no idea what to do, but there must be something. On TV, they always boiled water.

Claire nodded. "Grab me a load more towels and some washcloths from the linen closet. And Maddie's hospital bag from the main bedroom. Oh, and a clean pair of rubber gloves from the store. I'll holler if I need anything else."

No boiling water. It appeared a bit too late for the gloves, but he wouldn't ask.

"Sure." He lowered Jacob to the floor. "Let's go, L'il'un. How about you fetch Mommy's bag, and I get the rest?"

Jacob happily scurried off to get the bag while Ryan grabbed the linens and an unopened pair of dishwashing gloves he found in the closet. Claire didn't open the door much wider than before. Just wide enough to take the bag and the clean towels.

"Thanks." She loosed a long breath and sagged against the doorframe. Fatigue and stress turned down her lips and shadowed her eyes.

Concern for her twisted in his chest, and he rested his fingers on her hand, the one clutching the bundle of towels against her. "Is everything okay? What else can I do to help you?"

Instantly she straightened, pasted on a bright smile, and shook her head, giving her hand a little flick to shake off his light touch. She'd told him to go away as clear as speaking the words. "No problems here. Mother and baby are fine. The dispatcher talked me through what to do and what to watch for while we wait for the ambulance. You just keep Jacob entertained."

Claire hadn't said *she* was fine, and she looked anything but. He'd never seen her so wilted, so worn. None of the adrenaline-fueled excitement he expected from her after safely delivering her best friend's baby.

Something else bothered her.

He'd have to back off for now. This wasn't the time or the place to push the point. Maybe once everything was settled here, she'd let him walk her home. Then he could ask again.

"Sure. I can do that." He hoped his smile came across less faked than Claire's had. "Jacob and I can play a few more rounds of Animal Snap. Or we can make a Christmas card for the new baby."

"Cookies and milk usually help, too." Again, he couldn't see her, but Maddie sounded far stronger this time.

Jacob grinned. "I want it all, Mommy. Cookies *and* the game *and* making a card. *And* to say hello to my brother."

"We both need to have a wash. Then we'll bring him out to meet you. You might even get to see him before Daddy does." Laughter echoed in her words.

"Yay!" Jacob jumped and clapped his hands.

"Maddie, do you want me to phone Brad and see where he is?" Driving two hours from Spokane in the snow, then getting here only to turn around and drive an hour to the hospital would surely be the last thing the new father would want.

"Not yet." She chuckled. "I'd rather surprise him, the way this baby surprised me. He should be home any minute."

Claire raised an eyebrow, nodded toward the kitchen, and jiggled the bathroom door. Obviously impatient for them to go.

"How about we let your mom have her wash, L'il'un." He nudged Jacob. "You'll want to have that card ready to give your brother when you first see him, right?"

One day, maybe he'd be a proud father waiting to see his wife and his newborn child. And prickly and difficult as she could sometimes be, he wanted that wife to be Claire.

Two cookies, a large glass of milk, two noisy games of Animal Snap, and a Christmas card complete with a brightly crayoned nativity scene and a laboriously lettered greeting later, the bathroom door opened. Maddie, wearing yoga pants and a T-shirt, emerged, trailed by Claire carrying the new baby.

Phew. No nightclothes, and no blood. Mom and baby both glowed pink and shiny. His gaze skipped over them to Claire. Claire, unlike mom and baby, appeared pale and exhausted.

Though she cradled the baby carefully, everything about her drooped, even her usually bouncy braid. Wet patches on her jeans and sweatshirt suggested she'd dabbed at stains.

His brow furrowed. So she'd hate knowing his concerns. Still, he couldn't help worrying about her. Something had to be wrong when the new mom looked in way better shape than the person who'd assisted at the birth.

No mistaking the moment Claire noticed him staring at her, trying to figure what the problem was. Her head raised and tilted to one side as she assumed a tight and far-too-clearly faked smile. Challenge filled her eyes, daring him to ask.

Much as he wanted to, he'd learned enough wisdom to wait.

Jacob jumped up and rushed to Maddie and Claire, bouncing in excitement. "Mommy, Mommy, let me hold my brother!"

"Whoa there." Maddie smiled. "Sit on the sofa first. I'll sit beside you. Then you can hold him. We have to be very careful with brand-new babies. They aren't as tough as big boys like you."

He raced to the sofa and sat up straight, arms outstretched.

Claire scrunched up her face. "The ambulance dispatcher said to lie down."

"I don't need to go to bed. I feel fine. Sitting in here for a bit won't hurt. Then Peanut can meet his new brother properly."

Shrugging, Claire followed her to the sofa and laid the baby in her arms. Maddie gazed at her baby, love glowing in her eyes, before carefully nestling him in Jacob's lap. "His name is Nathaniel." Tenderness softened her smile. "Your daddy and I decided on that. It means God's gift. And he's a wonderful gift."

"He sure is." The baby didn't cry but lay quietly, indigo eyes wide open. "A brother. Wowee. This is the bestest Christmas present ever, Mommy."

Claire hurried into the kitchen and, by the sound of it, fired up the coffeemaker. Behind him, so he couldn't see her without making it too obvious he was turning to look. "I'll just set some coffee brewing. I know I could do with some." Her cheerful tone rang as false as her smile. Something was *really* bothering her.

Despite his concern for Claire, Ryan grinned at the cute scene. He barely resisted the temptation to turn and check her reaction. The hiss of the coffeemaker behind him offered the only suggestion she was even in the room. But no one could see this and not feel awe and joy.

After a minute, Jacob frowned at his brother. "So, does he do anything more than this? When will he walk and talk? You know, play with me?"

"Sorry, Peanut. That takes a little longer. Like, next Christmas? To start off, all babies do is cry, eat, and sleep. You were the same at his age."

"Awww. That's no fun." Jacob pouted.

Maddie laughed. "Sorry to disappoint you." As if on cue, the baby whimpered, turning his head side to side as if searching for something.

"He's ready to eat again, I think. Time to feed him." She lifted the baby from Jacob's arms and reached for the hem of her oversized T-shirt.

Before he got an eyeful of anything he shouldn't, Ryan hurried to push his chair back from the kitchen table and swiveled, so his back was to the sofa. At last, an excuse to look at Claire. He'd turned quick enough she couldn't pretend.

All her attention focused on Maddie and the baby, she showed no sign of registering his gaze. This time, he recognized the emotion darkening her eyes. A raw, desperate hunger. Like someone wandering in the desert would stare at fresh clear water, or someone starving at an all-you-can-eat buffet.

Claire wanted a baby, a family of her own. Longed for it.

While he ached to see her pain, it also gave him unexpected hope. For all her talk of not wanting to get married, he couldn't imagine her as the sort of woman who'd think she didn't need a husband for the baby-making part.

Could it finally be time to risk revealing how he felt about her? And if he did, would her response be his bestest Christmas present ever, too?

CHAPTER ELEVEN

Today ranked as the second-worst day of Claire's life. And she would *not* let Maddie's delivery force her into thinking about the worst one. As soon as either Brad or the ambulance arrived, she'd make her getaway.

In the meantime, since Maddie now lay in bed with Jacob, baby Nathaniel tucked between them, cleanup duty might be a teensy bit less triggering than watching Maddie nurse the baby again.

A *very* teensy bit.

The knock on the bathroom door she guessed must be Ryan came as a welcome relief. Someone she could snip and snark at without worrying he'd take offense.

She opened the door just wide enough to peek out and talk to him but slim enough to stop him from seeing in. No doubting his masculinity, but she had no way to know if he was one of those guys who fainted at the sight of a little blood. There'd been one in her prenatal class, a real macho man. Passed out at the first birthing video.

"There's not anything much I can do in there since I've washed up." He gestured toward the big open-plan kitchen and living room. "How can I help here?"

"Are you *sure* you're ready for this? It's a bigger cleanup than rinsing out the coffee cups." No need to hide her uncertainty. The man really *was* unoffendable.

His Adam's apple bobbed as he swallowed, but he nodded. "If having babies is messier than I thought, even more reason to help out."

Somehow switching off her emotional response, she surveyed the room again. "It's not too messy. Of course, I can't know how messy you expected."

She swung the door all the way open.

Ryan stood his ground. "Just tell me where to start."

Her usual practicality kicked in. "We'll need a pair of rubber gloves for you, a couple of rolls of paper towels, a scrubbing brush, some cleaning spray, and a bunch of trash bags. Don't bother asking Maddie about the stuff. Just grab it from the store. She can bill me for it later."

Chuckling, he headed for the stairs.

His help made all the difference. Not that she'd ever tell him so. Or why. Joking and snarking with him kept the memories at bay. In way less time than she'd expected, they had the bathroom sparkling again.

Nothing here to trigger her now.

And perfect timing, Brad pulled up outside the store as they dumped the last trash bag in the store's big trash bin. She raised a finger to her lips and winked. Hopefully, Ryan would guess to say nothing. Much as she'd love to see Brad's reaction, the new parents didn't need an audience when he found out.

She and Ryan ambled back into the building as if nothing unusual had happened.

Brad bounded in, victory punching as he did. "Made it! Home on Christmas Eve, just as I hoped. Hi, Claire, Ryan. I didn't expect to see you here. Where's Maddie?"

"Upstairs with Jacob." Ryan played along exactly right. "We've helped out here while you were away. How's your dad?"

"Home from the hospital today, with wife number six. He'll need to make some major lifestyle changes, but his doctors say there shouldn't be much permanent damage to his heart." Brad smiled. "One of those wake-up calls God gives us now and then. Thankfully, Dad's paying attention."

"Good news." Ryan clapped him on the shoulder.

"Well, we should get going since you're back. We're all done here." She hugged Brad. "Merry Christmas."

Minutes later, bundled up in their cold-weather gear, she and Ryan stood together on the store's wide porch, giggling like conspirators once Brad locked the door behind them.

A loud whoop from upstairs sent them into fresh laughter.

"We didn't get to see Brad's reaction, but I think we just heard it." Ryan grinned.

Nodding, she stepped out into the icy night.

A few inches of snow, fallen since she arrived at the store hours earlier, carpeted the street. Not too much to walk in. The clouds had moved on, leaving a bright clear sky. The mountains formed dark shadows against a blaze of stars.

Ryan stared up at them and smiled. "Don't you think the stars would have shone like this on the first Christmas Eve? 'Peace on the earth, goodwill to all, from heaven's all-gracious King.'"

Recognizing the quote from the carol Cee Cee Schaefer sang solo so beautifully on Wednesday night, "It Came Upon A Midnight Clear", Claire rolled her eyes. Since the accident, God hadn't felt as all-gracious as she used to think. "Sorry, I'm more interested in getting home than hearing the angels sing."

"Ever-practical Claire." He laughed. Then his face stilled, grew intent and serious. "Mind if I walk with you?"

Something in his gaze made her rush to look away. She shrugged. "Can't stop you. We'll be walking almost the same route, no matter what I say."

Not for anything would she tell him how glad she was for his company. While she'd joked with Ryan, all those memories she wanted to avoid receded. Though that sounded very like becoming dependent on someone else again. The last thing she needed.

He took her hand before they'd walked far. Somehow, even through their thick gloves, the contact felt warm and real. She shivered, knowing she should pull her hand away.

She should, but she didn't.

"Let's get you home, to your cat and your fire." His voice flowed over her, mellow and sweet as hot chocolate. She could get used to this.

And there was the trouble.

"Yes. Mrs. Mehitabel will be wondering where I am." Stomping the snow as if she could stomp down her unwanted feelings, she set off along Main Street.

They walked in silence for a few minutes. Then he stopped, outside the Gregorys' house, strung with Christmas lights. Ryan's grip tightened on hers, and she glanced at him, surprised. He grasped her other hand.

"Claire, I don't know how to pretty up what I want to ask you, the way some other men would. So I'm just going to ask you straight. Would you consider dating me, with a view to something more serious? I love you."

Pain as strong as labor pains engulfed her, clenching her tummy. As if everything else today wasn't enough, now she had to deal with this. The man she loved — okay, she admitted it — as good as asking her to marry him. Asking her to be the mother of his babies.

Not right now, of course, but in the future. His "something more serious" had to mean marriage and family.

If only he knew how much she wanted that. And how impossible it was.

Breathing deep and fast, emotion tightening her chest, she pulled her hands away from his and looked away. Breathe through the pain.

So all those prenatal classes came in handy for something.

When her feelings were buried again, deep enough for her to be sure the truth wouldn't show on her face, deep enough she could be sure of doing the right thing by saying no, she lowered her hands.

Snark. The safe response, especially with Ryan. She longed to be gentle but didn't dare risk it. Her resolve would be too easily shaken.

"You don't love me. You simply want a family, and that needs a wife. We're the only two singles the right age here. Propinquity. That's all it is."

It wasn't a defensive lie. How *could* he really love her? She'd hardly given him much encouragement.

His lips twisted. "You can't know how I feel. If that's all it was, me falling for whatever single girl happened to be available, wouldn't I have fallen for Sam Rose when she first moved here this summer? I didn't."

Rose... Did he have to say Rose? Couldn't he have called her

Novak since Sam was married now?

Claire shook her head, her heavy braid whipping from side to side, almost smacking him in the face. Serve him right if it had.

Why did he need to go stirring things up even more by telling her this now? Today of all days.

She had to cure him of whatever he felt for her, or living here would become unbearable. Bring on the man-repellent. "That proves nothing."

"It proves plenty. I want you, Claire, only you. You're the only woman I want to start a family with." In the glow of the Christmas lights, his face shone with sincerity.

Anger heated her cheeks. With him, for falling in love with her. With herself, for not being able to give him what he most wanted. And with God, for letting all this happen in the first place.

Ryan must *not* guess how her crazy heart had jumped at his declaration of love, how joy flooded her for a blissful instant. Until he went and mentioned the f-word.

Family.

The one thing she couldn't give him.

Though she died inside, she managed an almost-convincing snort and grabbed for the next convenient excuse to turn him down.

"So I'm supposed to believe you love me now, when this time last year the only woman you had eyes for was Maddie? I may as well not have existed, for all the notice you took of me." Her voice, supposed to emerge strong, confident, and one-hundred-percent off-putting, held a betraying touch of wobbles. "Well?" she demanded, achieving nearer the right tone this time. "Explain that away, if you can."

Ryan flushed, looked down, and shuffled his feet. "Well... uh...I..." A long breath escaped him, steaming in the icy air. "Look, I was stupid. I had a thing for Maddie before she left to get married. So when she came back single, I kinda slipped back into that. She was the only single woman near my age in town, after all."

"Right, and when I first arrived, I raised the count to two single women in Sunset Point. Yet you didn't even notice I existed." Her words didn't shake. Not one bit. Exactly as cool and unaffected by his declaration as she wanted to sound. Even if she didn't feel it.

"I'd been in the habit of thinking I loved Maddie. I was slower than I should have been getting over it."

"Sure." She rolled her eyes. "And Maddie's husband coming back might have had just a little to do with it, too."

"Okay, that helped." He spread his hands ruefully. "But I would have figured it out myself if he hadn't."

"Would you? I'm not sure I can believe that."

As she sniped at him about Maddie, she knew in her heart it wasn't the real issue. If things were different, she'd be ecstatic right now. She'd grab at him in a moment if she could give him the kids he wanted. His obvious crush on Maddie last Christmas wouldn't have crossed her mind.

But things *weren't* different.

Raising his focus from the snow his boots scuffed up, his brown gaze met hers. "I'm sorry. I guess...." He trailed off, his brow furrowing as he searched for words. "Okay, it's like this. The moon and the stars are still there in the daytime. We can't see them for the sun, right? But they're still there and still real, we just don't see them till after the sun sets, and then they make the night beautiful." He gestured to the blaze of the Milky Way overhead.

Unlike Ryan to be so poetic.

But he'd confirmed what she already knew. If she wasn't his sun by now, he didn't really love her. Or didn't love her enough to still want her when she dropped her bombshell. What man eager for a family would?

Hastily straightening her shoulders, drooped lower with each word he spoke, she raised her chin. "That's exactly the problem, Ryan. If I *did* choose to marry you, I wouldn't settle for less than being the sun in your life. Your moon and stars, too. That's the only way it can be when I love someone."

Hope lit his eyes. "You *are* my sun, now. I just meant when you first arrived. I was stupid and wrong, I admit it. So does that mean—"

"No!" Both her hands slammed into the air in front of her face like stop signs, to interrupt him.

Ryan jerked back as if she'd swung a punch at him.

Well, maybe she had. Good as, anyway.

Guilt and regret twanged though, sharp and painful. Hurting Ryan, the nicest guy she knew as well as the most irritating, had never been on her To Do list.

But he had to forget any thoughts that he loved her, now. If making sure he did meant hurting him, then she'd have to hurt him. Better to do it now than let him keep imagining they could have a future together.

She didn't love him. Not really. Nothing more than her pointless hormones, that's all.

Maybe one day soon she could actually believe it. When the ache of having to turn him down went away.

"Truly, Ryan, I'm not the girl for you. I can't give you the happiness or the life you deserve. I'd hate to let anything develop between us *then* have you realize that fact." Every word the truth.

"I love you, Claire. Nothing you tell me can change that." Smiling, he reached for her hands again.

She pulled back. Arm's length was the only safe distance. Though the other side of the lake might be an even safer distance.

"You don't know that for a fact. How could you?"

Maybe she should tell him the one thing sure to drive him away. But she couldn't face dealing with the mess she'd become if she tried.

"I'm pretty sure I *do* know. I'm sorry I was so slow to realize you were the woman I wanted to share my life with. I won't stop hoping you'll figure out I'm the man for you, too."

How could she make him understand, without telling him the truth? "Not everyone wants marriage and a family. My life is fine as it is." Time to lighten the mood. "Anyway, if your prediction is correct, soon I'll have six cats. Who needs a man when she can have that?"

He loosed an exasperated sigh. "Or, you could have the six cats *and* a loving husband who likes most critters."

"Sticking to cats would be way less trouble."

Cats would never make her have to talk about things she never wanted to even think about, things that would turn her into a bawling mess. She couldn't tell Ryan the truth. Not now and not ever.

Because once she started, she'd fly apart in a zillion little pieces and never get herself together again.

CHAPTER TWELVE

CLAIRE WANTED TO BLOCK HER EARS. Gabble meaningless words. Scream out loud if it would help. Anything to stop Ryan from saying more, talking about things she'd spent the last five years running from.

Love talk. Marriage talk. Family talk.

He stood eyeing her, lips quirked to one side, head shaking a little. More exasperated than hurt by her rejection.

Good. She didn't want to hurt him. But he looked too much like a man who hoped she'd change her mind and who knew how to be patient.

Better simply be her imagination, a trick of the light.

Because before she knew it, she'd weaken and melt into his arms, which could only lead to heartbreak for them both.

"Please, could we let it go now, Ryan? Let's not ruin each other's Christmas."

"As you wish."

Now it was her turn to shake her head, but with gritted teeth. He hadn't used that line from her favorite old movie accidentally.

Smiling, he raised his mittened hands in surrender. The man knew full well "As you wish" meant "I love you."

At least teasing was better than arguing or cajoling.

Ryan didn't say more, and he didn't reach for her hand again.

Though he'd done exactly what she asked, she missed the sweet contact. Longed for things to be different, so she *could* take his hands. Let him hold her.

Even cry on his shoulder and tell him exactly why today had been so hard for her.

Her gaze fixed on the blinking lights adorning the Gregorys' house. Anything to avoid his eyes.

"Let's get you home."

Still not looking at him, she nodded and turned.

They walked in silence through the quiet evening, the only sound the soft crunch of their feet on the snow. Near the corner where she'd turn off, her foot slipped. Unbalanced, she jerked, windmilled, and held her breath. Ryan grabbed her arm, steadying her.

Solid as a rock. A man a woman could depend on. Any woman but her.

She twitched her arm from his hold. "Thanks." The muttered word sounded and felt less than gracious.

He simply smiled. "It's okay. Guess there's some icy patches hidden under this new snow."

"Guess so." A glance measured the distance to her house. Time to let Ryan go. "I'm fine to walk the rest of the way on my own. And your mom will be expecting you home, too. Please let her know I'll be thinking of her tomorrow."

And I'll probably be thinking of you, too. Much as I wish I wouldn't.

"You could always come in and tell her yourself? She's still hoping you'll join us for lunch." He tilted his head toward the big house he'd grown up in.

Not a wise move. Either going there now or for Christmas

lunch.

Much as she wanted to support Ryan, and Jeannie too, in their first Christmas since Hank died, spending the holiday with them felt too risky. They both might see it as encouragement she'd be wrong to give.

Especially when she already longed to grab his coat and pull him close to kiss him.

Refusing him hurt — an icy boulder in her chest. But he'd thank her one day when he found the girl who really *was* right for him. Ryan deserved a wife who could give him what he wanted.

She shook her head. "Jeannie's kind to ask me, but I probably won't. I have a date with my cat, my flannel PJs, and a bunch of old movies on Netflix. My idea of a happy Christmas."

Ryan huffed. "Hope you enjoy it. If you change your mind, you can simply turn up. It's an open invitation." He gazed at her, brow furrowing a little, doubt darkening his eyes. As if undecided whether to say more.

"Go on, say it." Probably risky, but this day couldn't get much worse. Even though he only imagined he loved her, his day hadn't been exactly a barrel of laughs, either.

"Okay." He took a step back, suggesting he already guessed she wouldn't want to hear whatever it was. "I'm thinking I should tell you something from a book Pastor Roberts gave me not long after Dad died."

She folded her arms across her chest. A book on grieving, for sure. Maybe even the same book her pastor had given her, donated to the Goodwill unread.

Ryan guessed right. This *wouldn't* be anything she wanted to hear.

He took a deep breath and straightened his shoulders. "It said some people get angry with God and other people when something bad happens. They switch off to letting in the things that are still good in their lives."

Not responding to that. Not meeting his warm, brown eyes. Not letting his well-intentioned words settle in her heart and mind.

Not letting herself retort that he had no idea of how bad "bad" could really be.

Instead, she simply shrugged and focused on the way each word puffed visibly from his lips, steaming in the frozen air. Let it trigger safer memories. How she'd loved pretending to be a dragon as a kid, on the rare winter days cold enough for her breath to steam.

And now, she really *was* becoming a dragon. Before too long, she'd be like Mrs. Parks. Except with cats instead of a yappy little dog.

"I'm getting nudged to tell you a verse that book quoted," Ryan continued. "A different version to the one everyone usually quotes. I don't know if it's a God thing or not, but here goes. 'Stop fighting, and know that I am God.' You don't need to keep fighting, Claire."

Fury swelled in her, hot and quick. Her hands clenched, and she closed her eyes, struggling to contain the volcano of rage, stop it erupting. She didn't need anyone, especially someone who hadn't been through what she experienced, telling her how she should feel.

Ryan had grieved, sure. He'd lost his dad.

But she'd lost more, so much more. She'd *had* to fight, every day since the accident, simply to hold herself together.

"Whatever that bad thing was, God is still there for you. He won't let you fall. And I won't, either." Emotion roughened his low voice. Almost tenderness. "That's all I wanted to say."

If she let his tenderness in, she'd break her heart even more. And his, too.

"Thanks, Ryan. I need to go now." Her words emerged clipped and tight. She clamped her mouth shut to stop saying more.

He wanted to help. She got that. He simply didn't understand. How could he? No one understood because they'd never been where she'd been.

Stomping away, she didn't look back, didn't sneak a backward glance. Knowing Ryan, he'd be standing where she'd left him, waiting till he saw she'd made it safely home before he went home himself.

His care for her lit a warm, gentle glow deep inside her, totally unlike the heat of her fury. Ryan was a good man. One of the best. Her anger wasn't aimed at him. He didn't deserve it.

God did.

Her tense shoulders and rigid back sagged as soon as she shut her front door behind her. Leaning on the door, she pressed her gloved hands hard against her eyes to hold back tears.

Help me, God. Why don't You help me? You really don't care, do You? If You did, surely You'd show me You do. Like Ryan does, in so many little ways.

He was right about one thing. She *was* fighting God. And in the last five years, God hadn't given her a single reason not to.

Mrs. Mehitabel twined around her legs meowing. Sniffing a little, Claire bent to pet the tabby. "Are you telling me *you* care,

Mrs. M? Or do you only care for the dinner I'm about to feed you?"

The cat didn't answer any more than God did.

Peeling herself away from the door, Claire took off her boots and coat then padded out to the kitchen. The expectant cat loosed a string of pitiful meows as Claire opened two pouches of Mrs. M's favorite food and emptied them into a bowl.

"No good pretending you're starving, Mrs. Not when there's still half a bowl of your crunchies left from lunchtime."

She should get herself something, too. A hot chocolate. Cheese on toast. Then turn on the TV. Pretend today simply hadn't happened and everything was fine.

It didn't help. *A Christmas Carol*, a film she normally loved, was mere light and noise. Nothing to distract her from the memories, hitting full force, impossible to suppress.

The excitement when the contractions became strong enough to ask Karl to take her to the hospital. The joyful anticipation that soon she'd see her baby. The moment the car spun out of control. Her desperate prayers, hands clutching her belly as if somehow she could keep her baby safe. Then the crash and the terrible pain and slipping into darkness. Waking in the hospital to more pain, tubes in both arms, and a flattened belly.

The doctor's explanations — he'd tried to save her baby, but by the time they'd arrived in the hospital, it was too late. He'd tried to save her womb, but the damage was too much. Oh, and he was sorry, her husband died, too.

Next, the nurse wheeling her baby to her, washed and dressed in pink. Perfect and beautiful, with ten fingers, ten toes, the cutest little button nose. But so quiet, so still.

She'd walked out of the hospital six days later, with a red angry wound running vertically up her belly and five pints of other people's blood in her veins. Gone home to an empty, quiet house.

People told her over and over she was lucky to be alive. That she should feel glad her husband didn't suffer. That she could be thankful her baby was with Jesus. She didn't feel lucky or glad or thankful. She just wondered why she hadn't died in the accident, too, when so much of her died that night.

Her hands formed fists, hit again and again on the arm of her couch. Hot tears burned her eyes. Tears of anger at the unfairness of losing Karl and Rose and the other children she might have birthed. Losing everything she'd hoped and dreamed and planned.

Why, God? Why? Why do that to me — and to them? How can You claim to love us when things like this happen?

She asked Him, over and over again. God never answered. He didn't care, and the proof was — He hadn't *shown* He cared. Not once since the accident five long years before. This time wouldn't be any different.

But this time, the verse Ryan quoted echoed in her mind. "Stop fighting, and know that I am God." Along with a gentle whisper. "Trust Me."

Was this her answer?

Could it be that, the same as she hadn't noticed or she'd been irritated by the small, everyday ways Ryan showed he cared, she'd been the same with God? Had she really refused His help, the way she'd refused everyone else's help, from her family to her pastor to the grief counseling the hospital offered her?

Maybe if she stopped fighting Him and flinging anger at

Him, she'd find He'd been answering and trying to show how much He cared all along.

Suddenly, she knew. The answer was right in front of her, in the Nativity scene on her mantelpiece.

Christmas was the proof she'd asked Him for.

The Nativity wasn't just a nice story to tell the kids and get them to act out once a year. The Baby in the manger wasn't just a doll. That was a real, live, flesh-and-blood baby, as real as Maddie's new son. God's gift to us, as surely as Nathaniel was to Maddie and Brad.

God answered. He always answered. He answered right there — Jesus, God's Son, a baby resting in the hay.

God knew exactly what she felt because He'd lost a child, too. Letting His Son be born a baby, knowing the terrible way He'd suffer to bring life and redemption to all who chose to accept it. When Jesus cried out "My God, my God, why have you forsaken me," right before He died, what father wouldn't have wept tears of blood for his son?

God's answer wasn't like the ones other people tried to give her after the accident. Not an easy-to-say canned answer, like "But you can adopt" or "It's all God's will and you need to accept it."

God had suffered just as she had. He knew her pain. And He gave her what He could to help.

God's answer in Jesus was far from easy. Nothing pat or throwaway about it.

But Jesus was the answer that made all the difference. An answer to meet her where she was, right there, crying and punching her couch. An answer to stay with her for a lifetime.

All those prayers she thought weren't answered, when what

she needed to do was stop fighting long enough to open her eyes and see Him standing there, arms outstretched, ready to help her.

Please forgive me, Lord, for blaming You so long. I'm willing to trust You again. I'm willing to trust that You will heal my pain. I'm even willing to trust that You can bring good out of the most terrible things.

Memories washed over her again, this time her ghosts of Christmases Past.

All those good Christmases with Mom and Dad and her sister, secure in the knowledge she was loved and cared for. The years she'd shared with Karl, full of hope and joy and dreams of the life they'd have, the children they'd raise, the family they'd make.

And then the wonderful Christmas when she'd been expecting Rose. She'd felt the first flutters of the baby moving inside her on Christmas Day and called it the best Christmas present ever. She'd been so truly happy. Those memories weren't the curse she'd seen them as when she'd lost it all.

They were still a blessing. They always had been.

Thank You, Lord, for giving me a good family and Karl's love. Those years were wonderful gifts. And thank You for the privilege of carrying Rose. I felt her grow inside me. I felt her move. I saw her lovely face. Open my heart and mind to trusting she's now safe in Your hands.

She imagined literally taking all those hopes and dreams and handing them over to God. And holding her beautiful perfect baby in her arms, hugging her close for a moment, and then passing her over into God's tender care.

Tears streamed down her face. Different tears from the angry ones she'd cried since the accident. This time, her tears would bring healing. Begin to wash away her grief and pain.

Instead of holding them back, she let them fall.

Then there were more Christmases to remember. The ones since the accident. Angry and alone. Refusing to find what joy and comfort she could with friends and family because she couldn't have the Christmas she really wanted, with Karl and Rose and the other babies she might have had.

It didn't take much of a jump to imagine what her ghost of Christmases Future might be. Isolated, bitter, and making an idol of not needing anyone. Refusing to accept God's gifts.

Did she really want to keep living like that?

Time to let go of her rage over losing the life she'd wanted and start living the life she had. To trust that He kept her alive for a purpose. To take her anger and resentment, a misshapen, basketball-sized lump, and offer it to Him, too.

This must be what that verse about making our lives a living sacrifice really meant. Not just giving Him the prettied-up parts of us for a few hours a week at church or a few minutes a day of Bible reading, but giving Him *all* of ourselves. The ugly parts that came with being human, too. The anger, doubt, fear, envy, and all the rest.

Take my sacrifice, Lord. I place it into Your hands.

She sat, still and quiet, as the beginnings of peace seeped into her soul.

And now, one more thing to do. She needed to decide the best way to change her Christmas Present from what it was, into what God wanted it to be.

CHAPTER THIRTEEN

AFTER WASHING UP THE DINNER DISHES, Ryan sat in the living room with his mom, only half-watching the Christmas Eve movie. A Christmas Carol, one of his favorites. One of Dad's favorites, too.

As always, when he thought of Dad, the loss ached, as real as the ache of a pulled muscle. Last Christmas, no one could have guessed the man who'd always seemed as strong and solid as the mountains he loved wouldn't be here this year.

Thankfully, Mom seemed to be managing okay so far, even laughing in places, though he knew she'd be missing Dad as much as he did.

Help Mom to get through tomorrow, Lord. And please, help Claire to know You're with her, too. I'm so sorry I upset her, earlier. I don't know what I can do to make it right. Maybe I can't fix whatever's made her feel she needs to fight everything and everyone, and maybe it's not up to me to try. But You can.

Knowing he'd messed up gnawed at his conscience, ever since Claire marched away from him on Main Street. He'd stood, praying for her, watching till she disappeared into her house. He hated causing her distress. But he couldn't ignore that quiet voice of the Spirit, prompting him to say what he had.

All he could do now was let go of wanting to fix things and

leave that to the Lord. But even when he *had* handed that worry over to God, thinking of her and hoping she was okay made concentrating on the movie difficult.

When the doorbell rang, he jumped up and waved for Mom to relax in her seat. "I'll get it."

Claire stood at the front door, eyes red-rimmed and puffy. Jaw tightening, he winced. Had his words caused this?

"Can I talk to you?" She peered up at him, hesitancy replacing her usual feisty tone.

His heart clenched as he swung the door wide to invite her in. He'd never heard her sound or look so troubled and quiet. "Of course. Come on in. Mom's watching a movie in the living room, but we can sit in the kitchen."

As she took off her coat, hat, and gloves, he prayed.

Help me do whatever's best to help her, Lord. Help me listen. And when it's time for me to talk, give me the right words to say.

Leading her down the hallway, he stuck his head into the living room to let Mom know. "It's Claire. We'll just be out in the kitchen."

"Sure, son." She nodded, though a concerned frown creased her forehead. Claire's only visit to the house, in the year she'd lived nearby. And Mom probably heard the un-Clairelike note in her voice, too. She'd have figured this wasn't a good time to come out and be neighborly.

He smiled reassurance he didn't fully feel.

In the kitchen, he pulled two chairs away from the table. "Can I get you a coffee? Mom's got a cinnamon latte blend you might like."

Claire waved a hand in refusal. "It's okay."

As soon as she sat, she bowed her head, shut her eyes, and

steepled her hands in front of her mouth. So clearly praying, he quickly swallowed the "What's wrong?" he'd been about to ask.

After a minute, she raised her head with a watery smile. "I guess you're wondering why I'm here. I came to tell you you were right. I *have* been fighting God."

"Uh-huh." He wanted to see Claire happy and at peace with God far more than he wanted to be right. "And...uh...are you still fighting Him?"

Her smile widening, she shook her head. "Not anymore. Thanks to you. I'm grateful now you said what you did. You made me stop fighting long enough to recognize the ways He cares for me and blesses me. He gave me a loving family to grow up in. He brought me here, a supportive community filled with good people. He gave me a home of my own, children who need a teacher, and good friends like Maddie and Brad and Sam." She stopped for a moment, something he didn't dare to hope was love gleaming in her steady gaze. "And a friend like you."

Though he longed to tell her again how much he wanted to be more than a friend to her, the wisdom Dad taught him said to hold back.

One blessing at a time. One step at a time. This less defensive, more open Claire was a huge step in the right direction. And if she only ever wanted to be friends, he loved her enough to be okay with that.

He hoped.

"I'm glad you see me as a friend." He was glad, truly glad.

"I do." Again, a brief flash in her eyes, suggesting she also wished they could be more, mingled with unmistakable sorrow. She glanced away, her face stilled, her beautiful lips drooped.

"God gave me other blessings too, though they aren't part of my life anymore. That's what I need to talk to you about."

Shifting forward in his chair, so their knees almost but not quite touched, he reached out both his hands and left them open on his knees. It had to be her choice to take them or ignore them.

Though she kept her gaze averted, she rested her chilled fingers in his. Despite his concern for her, joy burst like Fourth of July fireworks in his chest. He clasped her hands in a warm hold. Firm enough to make sure she'd feel how much he cared for her and wanted to be there for her, loose enough she could pull away whenever she wanted.

"I'm listening."

She released a long breath, almost a sigh. "When we walked home from the store tonight, you were honest about how you felt for me. God made me realize you deserved the same honesty from me. I came here to tell you the reason we can only ever be friends, nothing more."

Her serious tone and the grief shadowing her eyes when she lifted her gaze to meet his clutched at his heart. Fireworks to heartache in the space of a few seconds. That's the way it was with Claire. Maybe the way it would always be.

And his job was to forget his own heartache and be here for her.

Whatever she planned to tell him would almost certainly be big and almost certainly be bad. The "bad thing" he'd guessed might have happened to her and challenged her about on their way home.

Probably, she'd never spoken of this to anyone else here. Listening and supporting her in whatever way she needed was a responsibility he had to be man enough to handle right. Even if it meant giving up his hopes of someday marrying her.

He'd told her he'd be there for her, and he would. With God's help.

Staying silent, he waited for her to speak.

"You were right not just about me fighting God but about the reason why, too. There *was* something bad that happened to start it. I married my high-school sweetheart as soon as we finished college."

Claire was married? He'd never considered that. If she was still married, he needed to adjust the way he felt for her — and fast. His hands tightened on hers, but he said nothing, knowing she had more she needed to say.

"We found jobs, bought a starter home together, and after a couple of years, we started trying for a family. I was in labor with our first child when we were in a car crash on the way to the hospital."

Her voice stayed matter-of-fact, but tears began streaming from her eyes. Dreading what might come next, he released one of her hands just long enough to reach for the roll of paper towels and place it where she could reach it.

"My husband died. My baby girl died. And I lost the ability to have more children." Her hands quivered in his clasp, and her tears kept falling.

His heart contracted painfully. All those losses. No wonder she'd been so angry.

And no wonder she'd watched Maddie and Baby Nathaniel with such a hungry, longing expression. Maddie had something Claire would never have. A huge thing for a woman like Claire, who was so great with kids and clearly loved them.

A huge thing for a man like him, too. But this was about her, not him.

"Oh, Claire. I'm so sorry." Inadequate words for all she'd suffered. Take what he'd felt over losing Dad and multiply by three. Maybe more. The salt of his own tears stung his eyes as pain for her twisted through him.

Lord, help me to help her. I don't know what to say.

Letting his hands go, she tore off a paper towel, mopped her face, blew her nose, and then met his gaze with swollen, tear-bright eyes. "That's why I secretly raged against God. And that's why I'm totally the wrong girl for you to fall in love with. You've made no secret of how much you want a family."

He hadn't. He *did* want a family. And he wanted Claire, too. But choosing her, no matter how much he loved her, would mean letting his hopes of a big family go. Maybe letting his hopes of *any* family go. Could he do that?

The decision he needed to make weighed heavy on him.

Impossible to give her false reassurance by saying he didn't want children. Foolish to hope some miraculous healing or a medical breakthrough might cure the reason she couldn't have more babies.

She raised her hands, stopping words he hadn't said. "Please don't tell me we could adopt. I can't tell you how many people back in Texas said that — like it was a quick and easy solution that fixed everything. Like they were saying I had no right to grieve over never having children of my own. Getting away from that was what made me decide to move somewhere no one knew me and no one knew what happened. I was ready to scream 'And you could get some sensitivity' at the next person who said 'But you could adopt' to me."

The sharp edge in her voice sounded far more like the Claire he was used to. Good thing he'd held back from asking if adopting would be an option.

Slowly, he nodded, taking time to find the right words. "I can see how tough that would have been. The way I'd feel if anyone told me not to mind Dad dying and not to miss him because Mom could remarry and give me a new dad."

"Exactly. No matter how good the man was, or how happy he made your mom, the loss of your father would still be there." Her smile held gratitude, not happiness. "Thank you for understanding what I meant. I know I won't be able to be a good mother to another woman's baby until I've stopped feeling so sad and angry about not being able to have babies of my own. And I don't know when that will happen. I don't know if it will ever happen."

Her total honesty demanded honesty in return. And he knew what he needed to tell her.

The truth.

Reaching for her hands again, he took them in a firm and hopefully reassuring grip. She didn't try to pull away. "Nothing you've told me makes you the wrong girl for me. I still love you, Claire. Even more than I did earlier since I know how brave you've been dealing with all this."

Her gaze shot up to meet his, and her mouth sagged open. She stared at him for a long moment, hope and disbelief battling in her eyes. "You do?"

His nod this time was a lot more decisive. "I do. I still want to marry you. I know choosing you, if you'll have me, means letting go of my hopes to have children of my own." He shrugged. "I'll need some time to grieve that, too. But life never comes with guarantees we get what we want. God might have something far better planned for us. We just need to trust Him."

He stood, then drew her to her feet. "Will you have me, Claire, and help me discover what that something better might be?"

Her response was instant. She let his hands go, but only so she could grab the front of his shirt and pull him closer. Hoping this meant what he wanted it to mean, he wrapped his arms around her, gently and tenderly, demanding nothing. His heart thumped uncomfortably as he gazed at her, waiting. The next move was up to Claire.

He'd made his choice. Now she needed to make hers.

Green eyes glowing with emotion, she clasped his face in both hands. Even tear-wet and puffy-eyed, she stayed as beautiful as ever. Her face tilted toward his, her eyelids fluttered shut, and her lips parted, inviting his kiss.

Slowly, carefully, giving her time to pull away if she wanted, he lowered his lips to brush hers, and his arms tightened around her. His mouth moved to her forehead, her cheeks, her poor swollen eyes, kissing away the salt of her tears. As inevitably as a compass needle pointing north, his lips drifted to hers again.

And Claire kissed him back. The soft eagerness of her lips suggested she'd been longing for this moment as much as he had. The kiss deepened, setting the blood pounding through his veins, leaving him breathless and wanting more.

Finally, he ended the kiss and drew back. Letting things get this intense wasn't wise. Especially when she hadn't spoken yet.

Even if the wonder of her kiss was her reply, he still needed to hear her say it.

As they gazed at each other, and tears filled her eyes again, awareness shimmered between them. This didn't feel one-sided. He asked the question he'd implied but hadn't voiced outright. "Claire, will you marry me?"

Her forehead furrowed, and her lips tensed. Surely, she wouldn't say no after kissing him like that. "I love you, too." She chuckled. "I guess you might have already figured that out."

The words he'd been waiting to hear. Gratitude flooded him, warm and sweet.

Thank You, Lord!

"I hoped, but I couldn't be sure." And he still couldn't. Something told him her next word would be a "but". Better not get excited too soon. His contrary Claire could still say no.

Despite her tears, threatening to overflow again, she grinned and nodded. "You can be sure. But I've only taken the first step today. There's still a long way to go before I'm truly healed. I'm not ready for us to get engaged yet. Could we try what you suggested earlier? Dating seriously, with a view to getting engaged?"

A pulse throbbed in her pale throat, and her eyes asked the question, too. A hint of fear still lurked there. The fear he'd pressure her for all or nothing.

"I love you enough to wait for you." That he knew, as sure as he knew the sun would rise tomorrow, as sure as God's grace.

Grateful joy drove the fear from her eyes. Now, they shone with relief. "Good. I'm calling Pastor Roberts after Christmas to ask if he can recommend a good Christian grief therapist. I'm warning you now, it won't be an easy process. I'll cry. I'll rage. I'll snipe and snark at you when it's not you I'm really angry with. And I can't give you children. Are you *sure* you still want to marry me?"

Her adorably quirked eyebrow showed she knew the answer. No uncertainty remained.

"I'm sure."

Mischief gleamed in Claire's eyes and her smile. "I'm starting to believe you. But before we go tell your mom I'll be here for Christmas lunch tomorrow, I think I need you to prove it."

Drawing her back into his arms, he held her in a warm embrace. "Only one way to do that." His lips lowered to hers again, in a sweet pledge of love he intended to last the rest of his life.

As they kissed, his heart sang a Christmas carol of joy and thanksgiving.

For God's amazing love. And for Claire's.

EPILOGUE: FIVE YEARS LATER

As she watched Ryan and Claire laugh while their adopted son opened his Christmas gifts, gratitude warmed Jeannie. A grandchild at last, and a loving wife for her son. Their wide smiles suggested Claire's parents, here for the holidays, felt the same joy she did.

Crumpling the brightly printed wrapping paper in his chubby fists, eight-month-old Caleb grinned and chuckled with glee. Like most babies, he'd been far more interested in playing with the packaging than the actual toy inside it. She adored sitting with him while Claire taught school and Ryan worked. And she cherished seeing how much Claire loved her son.

Thank You, Lord, for this answer to prayer.

When I asked You to bring Ryan a wife he could start a family with and suggested Claire, I had no idea of the heartbreak she needed to overcome. But they've come so far since that first Christmas Day she joined us for lunch.

I can see their love growing deeper all the time, just as it did for me and Hank. I'm so glad you blessed Ryan with a love as strong as ours was.

You really do work in amazing ways. And always for our good.

Ryan stood and picked up his son. Claire snuggled her arms around them both, kissing the top of Caleb's head, then smiling at Ryan. The love in her eyes glowed brighter than the lights on the Christmas tree or the star that led the wise men to Bethlehem to worship the newborn King. And Ryan's love shone just as bright.

A love to last a lifetime. Exactly as it should.

THE END

PEPPARKAKOR RECIPE

These thin and delicious spiced cookies are a traditional Swedish favourite, often cut in the shape of men, women, hearts, stars, flowers, and even pigs! There are many different recipes, often handed down within families. Though pepparkakor are often called ginger cookies, they contain other spices not usually used in American-style gingerbread.

One change from the traditional version is the sweetening syrup used. Swedes normally use *sirap*, a uniquely Swedish sweetener made from sugar beet. Either dark or light *sirap* is used, depending how brown the baker wants the cookies to be. You may be able to purchase authentic *sirap* from a Swedish grocery store, or IKEA (they also sell ready prepared pepparkakor dough). Or use the suggested sweeteners as an alternative. Golden syrup and molasses will give the closest taste to the original, but can be substituted with corn syrup if needed.

The dough should ideally be made the day before baking. Makes 6 dozen cookies, depending on the size of the cookie cutter used and how thick or thin the dough is rolled.

This recipe is a combination of several found on the internet. The original recipe can be found here (in Swedish, so I'm grateful for Google Translate!):

https://sv.wikibooks.org/wiki/Kokboken/Recept/Pepparkakor

Ingredients

1 1/2 teaspoons cardamom pods (or 1/2 teaspoon dried

cardamom)
- 3/4 stick (75 g) butter or margarine
- 1/2 cup (125 g) sugar (white, brown or a mixture)
- 1 1/2 tablespoons (25 g) golden syrup (or light corn syrup)
- 1/2 tablespoon (10 g) treacle (or dark corn syrup)
- 1 1/2 teaspoons ground ginger
- 1 1/2 teaspoons ground cinnamon
- 1/2 teaspoon ground cloves
- 1 1/2 teaspoons baking soda (bicarbonate of soda)
- 3 1/2 tablespoons (50 ml) water
- 1 3/4 cups (225g) all-purpose (plain) flour

<u>Instructions</u>

Lightly crush the cardamom pods and empty the seeds out. Grind the seeds in a mortar and pestle or spice grinder and discard the pods. Set ground seeds aside with other spices.

Mix the sugar, all the spices, and the sweetening syrups in a saucepan over a moderate heat, stirring until the sugar is melted.

Remove from heat, add the butter while mixture is still hot, and stir until it is melted and mixed into the sugar syrup.

Add the baking soda and mix thoroughly.

Add the water and stir in.

Add the flour and mix until it is completely combined with the wet ingredients.

Empty the mixture into a bowl and allow to cool. When completely cool cover with food wrap (cling film). Leave the dough to rest in the fridge overnight.

Preheat the oven to 400°F (200°C, gas 6, fan oven 180°C).

Break off a small portion of the dough, leaving the rest in

the fridge. The dough should be stiff, but not crumbly. Knead it a little to soften, and then roll out thinly (1/8 to 1/4 inch or 3 to 6 mm thick) on a lightly floured surface or on baking paper. If the edges crack, gently rub the cracked area back together with your fingers.

Cut the dough into shapes using a cookie cutter, or cut to the desired size and shape using a sharp knife. Leftover dough can be combined with the next batch. Transfer to cold cookie sheets (baking trays). If not using baking paper (recommended!) the trays should be lightly greased.

Bake for 5-8 minutes until evenly browned. Check frequently during baking, as they burn easily. Traditionally, the cookies are baked till crisp, but if you prefer a softer cookie, remove from oven when edges are browned.

Leave to cool a few minutes, then lift on the baking paper to a wire rack to cool completely. If not using baking paper, allow the cookies to cool longer on the cookie sheets — they break easily when hot.

Continue baking in batches until all you have enough cookies or all the dough is used. Unused dough will keep well for at least a week in the fridge if covered.

Though plain cookies are more traditional, once cookies are completely cool, they can be frosted (iced) in whatever pattern you wish.

Cookies should be stored in an airtight container and will stay good for up to 4 weeks.

Enjoy!

BIBLE VERSES AND OTHER REFERENCES

<u>Prologue</u>
The Lord God said, "It is not good for the man to be alone. I will make a helper suitable for him." Genesis 2:18 NIV

<u>Chapter 4</u>
For I know the plans I have for you," declares the LORD, "plans to prosper you and not to harm you, plans to give you hope and a future. Jeremiah 29:11 NIV

But the fruit of the Spirit is love, joy, peace, forbearance, kindness, goodness, faithfulness, gentleness and self-control. Against such things there is no law. Galatians 5:22-23 NIV

And we know that in all things God works for the good of those who love him, who have been called according to his purpose. Romans 8:28 NIV

Each one of us has one body, and that body has many parts. These parts don't all do the same thing. In the same way, we are many people, but in Christ we are all one body. We are the parts of that body, and each part belongs to all the others. Romans 12:4-5 NIV

<u>Chapter 11</u>
IT CAME UPON THE MIDNIGHT CLEAR
It came upon the midnight clear,
That glorious song of old,

From angels bending near the earth,
To touch their harps of gold:
"Peace on the earth, goodwill to all,
From heaven's all-gracious King."
The world in solemn stillness lay,
To hear the angels sing.
Still through the cloven skies they come,
With peaceful wings unfurled,
And still their heavenly music floats
O'er all the weary world;
Above its sad and lowly plains,
They bend on hovering wing,
And ever o'er its babel sounds
The blessèd angels sing.
Yet with the woes of sin and strife
The world has suffered long;
Beneath the heavenly hymn have rolled
Two thousand years of wrong;
And warring humankind hears not
The tidings which they bring
O hush the noise and cease your strife
And hear the angels sing.
And you, beneath life's crushing load
Whose forms are bending low,
Who toil along the climbing way
With painful steps and slow,
Look now! for glad and golden hours
come swiftly on the wing.
O rest beside the weary road,
And hear the angels sing!

For lo!, the days are hastening on,
By prophets seen of old
When with the ever-circling years
Shall come the time foretold
When the new heaven and earth shall own
The prince of Peace their King
And all the world give back the song
Which now the angels sing.

(Edmund Hamilton Sears, 1849)

Chapter 12

God says, "Stop fighting and know that I am God! I am the one who defeats the nations; I am the one who controls the world." Psalm 46:10 ERV

So I beg you, brothers and sisters, because of the great mercy God has shown us, offer your lives as a living sacrifice to him—an offering that is only for God and pleasing to him. Considering what he has done, it is only right that you should worship him in this way. Romans 12:1 ERV

And we know that in all things God works for the good of those who love him, who have been called according to his purpose.
Romans 8:28 NIV

THANK YOU FOR READING…

Though an intense and emotional experience, I loved writing this story of love, renewed faith, and truly surrendering to God. I hope so much that you enjoyed reading it!

If you did, please consider leaving a review. Reviews help other readers like you find the books they'll want to read. Your opinion counts!

Plus, if you liked this story, you'll probably enjoy my other books. All include love, faith, characters overcoming real issues, and a happy ever after!

You can see all my currently released books on my website www.FaithHopeandHeartwarming.com While you're there, you can also sign up for my reader newsletter to get all my book news, exclusive subscriber giveaways, and freebies!

I'M GRATEFUL TO...

Marion, Cecelia, Jan, Clare, and Mary — the wonderful authors in the multi-author set I originally wrote this story for. It's a privilege to work with such a friendly and harmonious group of dedicated, God-focused women. Special thanks to Marion for the lovely cover and formatting and to Cecelia for being our financial administrator. You are appreciated!

My superb editor, Dee at Brilliant Cut Editing, a true sister in Christ who always shows me how best to polish my words. Any grammatical errors in the story are all mine, added after she edited.

My writing buddy and dear friend Shannon Marie, who is such a blessing to me. Her story suggestions and friendship make all the difference!

My beloved husband Arthur, for trying his hardest to understand what it is I do when I write, and why I have such a passion for it.

As always, my deepest and most heartfelt thanksgiving and praise to God, who makes it all possible. Without Him, I would be nothing.

And thanks to you, dear reader, for coming this far with me. I truly pray this story blessed and uplifted you.

WANT A FREE CHRISTIAN ROMANCE?

Would you like to be one of the first to know when my new books are published, access subscriber only giveaways, and get my future subscriber freebies? Sign up for my newsletter at www.autumnmacarthur.com or go straight to my sign-up page by using the QR code.

Subscribers have access to exclusive freebies, contests and book giveaways, as well as being first to know about new releases and special offers. Emails rarely arrive more twice a month, unless I have special news to share I think you won't want to miss; your email address will never be shared; and you can unsubscribe at any time.

Made in United States
North Haven, CT
21 November 2022